REBECCA RAISIN is a true bibliophile. This love of books morphed into the desire to write them. She's been widely published in various short story anthologies, and in fiction magazines, and is now focusing on writing romance. The only downfall about writing about gorgeous men who have brains as well as brawn, is falling in love with them – just as well they're fictional! Rebecca aims to write characters you can see yourself being friends with. People with big hearts who care about relationships, and most importantly, believe in true, once-in-a-lifetime love.

Also by Rebecca Raisin

Christmas at the Gingerbread Café
Chocolate Dreams at the Gingerbread Café
The Bookshop on the Corner
Christmas Wedding at the Gingerbread Café
Secrets at Maple Syrup Farm
The Little Bookshop on the Seine
The Little Antique Shop under the Eiffel Tower
The Little Perfume Shop off the Champs-Élysées
Celebrations and Confetti at Cedarwood Lodge
Brides and Bouquets at Cedarwood Lodge
Midnight and Mistletoe at Cedarwood Lodge
Rosie's Travelling Tea Shop
Aria's Travelling Book Shop
Escape to Honeysuckle Hall
Flora's Travelling Christmas Shop

Elodie's Library of Second Chances

REBECCA RAISIN

ONE PLACE. MANY STORIES

HQ
An imprint of HarperCollins*Publishers* Ltd
1 London Bridge Street
London SE1 9GF

www.harpercollins.co.uk

HarperCollins*Publishers*
1st Floor, Watermarque Building, Ringsend Road
Dublin 4, Ireland

This edition 2022

1
First published in Great Britain by
HQ, an imprint of HarperCollins*Publishers* Ltd 2022

Emoji(s) © Shutterstock.com

ISBN: 9780008457013

MIX
Paper from
responsible sources
FSC™ C007454

This book is produced from independently certified FSC™ paper to ensure responsible forest management.

For more information visit: www.harpercollins.co.uk/green

This book is set in 10.5/15.5 pt. Sabon by Type-it AS, Norway

Printed and Bound in the UK using 100% Renewable Electricity at CPI Group (UK) Ltd, Croydon, CR0 4YY

This one is for you, Joanne Mateljan

Chapter 1

I turn the page of my book as I'm gently poked and prodded from every angle while my hairdresser works his magic, taking me from average thirty-something woman to red carpet ready. You'd think it'd be exciting, but after years of these events it's just another chore to add to the list.

I squirm sideways in an effort to see the words on the page. 'Stop fidgeting, Ellie,' says Jonas, who tabloids have coined *coiffeur* to the stars, a fancy term for hairdresser. He's as flamboyant as he is talented and the best in the biz. He's been doing my hair and make-up for years now and we've grown close.

'Thirty minutes until the limo arrives to transform this sweet thang into a goddess,' he says under this breath.

'Did you just call me *sweet thang*?' Only Jonas could make that expression sound right.

'I did.'

I shake my head with a laugh and continue reading, only stopping every now and then to ponder what I'd do if faced with the same scenario my characters are.

'We're a little behind schedule here.' Jonas grimaces as he glances at his watch.

'Just put my hair in a topknot.'

He raises well-groomed brows. 'Oh, no, no, no can do. Your mother wants loose Hollywood curls.'

'Again?' I say with a what-can-you-do shrug. I don't get a say in these things. Besides, allowing Mother to arrange the styling gives me more time to read while everyone else fusses behind the scenes.

'Your look today is old Hollywood glamour.' While my life might seem exciting from the outside, it's empty on the inside. I'm ferried straight from the office of Astor News and Media to nightly events, which doesn't leave a lot of downtime. Usually after a twelve-hour day my rigor mortis smile is fixed into position, giving me lockjaw, and I pine for a life other than this. Reading is my happy place, my go-to where I can forget the world and relax no matter how short a time I have to get lost in the pages.

'Speaking of glamour . . . where the bloody hell is Holly?' Jonas asks. 'She's supposed to have the frock ready to go! If she comes traipsing in here with the wrong dress again, I'm going to need a stiff drink and a long lie-down.'

'Don't worry, she'll be here soon.'

Jonas puts the finishing touches on my curls and moves on to my make-up. He's a man of many talents but gets worked up when he knows the likelihood of bumping into my mother is imminent.

'OK, OK. My nerves are shot is all.'

I give him a supportive pat on the hand. 'You need to lose yourself in a good book every now and then to help you relax.' I'm rewarded with a dramatic eyeroll. 'I have tequila if all else fails.'

'Now *there*'s a book I could get into . . . *Tequila Mockingbird*.'

'Jonas!' I throw my head back and laugh. 'Sounds like the name of those ultra-hip cocktail bars you frequent on a Friday.'

'*Thursday* is the new Friday, darling. But you wouldn't know – you're too busy strutting the red carpet.' Jonas is a bit of a celebrity himself these days and is always getting write-ups in the press as he hops from one bar to the next with his fabulously fashionable entourage.

'Is it? I have *no* clue. If I have a night off the last thing I want to do is head out.'

My gaze wanders back to my book. *The Last Days of Rabbit Hayes* is heart-wrenching, but I can't bear for it to end. An ugly cry every now and then is good for the soul but now is not the time for that sort of thing. Still, I really need to know what happens . . .

Jonas glances at his watch again. His worry is contagious, and I only hope Holly *is* on her way here. I don't like being late – it screams diva and that is something I'm not. Plus, I don't want to put any more pressure on my anxious *coiffeur*.

'Tilt your head to the side, darling,' Jonas says. I give in to it and forget about the dress, and my assistant who is MIA. Poor Holly will be running all over London trying to find the right garment, one specifically requested by my mother, with only a vague description of where it actually is – Mum can be very Miranda Priestly at times.

I get to an emotional scene in the book and despite my trying to hold it in the floodgates open. I thought there'd be a miracle, something, anything for it to end another way. I swallow back tears, knowing I'm only a moment away from a sob fest I might not recover from. The shattering of my heart is almost audible, like the splintering of a thousand shards of glass.

'Darling are they *real* tears?' Jonas scrutinises me. 'Is my queen *crying*?' He peers closer, which only make the tears fall harder. Jonas's expression appears positively worried.

'Sorry! It's this book.' I wave it in the air as I try to swallow my heartbreak and compose myself. 'It's. Just. So. Devastating.' The words come out haltingly. I take a deep centring breath and expel some of the grief. 'Yet it's somehow uplifting. I don't think I'm going to be able to sleep tonight thinking of it.' My bottom lip wobbles as I put on a brave face.

'You're too good for this world, with a heart bigger than Texas – that's you. It baffles me because you're the *opposite* of your mother. I often wonder where you get your empathetic streak from, but that's a conversation for another day. Can I get you a tissue, a . . . tequila?'

'I'm good, I'm fine. Have I ruined the make-up? Sorry, I know we're already pressed for time.'

Jonas shakes his head. 'It's not a problem, darling. Nothing these nimble fingers can't fix.' He dabs under my eyes to repair the damage. Really, I should know better than to read such an emotional tale before a red-carpet event.

With that my brother Teddy wanders in. 'Elodieeeee.' He draws my name out as if it's a song lyric. He's the only person who doesn't call me Ellie. I'm sure he does it just to annoy me. Kid brothers, eh?

'What's with the tears?' he says, his eyebrows pulling together.

I sigh. 'A deeply moving book that I've been emotionally invested in.'

'This?' He takes it from my hands but trips on the hair curler cord and drops it. The novel lies forlornly on the carpet, its pages mussed, as if it's suffered an injury.

I motion for Teddy to pick up the book before its pages are indelibly wrinkled.

Teddy rescues it and straightens it out. 'What's so earth-shattering about this particular tome?'

'It's too hard to explain – you'll have to read it. My heart . . .'

'Ellie *felt her feelings* and is a little fragile now.'

'Unfortunately I felt my feelings all over my make-up so now poor Jonas is back to square one.'

Teddy tuts. 'Must be a good book.'

'The best.' I sniff, thinking of Rabbit, Molly and Juliet. 'They felt so *real*. It's as though I've just closed the door on my best friends and the innermost workings of their lives.' I double blink in an effort not to weep. 'What I need is to throw myself onto the sofa to process it all. Not a red-carpet event and a hundred flashing cameras pointed at me.' I hold a hand over my heart, knowing those characters will stay in there for the rest of my life.

'I wish I could take your place,' Teddy says lightly. 'I'm not tired of the spotlight, or red-carpet events. I don't think I ever will be.'

For a very brief stint, Teddy worked alongside me at the family biz. He didn't take his role seriously, made a splash being papped doing silly things like guzzling out of magnum bottles of champagne or dancing on tables. Nursing a sore head, he'd call in sick time and again. I covered for him as long as I could but even I couldn't magic away those awful paparazzi pictures of Teddy in our rivals' glossies. When Mother found out she was furious and fired him on the spot. He's been trying to claw his way back ever since, but she won't hear a word of it. It's a shame because Teddy could charm the socks off anyone, and he's made progress sorting himself out.

'I'd trade places in a heartbeat.' I give him a sad smile. There's no convincing Mother when she's made up her mind. She's steely, at the best of times.

That's why I'm grateful for my brother, wayward as he can be. We're close and rely on each other a lot, especially when it comes to speaking up for each other. Our parents subscribe to the stiff upper lip style of parenting, and don't always understand when I quite readily *feel my feelings*. My mother claims those kinds of *histrionics* are not necessary. If she caught me crying over fictional characters, she'd give me another talking-to about learning the art of regulating one's emotions. We're different, that's for sure.

Teddy cranks some happy music on his phone, no doubt to distract me.

'That's more like it,' Jonas says, and softly sways to the music as he highlights my cheeks with an angled brush. 'My blood pressure is through the roof knowing your mother is about to sneak up at any moment while I've got her golden child sitting here with red-rimmed eyes clutching her heart. It doesn't look good.'

'I don't blame you for being worried, after that last fiasco with the small hair fire,' Teddy blurts out and I swear Jonas's complexion turns a radioactive shade of green.

'I'll handle her,' I quickly reassure him, giving him a sunny smile. Mother was incensed about the small hair fire – you'd have thought *her* locks went up in flames. At the time, I'd been so engrossed in Joan Didion's *The Year of Magical Thinking* that I leaned too close to a scented candle and next minute my hair caught. Jonas managed to stamp it out fast, but my mother walked in at that exact moment and all hell broke loose.

Since then, she's been wary about Jonas, but I've explained

a million times it was *my* fault and an accident at that. It's only hair, but she's all about aesthetics, that woman. I quite liked having an excuse to chop my long locks off, but a pixie cut was vetoed by Mother as not the right look for Astor and now it's grown long again anyway. I mean, seriously. I have a degree in librarianship and here I am still needing permission for a hairstyle! Just how did I let this happen to me?

'Louise is going to be there tonight,' Teddy says. Aha, now his impromptu visit makes sense! He's not here to commiserate with me, he's here for intel.

'Yes, I know.' Teddy has been in love with actress Louise for years, but she won't give him the time of day. They'd make a lovely couple if Teddy did manage to settle down. The thing is, his reputation precedes him, even though he's managed to get his act together over the last year or so.

'Why not invite her to an intimate dinner party you're hosting?'

'Erm, what dinner party would that be?' I cock my head.

He stares down his nose at me. 'Do it for your baby brother, Elodie . . .'

I cross my arms. 'Louise will see right through me, you know.' She knows full well I do my brother's bidding for him! He's got me wrapped around his little finger.

'Yes, she's certainly got my measure.' He grins. 'That's what I love about her. She's so clever. It's not just the way she looks – she's the whole package. I *adore* her. And I always will.' His eyes are bright as he drifts off to dreamland . . .

'I'll see what I can do.' As usual Teddy's puppy-dog eyes get to me. The poor fool adores a woman who doesn't even give him a second glance. It's so like Teddy to choose the hard road.

'I've heard she's shooting a movie soon with Dillon Hollander,' Jonas says, voice lilting like it does when he's sharing gossip.

'That slimy so-and-so?' Teddy says, his voice full of disgust. 'Really?'

'Yep. But methinks Louise will make short work of him if his hands do go a-wandering. Why he's still in the movie business is beyond me.' Jonas always has the inside scoop on celebs. 'Proves it's not what you know, it's who you know.' Dillon is the progeny of a famous director who mainly does superhero movies. That'll open doors, like nothing else will. Talk about nepotism, though who I am to judge?

'Does Louise know what he's like?' I ask.

'I better text her and give her a heads-up,' Teddy says. 'Do my civil duty.'

I smile. 'You do that.'

Twenty minutes later my assistant Holly appears, sweat beading her brow, slinky dress held aloft. 'Don't ask,' she says. 'Let's just get this on you. Your mother's on her way up!'

At the mention of my mother panic reflects in Jonas's eyes. He moves quickly and finishes spritzing the setting agent for my make-up. 'Get out of here, Teddy, so we can dress our queen,' Jonas screeches. 'She's got to be ready on time! I really can't cop another bollocking from Dorothea – I'm still traumatised over the last one!' Mother can be downright terrifying if you're not family – it's all smoke and mirrors but most people don't recognise that.

'Knock 'em dead, Ellie,' Teddy says. He makes a hasty exit with a backwards wave and shuts the door behind him.

Once he's gone Jonas slips off my robe – he sees me as nothing more than a mannequin, a job, not a red-blooded woman. Holly pulls the satin bias-cut dress over my head. It floats down in liquid rivulets and my hair and make-up remain pristine. As the drape of the golden dress touches the marble floor, my mother appears wearing her supercilious trademark look, better known as: resting bitch face.

Mother gives me a slow once-over. 'You didn't fast today, dear?' she asks, her gaze settling on my stomach.

'No, of course I didn't.' Her rules for red-carpet appearances are antiquated to say the least.

She raises a brow as if I've let her down. 'You know what the press are like with their camera angles.'

I let out a sigh. 'Well, bad luck.' High heels are the work of the devil and I won't be convinced otherwise. Trying to keep my energy levels up all night is even worse. Tonight I'll be strutting down the red carpet to promote a documentary the family company has produced and then attending an after-party.

'Your eyes are slightly bloodshot, Ellie. Are you getting enough sleep?'

I dart a glance at Jonas who looks as if his head is about to explode.

'Probably not,' I say. 'There's never time for rest, is there?'

She shakes her head. 'Don't start with all that blather about downtime again. You don't know how lucky you are; millions of women would swap their lives with you in a heartbeat.' Mother heads towards the door, calling over her shoulder, 'The car will be here in five. Don't keep me waiting.'

'I'll do my level best.' We collectively let out a breath as she leaves. Dorothea Astor has that effect on people. As if on cue my stomach starts to rumble. I really should have eaten something before now; lunch seems like light years ago.

'I don't know how you stand it,' Jonas whispers and goes

to the fridge, before returning with a plastic-wrapped Reuben sandwich. 'Have this. You need to eat.'

'Thanks, Jonas. You're a lifesaver but I'll only have half.' Jonas is forever eating on the run between clients and stashes his booty in the small bar fridge alongside the bottles of bubbles I keep on hand in my dressing room for my team.

'Don't be silly.'

'What's tonight's premiere about again?' Holly asks, as she riffles through her Mary-Poppins-sized tote bag before brandishing her phone and taking arty snaps of me for the Astor social media pages. I really hate these candid pictures – they seem so self-aggrandising but my mother won't be told.

I unwrap the sandwich and wonder how I'm going to eat without messing up my lipstick as my stomach rumbles in protest. 'It's a documentary called *Eyrie*. Focusing on the lives of free solo climbers and the reasons they take such huge risks, without ropes or safety equipment.'

'Why do they?'

I take a moment to reply. 'It's just them and the mountain; they're not chained to anything. They're driven by this indelible need to escape and when they get to the top, the eyrie, it's only them and the stunning view. I expect it's liberating. They're totally *free*.' How I wish I was too.

'Right,' Holly says with a shake of her head as if it doesn't make any sense to her. She glances out the window. 'The car is here.'

Jonas fluffs my hair before air-kissing me. 'Enjoy the night, darling.'

Holly motions for me to take a bite of my sandwich before she snatches it away, as this duo have managed once again to transform me into something I'm not.

Chapter 2

The next morning I'm feeling anything but enthused at the latest Astor News and Media executive meeting. Part of me is dreaming of bed. I've been burning the candle at both ends, with long workdays, followed by night-time events. This morning Mother is leading the team, jabbering on about KPIs and how she needs us to 'demonstrate more forcefully key business objectives'. Read: make money aggressively without spending more to do so.

An exasperated sigh escapes me, and the boardroom falls silent.

'Care to share what's on your mind?' my mother says, giving me her signature glare. It bounces right off me, but I know it burns other mere mortals into the ground.

'It's just that we're always so focused on the money side of things. I've been reading this amazing self-development book by Simon Sinek called *Start with Why* and it's really got me thinking about WHY we do what we do and WHAT we could achieve if we thought in those terms. Astor's profits are up almost fifteen per cent compared to this time last year, yet we act like the sky is falling down and we're all about to be unemployed.'

'And do you know *why* it's up fifteen per cent, Ellie? Because we don't take our foot off the gas; we don't rest on our laurels. It's not the Astor way.'

I'll never be able to convince her otherwise, and it's true, she's built this business from the ground up. But there's no sense of giving back, of appreciating what we have. She just raises the bar higher and expects everyone to work longer hours to achieve more.

'Since you're so sure Astor is infallible what do you suggest we do to increase revenue this quarter?' she says with a glint in her eye that suggests she thinks I'm going to zip my lips and pretend I'm not here like I usually do.

I fidget with my pen. 'Well, it's not exactly revenue-raising but I've been approached by a librarian from a school in a lower socio-economic area about donating some of our returns for their library. And that got me thinking – a small percentage of our returns could essentially be donated to places in need, rather than letting them be destroyed. I hate to think of those books going to waste, and this way they'd go on to fulfil their destiny and be read by people who genuinely need them. I was thinking hospitals, rehabilitation centres, schools, the list is endless. Wouldn't it be nice to give back instead of—'

Mother interrupts with a guffaw. 'Let me get this straight. Your idea is to *donate* our returns to help us reach our KPIs? Ellie, listen to yourself! Giving away books does not lead to profit! Add in the cost of extra freight, it makes no sense. And it goes against everything we stand for. Your energy could best be spent working with sales to help keep returns as low as possible in order to prevent wastage. Apologies, team. Ellie's had a lot of late nights and isn't herself. Now, Marco, where are you at with the expansion plan for the Paddington bookshop bar?'

Normally, I'd sink back into my chair, knowing I'm defeated, but today I don't feel like giving in. 'Wait, I don't think you're hearing me. Of course I understand that giving books away wouldn't lead to more profit. But business isn't *just* about profit margins, is it? What about good PR? Instead of sending me to every red-carpet event, I could be liaising with community groups who need *our* help. I could *personally* deliver some of those returned books to places who need them, thus putting a name and face to Astor with a hefty dose of goodwill. We're *always* going to get returns; it's not a perfect science knowing exactly how many books will sell in any given shop. I know it's important to focus on the bigger picture, strategic growth and all that jazz, but why not let me try this one charity initiative? Wouldn't it do the Astor name a world of good . . .' The room is deathly silent – will this be the day I convince my mother to take me seriously? When she doesn't speak, I quickly add, 'Which in time might lead to more profit if people associated Astor with being benevolent and helping out in the community.'

'Darling,' she says, gently. 'We will *never* give away our product, never in a million years. It's the basic rule of economics. If we start, where will it end? Next minute you'll be giving away free drinks in our book bars to promote lengthy conversations or something equally impractical. No, that way lies madness. Now, back to you, Marco.'

Marco spends the next hour highlighting expansion plans for the five-level Paddington bookshop and bar, while I quietly seethe. My mum and I are two different people and it feels as if we'll never be on the same page. One thing is certain, this isn't the life I dreamed of, and something needs to change . . .

Chapter 3

Willow Grove library at risk of closure

The Chronicle by Finn Ford
Posted Friday July 8th at 10.55 a.m.

Local city councillor Jason Stephens announced the grim news this morning that Willow Grove library is at risk of closure due to dwindling memberships and an increase in running costs. He warns that unless library memberships double, thus making the library eligible to apply for council funding, the doors will close at the end of the year. When the minutes of the meeting were published head librarian Agnes Bitterweather chose to take a redundancy package effective immediately, leaving Willow Grove library after a tenure of ten years. 'It's not the same anymore,' she says. 'People want to stare at screens like zombies. The sad fact is, the library just isn't saveable.'

What will a town without books look like? Where will those who seek comfort in reading go? What about those who find joy in walking along the colourful racks in search of a fictional friend? Job applications are open for the position of head librarian. The successful candidate will have a monumental task on their hands to save Willow Grove library. Go to www.willowgrovelibrary/ jobs to apply for the position.

A town without books?

The idea pierces my heart. And in sleepy little Willow Grove, no less. Teddy and I went to boarding school in Buckinghamshire, not far from there. I can still picture the library as it was when I was younger. Those hallowed halls full of the citrusy perfume of musty books. Shadowy recesses where I'd pull up a chair and discover secrets between the covers of hardback books. The many adventures I took, surrounded by soft-bound stacks. I loved the sheer escapism as the real world faded and I was lost inside a story.

Libraries are the lifeblood of communities, a safe space where residents converge, and literature is free for one and all. I imagine a despondent librarian shutting off the lights for the last time, the books thrown into darkness abandoned on shelves gathering dust for eternity. In the dim light of a forgotten library, I imagine the tomes murmuring sadly: *Where did the readers go?*

A sudden thought hits. There must be a reason I stumbled on this article on social media – I have to save Willow Grove library! But how?

'Look at this.' I hand my phone over to Teddy, who gives the news piece a cursory look. Outside, rain drums at the windows of my London townhouse, but I barely notice it. I'm already there in spirit at Willow Grove library, running my hands along the spines, making silent promises to them: *You will be borrowed again . . .*

Teddy runs a finger over the screen as he speed-reads and shrugs. 'So what? It's a tiny little concern in some forgotten town. I hated having to go to Willow Grove as a child. Talk about dull.'

Once a month we'd had school excursions to Willow Grove, the boys' school on the opposite side of the road to us. I used to sneak into the library while everyone else gambolled by the river. And don't even ask about Teddy – he got up to plenty of hijinks and was always being reprimanded for it.

I remember the scent of the well-thumbed books and the promise of escape trapped inside them. We had our own school library, but Willow Grove had an almost magical air about it. Back then it was dusty and disorderly as if the librarian would rather read than wander the aisles cleaning and sorting – I loved the idea of that. There were countless times I caught her, feet propped up underneath her as she read the day away. That sort of thing would be frowned upon these days, but back then it seemed fitting; after all, how could she recommend books if she hadn't read them?

Even back then the library had an abandoned air to it, as if I were the only one who knew of its existence. I studied librarianship because I'd been so inspired by that place and its quirky librarian. It had been so different to the more sterile Astor News and Media, a corporate world purely run for profit as opposed to a library that's there for the community with an emphasis on educational initiatives.

I've always dreamed of working at a slower pace, concentrating on people's love of reading, rather than the nuts and bolts of publishing, spreadsheets and number crunching, done under blinding fluorescent office lights. How had I forgotten my dreams for so long?

'How did the premiere go last night? Was Louise there?'

I roll my eyes. Louise did the narration for *Eyrie* and Teddy is still upset he didn't get to strut the red carpet – so he's not listening to a word I'm saying. Last night Louise admitted to me that Teddy just doesn't take life seriously enough for her, but I haven't got the heart to tell him. He's trying – he's back on track at least, but there's still those who doubt it'll last, I guess. '*Seriously*, Teddy? Forget Louise. She's off to Spain to shoot that movie, but she did mumble something about catching up for drinks when she gets back.'

'Well, that's something to look forward to.' He grins. 'Now what were you on about?'

'Willow Grove. It's more important that the library *is* in a small town. A town that was very good to us once upon a time. *Everyone* needs books – you of all people should appreciate that.' I sigh. Sometimes my brother can be so blasé. Not hard to see why, the way we've grown up. Privileged is an understatement.

He gives me a blank stare, so I continue, 'Imagine saving Willow Grove library. Achieving something that *matters!*' From right back when I wore my hair in plaits I wanted to be a librarian. Even though books were always readily available to me at Astor I spent my formative years visiting libraries, feeling a kinship there. As though I belonged. I idolised those bespectacled women who seemed to float through the aisles, righting fallen volumes as they matched a novel to its reader.

They seemed to have the ability, this fine art of being able to look into your eyes and instinctively *know* which book you needed before you even did. That's why I first believed working at Astor would be magical. We *are* publishers, producers of literature, but it was soon evident my mother only had one goal for me, and it didn't include any of the things I'm passionate about. I thought I'd have more leeway, be able to make changes so we highlighted the love of reading, helped those in need by offering literature programs and funding university scholarships, but none of my ideas have been taken seriously. My mother is an astute businesswoman – there's no question – but we are so very different. She could be in any industry and she'd make money, but surely life is about more than that?

Teddy closes the article and hands my phone back and stares at his reflection in the gilt mirror, fixing his already immaculate hair. 'Saving Willow Grove library would be quite the philanthropic spectacle and good for the Astor name, but the gatekeepers would never agree.'

Frustration pulses. 'I don't want it to be a philanthropic spectacle and I definitely wouldn't want the Astor name tied to it.' The funny thing is, we aren't even technically Astors. Teddy and I are Halifaxes. In the early days, the press incorrectly assumed that our family name was Astor because my parents were married, not knowing that my mother kept her maiden name and used it for her publishing empire. My mother never corrected the media and now it's stuck.

'Anyway,' I continue. 'This would be me stepping from the shadow of the Astor name. Going out alone and doing what I've always wanted to do.' Sure, my name opens a lot of doors, but that in turn really bugs me. I always wonder what it'd be like to be unknown – those doors would soon bang shut in my face, and I'd revel in that. Whatever I wanted, I'd have to earn.

Pity dashes across Teddy's face. 'They'll never let their golden child go. You're stuck in this gilded cage forever.' Stuck at Astor News and Media. The thought is enough to steal my smile. His voice turns wistful as he says, 'Unlike me, the great disappointment who could disappear off the face of this earth before anyone would be any the wiser.'

Our parents have washed their hands of Teddy in the business sense and probably wouldn't notice if he up and left. They'd put it down to him going on one of his drunken jaunts with his merry band of friends, other trust fund babes from billionaire families who don't have the drive or ambition to work, and certainly no need for financial reward.

'*I'd* notice if you disappeared,' I say gently. 'I'd scour the earth until I found you again.' We're as close as siblings can be, and I love my little brother even though he's a handful at the best of times. He's got a big heart when it matters.

'Shucks.' Teddy pretends to wipe a faux tear. He acts as though our parents ostracising him from the biz doesn't bother him, but I know it does. In return he plays the cliché party boy they think he is. If only they looked closer, they'd see that inside he's still got a touch of that lost little boy from childhood who so desperately wanted love and attention from parents who lived by the adage: children should be seen and not heard.

They underestimate what he *could* be if given a second chance. Unlike me, Teddy yearns to be back working for the great Astor News and Media Corporation, which handles news, media, film, print and publishing and now book bars and restaurants too. My mother has her fingers in so many pies, she's run out of hands. That's where I come in. I'm all for women in business, but I'm only a ribbon cutter. A commodity. She says I'm the face of Astor and that's what sells. When my mother sees people, she sees dollar signs. My father is her faithful sidekick and much the same, but it's the formidable Dorothea Astor who calls the shots. Don't get me wrong, they're great people, visionaries in a way, but I always wished they were a little more loving. A little more switched on to the nuances of our lives *outside* of Astor. Mother always says I'm too whimsical, with my head in the clouds, and maybe that's the case. It's ironic really – she blames my love of reading for that whimsy. Says if I keep getting lost in books one day I won't find my way back. It's true I don't have her eye for the next big money-making thing. My passions lie elsewhere.

Lately my desire to flee has grown. After watching the *Eyrie* documentary again, envy washed over me. Their need for escape was so relatable. Those free solo climbers are living life on their terms. At the summit of those mountains it's only them in nature wearing their big, free smiles. *I want that.* In my own little corner of the world. Not on a mountain but perhaps in . . . a library.

I always hoped I'd grow to enjoy my work at Astor, but if anything each day it becomes harder to motivate myself to participate. Donning the fake smile and launching yet another branch with no space to pursue my own passions there. Again, I'm reminded of Teddy who would relish my role, and I wish things were different so he could take my place.

Could I dare up and leave? My parents would never forgive me. Each day they remind me they're close to retiring and I'm to take the helm. But it's an empty threat. My mother will die at her executive chair; there's no way that woman will hand over control. If I don't leave now, I never will and I'll be stuck for good. My own purpose in life evaporated.

Soon, the daydream swirls . . . me, switching on the lights at Willow Grove library. The books shimmying and shaking in anticipation of being read once again, of their pages being turned, the words soaking into a reader's heart.

A town *with* books now and forever.

I lean back into the plushness of the sofa. 'Libraries are magical places, Teddy. Sacrosanct. They need to be protected. Fought for. What's more important than literature for young and old? It's absurd to think of a town with no books. Not everyone can afford to buy the latest novel, or the next edition of a school textbook. Or newspapers, magazines, ebooks. And what about the book clubs they host? They're crucial for authors as well as readers, are they not? Don't forget about all those lonely elderly people who go to their local library for company, a chat before they take their book haul home and lose themselves in the pages of a novel. What about them? Mark my words, there'll be a range of people just like that and many more who use Willow Grove library for more than just borrowing books. The library is the heart of a community.'

Teddy frowns. 'You speak as if it'll be an easy fix. It can't exactly be the heart of the community if memberships are down and no one's using it. From what I remember it was a ramshackle building that looked as if the wind might blow it over at any moment.'

It did look like that, like something out of a fairy tale, but where I see that as magical Teddy sees it as dilapidated. 'There could be any number of reasons for memberships dwindling.

Maybe they haven't got enough books. Maybe the place needs some rejuvenation. If one library closes, then how long before it happens in the next town, and the one after that? Suddenly books *aren't* accessible to everyone. And that's just not fair; in fact it's downright terrifying.'

My mind's eye sees lights being switched off, and books plunged into darkness from one town to the next and we quickly become *a world without words*.

'It's the most boring place on the planet, old Willow Grove, but I can see your point. Would you really give all of this up on a whim?'

All of what exactly? I'd leave in a heartbeat to follow my dream, if only I knew my parents would be OK with it. 'I would.' I shake my head, considering what closure would mean for Willow Grove and how quickly it could domino if funding dried up and libraries began to shut across the country. 'I *need* to save this place. I can feel it in my bones but there's one major problem – despite being the scion of a publishing family, I haven't really used my degree in that capacity. Will I even remember how to do it?'

There's a twinkle in Teddy's eye that I know all too well. It means he's going to encourage me no matter what the risks are. 'How hard can it be? It's not like you're taking over a place the size of the British Library. You'll dig out your course notes and have a refresher.'

I consider the pros and cons. 'No one would take me seriously if they knew who I was. Expert ribbon cutter and speech maker, that's me. If the press got wind of it, they'd presume Astor was moving in and expanding.'

The rain against the window softens to a pitter-patter. 'Why would they have to know who you are?'

'Well wouldn't they recognise me from all the tedious red-carpet events. My gigantic head on all those Astor billboards?' When Mother said I'd be the face of Astor, she wasn't lying. I cringe every time I see myself blown up on a poster plastered somewhere. 'The Ellie Astor presents column.' Which I don't even get to write myself.

'But you're *not* Ellie Astor, not really. You're Elodie Halifax. You go undercover. Your degree is in your real name; you have the credentials. Cassie in HR can be a reference for you. You have experience from when you took on that role sorting the archives for the historian Henry Ackley ahead of the publication of his memoir,' he says.

'Cassie would definitely keep it secret too. I'm the one who hired her and then approved her raise a few months after Mum denied it.'

'Great! And Elodie Halifax is a good solid librarian name. All you'll need to do is commit to a mousy make-over, dye your blonde locks a few shades darker, don some specs, lose the executive uniform and develop a whole new persona. I'm thinking "single woman who rescues cats and doesn't talk much because she believes books are better than people".'

I laugh. 'Not that you're into clichés or anything.' I *do* prefer books to people, but that's a bookworm prerogative, right? I dart a glance out the window. The rain is clearing and filmy sunlight streaks through the sheer white curtains, brightening the room and my mood.

Finally, I *could* be my own person. And at thirty-something I've given corporate life enough of my time. I've tried to leave so many times, my protests falling on deaf ears – what if this time I don't take no for an answer?

'You should do it, Elodie. Why not follow your heart? What were the chances of you stumbling onto an article shared on Facebook about Willow Grove library? A place you used to sneak into, while the rest of us tried to get into the off-licence. It's a sign from the universe to get the hell out of here before you lose the will to ever make a change.' Teddy's thoughts mirror my own.

The idea is risky, but the truth of the matter is I feel like my life hasn't even begun yet. How sad is that?! I'm directed to attend gala charity events, which are usually just a poor excuse for the mega wealthy to dress in couture, quaff expensive champagne and gossip about each other under the guise of "giving back". I speak at all Astor events. From movie premieres, art gallery exhibits, book launches, TV ads, to bookshop openings.

But the only place I've ever felt like me is when I'm reading, like those free solo climbers who only felt alive when they were clinging to the face of a mountain. When I'm lost in a good book, I escape reality for hours on end and things don't seem as hopeless. I can relate to a heroine in a bind, a woman whose life isn't what she thought it would be. It makes me feel less alone, and how funny is it that my best friends are all fictional?

But it's more than that – it's the power of words and how they can save you when you most need it.

However, leaving my parents would be hard. They do rely on me for all the promotion. And if I were to get exposed as Ellie Astor who ran away, my mother would never forgive me for besmirching the Astor name. But I can't do it without hiding who I am or I wouldn't be doing it under my own steam and I'm eager to try that. How will the world treat me, if I'm just me and not my mother's daughter?

Willow Grove library, lights off, blinds shuttered, dust motes dancing for the last time as the pages of the books slowly . . . yellow with age.

I can't let that happen.

'I might not even *get* the job,' I muse as the idea takes shape.

Teddy scoffs. 'Yeah, I'm sure librarians around the country are lining up to move to nowheresville to take a job at a library that's months from closing.'

I lob a cushion at him and nearly hit a Ming vase. The ostentatious display of wealth I'm surrounded by makes me feel sick, like I'm stuck in the wrong life. Teddy and I live in neighbouring townhouses whose interiors were designed by a famous decorator, hired by Mum. It bothers me that we have so much, while others have so little and still our parents yearn for more. Why? To be on the cover of *Forbes* again? To beat their competitors? It's this relentless drive to be the best I just don't gel with.

At the risk of sounding like a poor little rich girl, I'm desperate to see how the other half live. I dream of a rustic little cottage that I can make my own, no fancy interior designer telling me this goes with that and screw the expense. I could learn to drive or catch the train. Discover the joy of cooking for myself. Run a hoover over some second-hand rug I picked up at a flea market. Double-stack rickety shelves with second-hand books that are all mine. Make friends with real people who don't know my famous name and won't treat me differently. *And I'd be free . . .*

'I'm going to apply,' I say before I can change my mind, when common sense invariably kicks in. 'What's the worst that can happen? If by some miracle I get the job, I can save the library and my own life at the same time.'

'Yes!' Teddy grins, slow and wide like a Cheshire cat. 'As long as you know you'll have to tell Mother straight away. They won't like you leaving no matter what, but it'll be worse if you leave it until the last minute. You'll need to give her time to sit with it and see you're serious about this.'

I deflate at the thought. 'Yes, I'll have to tell her. She won't be happy but hopefully she'll see reason.' What can Mum do – cut me off financially if I no longer work for Astor? Fine by me! A small price to pay; in fact I'll *insist* on it.

Teddy shakes his head vehemently. 'Ellie, you can't exactly tell her the truth. She'll convince you it's a terrible idea and you'll miss your chance at leaving. Or she'll figure out a way to buy the library and then you'll never get to try and save it.'

'Yes, true. And part of me wants to prove I can do this before I let her in on it. Maybe I'll say I'm taking a break from Astor for now. Going to find myself a job somewhere far far away and leave it at that?'

He considers it. 'Why not tell them you're burnt out, which isn't a lie, and that you need a good solid break? Time to reflect outside of London and decide your next steps.'

'OK, good plan. I'll say I'm quitting and if they baulk at that, I'll go for the burnout angle and say I need space.'

'Perfect.' He scrubs a hand across his face. 'Maybe I'll step up to the plate. Become the new you.' Doubt leeches from every word. It's as though he knows they won't even bother to hear him out. Teddy made a few mistakes in his twenties, mostly because there was no supervision, no one holding him account-able and he had money to burn – always a bad combination. They've been so busy with Astor they haven't noticed he's settled down, got himself back on track and hasn't touched a drop of booze in six months. 'Even though they still say I'm *bad for optics*.' He shrugs.

Really, he's no different to many of our family friends' progeny who did the same but now hold down successful jobs or at least play the part.

Teddy has charisma in spades and given the chance he could run the company better than I ever could because his heart would be in it. He's ambitious and has a head for numbers whilst I'm the daydreamer who lives and breathes books. This escape might just be the making of me, but could it also lead Teddy in the right direction?

'I can see you in a suit,' I say. 'Heading up the board, making changes.'

A blush creeps up his cheeks and hope reflects in his eyes. Too soon it fades. 'They'll never allow it. But let's show them that you're not their little solider anymore, eh? That you can use that big ol' brain in your head to save that backwater library.'

'You're a snob. But thanks, Teddy.'

Just who will the new me be? Will I be brave enough to pull it off?

*

A few short weeks later, I get an email about doing a Zoom interview for the librarian position. I tie my hair tightly back, wash my make-up off and wear some glasses so I don't look recognisable as me. When the call comes through, I take a steadying breath. I can do this! My whole future hinges on this interview.

On screen the face of a woman appears. She's looking down, shuffling paperwork.

'Hi! I'm Elodie.'

She looks up surprised. 'Sorry, Elodie I'm trying to do two jobs at once here, just like normal!'

While she appears harried, she seems to enjoy it.

'So I'll get to right to the point. Willow Grove library is in a dire position. There are just not enough members using it to warrant sinking more money into it. We have to be sensible about this, as sad as it would be to lose the library. It's not only new stock they need, it's building repairs and a whole host of other incidentals that tally up pretty quickly.'

'I understand,' I say as my pulse beats fast knowing this is going to be an uphill battle for whoever gets the librarian position. 'But can you place a price on a child who uses the library, a child who doesn't have access to books at home? What if that child, who used Willow Grove library, grew up to be the person who cured cancer? Wouldn't that be worth it then?' I ball my hands hoping I haven't gone too far.

'Well, Elodie, when you put it that way . . .'

'Sorry, I'm passionate about books being accessible to everyone, especially children. If we can introduce them to literature early on, the world is their oyster. They'll always have a friend waiting on their shelves to combat loneliness. Then there's the older members who use the library as a meeting place. If we take that away, where will they go? There's just so many reasons we need to save the library, and for me money is not one of them, although I understand the importance of not throwing more into a sinking ship. I believe I can turn the tide, if you will. If you gave me a chance to prove it, I think Willow Grove library could have a whole new beginning, a second chance.'

She raises a brow. 'Well, I was going to say you were hired

after the price on a child thing, but now you're doubly hired. When can you start?'

'Is next week too soon?' I consult my calendar, 'Monday 8th of August work for you?'

She grins. 'I was hoping you'd say that.'

*

I paste on a smile as I video-call my parents. I've timed it just right, so they only have a few minutes before they head off to a charity event hosted by their business rivals, Mogul Media. The families war like the Montagues and Capulets, without the star-crossed lovers part, but they keep up appearances by attending each other's parties as if nothing is amiss.

My father's face pops up on screen as he takes a seat at Mother's dressing table. 'Ellie, darling, to what do we owe this mid-week honour?'

'Just wanted to run something by you both – is Mum around?'

He turns and calls for her, and soon the great Dorothea Astor sashays over in a glittery slinky silver gown. I have to hand it to my mother, she looks like a million dollars, with a figure meticulously honed by a celebrity personal trainer who makes home calls twice a day. Mum keeps sending her to my townhouse in the hopes I'll start too, but I've seen how her torturous sessions play out and want no part in it. Mum is strict with her diet and wellbeing, living mainly on fresh air and green tea, but I'm built for comfort not calorie counting. Give me a creamy round of camembert and a classic romcom and I'm set. 'Ellie, how are you, darling? Why do you look so peaky?'

'You're right, Mother. I *am* a little peaky. There's never time to soak up the sun. I'm always at work or at a function *for* work. To be honest, I'm burnt out and in need of a bit of a life overhaul.' Her eyes narrow but I press on. 'My job at Astor, it's not fulfilling, it's not sparking any joy—'

'Oh, darling, don't start with that mumbo jumbo again. You sound like an ungrateful brat.' She rolls her heavily made-up eyes and studies her fingernails. I'm losing her as quick as that. When it comes to attention spans, Mother's is shorter than most, especially when I'm complaining. 'Go on a shopping spree – that usually sparks joy for me.'

'No, that's not my thing,' I hurry on, as my father stands up and wanders to the mirror to fidget with his lapels. 'If you could listen for a couple of minutes, please,' I say, voice brisk. They lazily swing their gazes back to the screen. 'I'm officially handing in my notice for Astor, effective immediately. You can use my built-up time in lieu for my notice period. I'm done. I need to start living life on my own terms.' I brace and try not to avert my eyes from her surprised gaze. She's downright intimidating when she wants to be, but that's the ace up her sleeve and I won't let her win this time. Deep down I know my mother wants the best for me; it's just that we see my future differently.

'And throw all your hard work away on a whim?' my mother says, her false lashes fluttering and giving her a slightly unhinged look.

'I've told you so many times I want to leave.' My resolve begins to falter so I remind myself what's at risk here. *A town without books.*

There's a ten-second silence. It drags on and on. 'You're not thinking straight,' my father says, shaking his head. 'Soon you'll take over Astor. You'll be in charge of it all. And we need you firing on all cylinders.'

I interrupt lest I'm subjected to some metaphor about pistons and engines. 'That's just the thing, Dad, I don't *want* to take over. I never have. Why not give Teddy a chance to prove himself? He's much better suited for the role.'

'Teddy?' My father guffaws. 'I hardly think so. That boy is nocturnal for a start. He's a liability. The amount of money we've had to spend keeping his exploits out of our competitors' papers – it's a disgrace!'

I manage to keep my temper in check. 'Do you ever think he might've been trying to get your attention? Why not give him a chance?'

My mother tuts and gives me a saccharine smile. 'Maybe you *do* need a holiday, darling. Clearly you can't think straight when you're overwhelmed and in need of a bit of R&R. Your father and I should have thought of this sooner. Not everyone can handle the pace we set, and that's understandable. Why not take a rejuvenating break and then we can meet and discuss this once you're refreshed?'

My shoulders slump. It's feels like I'm in the mafia at times! But I rally. I will not be controlled anymore. I deserve to decide my own fate even if I fail miserably.

'I'm sure we can come to an agreement that suits us all,' my dad says quickly while Mother and I commit to a stare-off. I won't be cowed, not this time. 'You *love* Astor News but we're willing to give you some time to clear your head. How about taking two weeks' holiday, Ellie?'

'No, you're not listening. This time I mean it.' I give them a sad smile. 'Enjoy your evening.' I shut the laptop on their disappointed faces. There's no other way to do it, except cut ties and leave and hope that they give Teddy a chance.

Later that night I pen a letter for them:

Dear Mum and Dad,

I'm sorry that things had to be this way and my most fervent wish was that you'd listen and let me go. Having my life orchestrated is getting me down. It's like being trapped in a very exotic cage and some days I find it hard to catch my breath. To get out of bed and put one foot in front of the other. I want to find out who I am and what I aspire to be.

I'm proud of how well you've built Astor and I know you've made sacrifices in order to do that, but I'm not the same as you. I want different things. As you know, I don't want to take over the helm. You've got Teddy who's itching to be part of the company if only you'll let him show you. Did you know he's been sober for six months? That he follows every move the company makes? He's more than up to speed and he'd be an asset if only you'd let him in. I'll be out of contact for a while, and I ask you to respect my choice. I've left my Astor mobile phone with Teddy. I'll check in when I can.

All my love,

Ellie

Chapter 4

The little town of Willow Grove is as picture-postcard perfect as I remember it. Weeping willow trees throw shade along the narrow roads, while pops of colourful flowers line the edges.

There's no time to meander – today is day one of my very new life! I just have to remember to introduce myself as Elodie Halifax. I'm out of practice using my real name, which seems as absurd as going under cover for a new job!

With my freshly dyed brunette locks, I've altered my appearance so much even I'm surprised when I see my reflection, so I'm sure that no one will recognise me.

Unless they're really into watching ribbon-cutting ceremonies, I should be safe.

As I turn the corner the library comes into view. It's still the same little ramshackle building that leans to the left as if burly weather has battered it sideways over its long and lustrous life. It's as cute as a button, despite the early signs of dilapidation. Roof shingles need replacing and a few windows need fresh glass. Most likely there hasn't been enough in the coffers to maintain it properly but that will have to be a priority for safety reasons.

By the front door I'm momentarily startled when I see

movement among a cluster of plastic bags. A dishevelled head appears, belonging to a man with a long mane of hair and a scraggly beard. He shoots me an apprehensive look, his eyes settling on my name badge.

'I'm going, I'm going,' he says and rolls up a frayed sleeping bag and quickly gathers the rest of his things. Before I can say a word, he limps off, as if every step is a painful one. Why is he sleeping rough like this?

I run a few steps after him. 'Hey, wait. What's with the rush to leave? I'm Elli . . . Elodie.'

The man stops and turns back to me, his eyes full of suspicion. 'I'm Harry. Apparently, I make the place look untidy.'

Untidy? His words are laced with hurt. I have to get to the bottom of this. 'How about we share a pot of tea? I've got biscuits,' I say and pat my handbag. 'I'd prefer not to eat them alone.'

'Thanks, miss, but the librarian's banned me. I'm not to step foot inside.'

Libraries are the last refuge, a place where everyone is welcome, where it doesn't cost anything to sit, read and keep warm. A place where you can find a friend in literature, or a librarian, and this man has been turned away simply because of his homelessness? Well, not on my watch.

'I'm in charge now and you're welcome here anytime. In fact, I insist you come in out of the cold morning air and share a pot of tea with me. These biscuits aren't going to eat themselves and, between us, I can see I'm going to be doing a lot of biscuit eating in this new job so you'd be doing me a favour if you helped me out with that.'

A dubious look crosses his face but he follows me inside slowly, as if he doesn't trust me. 'Pop your things in one of the lockers if you want to keep them safe and dry,' I say, noticing them to the left of the entrance. I try and recall the layout of the library from my visits as a student. From the looks of it, nothing much has changed including the carpets and curtains. It's like a time capsule and is quite a shock to the system. I'd have thought there'd be some improvements since I was a student, but it doesn't appear so. Even the computers are the old boxy type that take up most of the desk. Looks like I'm going to have to bring this place kicking and screaming into the present in terms of technology.

I know there's bathroom and shower facilities because the building formerly housed its librarians many moons ago. Would Harry use them if he was invited to or would he take offence at me suggesting such a thing? I want him to feel welcome, and I bet he'd like a long, hot shower after being out in the cold all night.

I hunt around behind the main desk, searching for a towel, but only manage to find some kind of chamois. Will that do? Maybe Harry has his own towel?

'Harry, I'm just trying to acquaint myself with the layout here and as soon as I find the kitchen I'll pop the kettle on. In the meantime, I found this poor excuse for a towel and I want you to know you can use the bathroom facilities any time if you need to warm yourself up. I haven't checked them out yet, so please let me know if they're not up to scratch.'

Tears spring to his rheumy eyes and he struggles to speak, just gives me a curt nod.

'Take your time. I'll get the tea on the go.'

As he limps off, another man appears. This one is dashing in a romance novel kind of way, with bright blue eyes and shiny white teeth, model handsome, as if he's just stepped off the cover of a magazine. 'I saw what you did,' he says and flashes a bright smile.

'Oh?' Somehow this stranger manages to dazzle me just by staring into my eyes, like he knows all my secrets. I remind myself to tread carefully.

'For Harry,' he says.

'Showed a small amount of courtesy? It was nothing.' I wave him away and pretend to be busy rifling through paperwork on the desk. The presence of this man has unnerved me for some inexplicable reason. He's familiar but I can't place why. What if he knows me as Ellie Astor and the game is up already? I talk myself down. It's first-day jitters. Of course he doesn't know me! And if he does, me acting strangely will be a dead giveaway, so I force myself to look up and stare right into his eyes. He's boy-next-door beautiful. The kind of guy who probably breaks a lot of hearts without even knowing it.

'It shows what kind of person you are.' He throws me another disarming smile. 'I'm Finn Ford, a reporter from the *Chronicle*. I'm hoping to do a story about you and how you plan to save the library.'

Ah, the hot journalist is the one who wrote the article that led me here! That's why he seems so familiar: his picture was next to his byline. My shoulders unknit. 'Thanks for the offer. I'll have a think about what I want to do and let you know when I come up with a solid plan to save the library.' I need to keep my face out of the papers so I'll have to spin it in such a way to Finn Ford (a reporter name if ever there was one!) that it's believable. I'll explain that I want the story to be purely about the library and how we aim to increase memberships.

'I've also been sent by the welcoming committee . . .'

I tilt my head. 'Oh, yeah?' I say, as a flirty smile plays at his lips. 'How many on the committee?'

'Just me so far.'

'Right.' I laugh, and feel my cheeks blush. I'm not the blushing sort, so this gives me pause. Just what magical powers does this man have? I bet every woman in town has a crush on him.

'If you're free on Friday the . . . welcoming committee would like to give you a tour around town culminating in dinner at one of its finest establishments. What do you say?'

I wait a beat and consider his offer. 'I'd hate to let down the welcoming committee after they've gone to so much trouble.' Who knew I could flirt like this? Shouldn't I be keeping a low profile . . . ?

'It would be cruel.'

We lock eyes again and I'm quite lost for words, which doesn't happen to me very often. There's a spark between us, and for just a moment I imagine what it could lead to, until I remember that beginning a relationship under false pretences wouldn't be very clever. It's not like I'm lying about who I am per se, it's more that I'm glossing over the truth. *Get a hold of yourself, Ellie, it's only dinner!*

He surveys me as if I'm a prize. I don't know quite where to look or what to say. 'I feel like we've met before,' he says.

'I bet you say that to all the librarians.' I shouldn't have said yes to dinner! My smile stiffens and I fight the urge to cover my nerves with inane chatter. If anyone is going to find me out, it'll be a nosy reporter and I'm already letting my guard down like a fool. I'm hoping I can save the library and *then* tell my parents what I've managed to do, thus proving to them this new life is the right course for me. If I mess it up in the first week I'll be red-faced and back at Astor with no chance of change on the horizon.

A red-headed girl lopes through the entrance, bag slung over her shoulder. 'Elodie?' she asks.

I breathe a sigh of relief that our exchange is interrupted so I don't put my foot in my mouth. 'You must be Maisie.' My one and only employee at Willow Grove library. Staff numbers were cut over the last few years, leaving only a duo to run the place. Maisie looks younger than I imagined with a bright shiny complexion as if she's fresh out of high school.

Finn clears his throat. 'I'll leave you two to get acquainted and I'll see you Friday, Elodie.' We shake hands and I feel a spark shoot through me. What is this? I'm used to meeting men, suave and sophisticated types that do absolutely zero for me, but Finn radiates a certain home-grown charm that is quite disarming. I have to tamp down the paranoia that I'm going to be found out or I'll never get anything accomplished.

'Friday it is,' I say and turn back to Maisie, trying hard to remember what I'm here for. I can't be distracted by the first guy who shoots a flirty smile my way, and yet . . .

'Right,' I say, giving my full attention to Maisie. 'It's so lovely to finally meet you. Let's have a sit-down. You can fill me in on what I need to know and we can make a plan about how we're to save these hallowed old halls.' There's still no sign of Harry but I keep an eye out so we can share the tea and biscuits I promised.

We head to the office. There are built-in Formica desks in Sixties brown and beige, with carpet to match. A fusty odour hangs in the air – nothing a good scented candle can't eradicate for now.

'It's great we get to save this place together, Maisie.' I take my notepad from my bag waiting for her reply, which doesn't come. I glance up at her, but she's staring at the door as if she's lost in thought. 'Tell me a little bit about the library. Why do you think memberships are dwindling?'

With her arms folded across her chest defensively, it almost appears as if I've inadvertently done something to upset her. We've been emailing back and forth since I got the position and while her emails have always been short and to the point, I figured that was because she was single-handedly running this place and too busy for small talk.

'Maisie?' I prompt.

She drags her eyes back to me. 'It's pretty obvious. There's no new stock; there's no money to buy new stock so why would anyone bother coming here?'

Her attitude comes across as defeatist, but it could be she's lost her enthusiasm working in a library that's flailing. I can understand how it feels. I need to do my best to inspire her.

'OK, that's good to know. Our first priority will be to sort the finances and see if there's a surplus that we can use for some new stock.' It strikes me that I could easily get stock from Astor returns without my mother knowing, but that would be cheating – I need to do this on my own and the library has to be able to stand on its own two feet. 'We need exactly 507 new members to be eligible to apply for funding. Yes, it's daunting, but we can do it if we have a solid plan to work towards.'

'It may as well be five thousand.'

With a lift of my brow, I say, 'Let's be grateful it's not.' I consult my notes. 'What about book clubs. Do we have collections to cover a group?'

'We don't have a book club.' She surveys her nails and looks downright bored.

'Let's make one then. Use our socials to invite locals to join the library and the book club.' If we can get a buzz happening early, surely people will be intrigued as to what's to come for their community library?

'Socials?'

Maisie is young, surely she knows what socials are? 'Social media. Doesn't Willow Grove library have social media pages to help spread the word about events and happenings?'

'No,' she guffaws. 'It's a *library* not a social club.'

Talk about living in the Dark Ages. No wonder the place is floundering. 'Well, that's something we can easily remedy. To get enough memberships in time we're going to need to offer all sorts of things to get people through the door. First up, I'd like you to start by making a Facebook, Twitter, and Instagram page. You could try TikTok but I'm not too familiar with that one myself. There's a subcommunity on there called BookTok . . .' Maisie yawns. Maybe I'm overloading her? I'm used to long meetings at Astor going over key points efficiently in an effort to get everyone up to speed so they can continue the workday. 'Anyway, we can work out our marketing plan once that's all up and running. Are there any local authors whose books we stock? We can invite them for an author talk and make a real event of it to kick things off.'

'Not that I know of.' Maisie plucks at the hem of her skirt, a tired expression on her features.

I frown and make a note to research the local area and see what creatives lurk among us.

'OK, how about kids' reading time? Rhyme time? Do we have an allocated day?'

'We don't offer that.'

'Let's target that next. We'll make a library schedule and timetable these. You can read to the children and we can also offer a rhyme time session for the littlies. Anything we can do that will help us get more members to join will be beneficial.'

'I'm not much of a public speaker.'

I take a deep breath. So far Maisie is coming across as a little negative and slightly jaded. Could it be nerves or the fact she's worried she won't have a job if things keep going the way they are? I give her some leeway. It's the first day after all and maybe she is suffering a bit of job ennui. It's not hard to see why with the state of the library. Once we get some systems in place she should spark up.

'I understand, but I'm sure you'll be OK. I can do the first session if you like and you'll see how fun it is. It's all about doing the silly voices and engaging the children in the story.' This is the stuff I've always wanted to do! Make the library a fun place for everyone. Interact with members and enjoy books. 'Our youngest bookworms are the most important as they'll be members for decades and we get to help foster a love of reading early. Besides, who doesn't love children's books?' Some of my best memories are my nannies reading to me and Teddy from a young age. Those magical, mystical places we escaped to from the safety of our beds, the nocturnal adventures we shared with Peter Pan, or traversing the countryside with Mole, Rat, Toad and Badger from *Wind in the Willows*. Those stories opened my imagination and I hope we can do the same for our littlest library members too.

'OK, but I don't fancy reading aloud. I'm more of a behind-the-scenes person.'

I do understand. If Maisie isn't used to being in the spotlight, then it's unfair of me to force her. But I'm sure when she sees how much fun the children have, she'll change her mind. 'Well, let's advertise it and we can go from there.' I scroll down my notes, looking for the easiest things to target first.

'What's he doing in here?' she says, her voice shrill. I turn to see Harry walking back from the bathroom. 'He knows he's not allowed in here and it looks as if he's gone and bloody had a shower!'

'Maisie, keep your voice down!' A blush creeps up my cheeks and I only hope he hasn't heard her. 'I invited him in and told him he could use the facilities.'

'What, why? That's a huge mistake,' she snaps. 'You'll have members leaving in droves if Homeless Harry is wandering about in here.'

I look at her sharply. 'Did you just call him Homeless Harry?'

She shrugs. 'That's his name.'

I bristle. 'His name is *Harry*. And it's not appropriate to call him anything other than that. Everyone is welcome here.' Have I truly stepped back in time when it was the norm to be so prejudicial?

Maisie crosses her arms tighter as if she's holding herself in check. 'You're not going to get many new memberships with an attitude like that.'

What on earth? 'Maisie, I'll let that go since it's my first day, but please adjust your way of thinking. Like I said, *everyone* is welcome here. Some people need our help more than others.' We've got to make miracles happen and I'd hoped when I arrived I'd be met by someone full of enthusiasm, keen to save their own job, but if anything it's the opposite. Targeting Harry is not on and I won't allow that sort of talk under this roof.

Maisie *will* settle into a new routine and we *will* save this library. It's just going to take a little more work than expected. But first, I have a very special tea date. I leave Maisie sulking and find the kitchen. It can best be described as an eyesore but it looks clean enough. I find the kettle and flick it on and search for some cups. Harry limps back, bags in hand, looking fresh-faced with rosy cheeks from the warmth of the shower.

'Just in time,' I say, bringing the tea things to the common area. As I pour, I surreptitiously steal a glance at Harry, wondering what his story is and how he ended up sleeping rough. I wish I had something more substantial than biscuits to offer him. Under his many layers, he's reed-thin and I'd bet he hasn't had a decent hot meal in ages.

Harry takes the proffered tea, but fidgets and keeps looking over his shoulder as if the previous librarian is about to storm in and kick him out. How to put him at ease?

'So, as I said, I'm new to Willow Grove and I'm going to save the library from closure. I'll need as much help as I can get and you look like just the man for the job.' If anything, Maisie has made me even more determined. This place needs a shake-up – that's obvious.

'Me?' he says, his voice incredulous.

'Yes, you, Harry! Why not you? Can you tell me a little bit about Willow Grove and why you think the library memberships are dwindling?'

He shifts in his seat as if he's not totally comfortable opening up.

I try again, 'Come on, Harry. I need an insider's opinion, someone who's not going to sugar-coat the truth, and you look like a straight shooter to me.'

'Do I?' He gives me a wobbly smile. 'Well here goes, and this is just my take . . . The previous librarian was a bit of a dictator to be honest, not only to me, but to everyone. Talk about rules! She was here for ten long years, and she scared people off. The librarian before her was this whimsical gentle soul.' As he reminisces, I picture the librarian I knew when I visited from boarding school, whose personality was more ethereal book nymph. Must have been a culture shock for locals when she was replaced by Agnes. 'Delilah moved on to greener pastures and Agnes took over. Don't get me wrong, Agnes tried her best, but she didn't have the people skills.' That reminds me of Maisie, but I keep my opinions to myself.

We're off and running! Harry settles into his story and tells me all about the little town I've come to live in . . .

Chapter 5

The next morning, I arrive at the library half an hour early. There's no sign of Harry and I only hope it doesn't mean Maisie's scared him off. I have a quick walk around but can't find him or his belongings. Perhaps he moves around a bit, depending on the weather? If he doesn't turn up at some point today, I'll make some discreet enquiries. I'd hate to think my presence has made him uproot his life.

There's much to be done and I'm filled with energy at the thought of my new job and sparkly new life. Day one had been successful, in that I got to know the place through Harry's observations and I made a rough plan with Maisie, and despite her sulky demeanour she managed to get our social media pages started and already we have a steady stream of followers liking our various pages.

The main problem is we have no new stock, but we can't apply for the funding grant until we've recruited 507 new members. It's the ultimate Catch-22! It's August already and the latest we can submit the paperwork is October so we need to get those numbers ticking over as a matter of haste.

I boot up the old computer, which takes an age to start. Eventually I'm in and I spend the next little while studying the finances. It occurs to me that I have a wealth of experience with the fiscal side of things thanks to my mother, who obsesses over every pound. I pore over the outgoings looking for anything that can be cut back. From the looks of it, the bookwork has been meticulously kept but it's disheartening to see there's not a spare penny to be found no matter how hard I search.

The library is dangerously in the red. What did I expect though? That I'd find a bag full of money that Agnes had put away for a rainy day? As I dig deeper into the money trail, I see they haven't purchased new books in years. With wages and other outgoings there's been nothing left. We need the funding as a matter of urgency, or this place will continue to sink into bad debt that will be impossible to recover from. I sympathise with Agnes Bitterweather: she really had her hands full trying to balance these books.

My phone beeps with a text and I'm happy to see it's from Teddy. Just the distraction I need.

Puppet masters not too happy to find you MIA. Guess they didn't take you seriously, but are we surprised? I told them you're in an ashram in India seeking enlightenment. Namaste.

Will they buy the ashram idea?

Leaving my Astor mobile phone at home has been a weight off my shoulders. If I'd taken it my parents would be calling me every five minutes and my resolve might have crumbled already. A clean break was needed, and it's been bliss having a phone that only Teddy knows the number to so far.

I hit reply: *Tell them I'm meditating and searching for enlightenment, which might take some time as I have a lot of past lives to work through. Have they let you return to Astor?*

A few moments later another text appears: *Not back at*

Astor yet, but I'm working on it. There's a big shiny office overlooking the Gherkin with my name all over it. Have snuck in for a recon and honestly, Elodie, what were you thinking with those chairs? Ergonomic or not, they're utterly hideous.

I laugh. They are the worlds ugliest chairs. *Oh dear brother, as if I get to choose important things like office furniture! That was Mum, who I'm sure purchased them because they're the only chair that make you want to stand rather than sit ever again! They were frightfully expensive, and absolutely useless in practical terms. Make a nice coat rack, maybe?*

Teddy replies: *Make good firewood, more like. Enjoy your day and keep me in the loop with what's going on in Snoresville.*

The front door opens and Harry peers in.

'Harry!' I say brightly, so relieved to see him back. 'I was worried when I didn't see you here earlier this morning.'

'The wind was howling through the eaves, so I had to move. Didn't get a wink of sleep last night.' Fatigue is written all over his features. I question how often he gets a decent night's rest. While the days are bright and summery, the nights have been cool.

'I'm sorry to hear that. It certainly was a windy night. You look like you were blown away.' Harry's long mane of hair stands up in places as if the wind took hold of him and didn't let go. 'If you want to stash your things in the locker go right ahead or put your feet up in one of the cubicles – you're more than welcome.'

'Thanks, Elodie. I'm OK. But I wouldn't mind offloading these bags for a bit.'

Harry stores his belongings while I go to the shower facilities and deposit some goodies for him that I bought at the local supermarket this morning. When I return, I take a container from my bag and hand it to him. 'I'm not used to cooking for one—' *or at all!* '—and I made far too much so I thought you might like to try this and tell me what it's missing? I'm new to cooking, and I'm not sure I'm any good at it.' My first attempt at making a stir-fry went well, if you don't count the burn on my little finger and the fact the onions are on the wrong side of charred.

'Oh? New to cooking?'

'Yeah, I'm an expert on frozen meals, but cooking from scratch, not so much.' Lies, lies, lies. I've never had a frozen meal in my entire life, but Harry doesn't need to know that. I feel like you haven't lived unless you've tried a frozen pizza and I plan to do a lot of real-life living while I've got the chance.

'Sure, I can tell you what I think but I'm no expert either.'

'Two heads are better than one. I've got enough cookbooks in here to figure out what to cook next.' Although by the looks of the stock, I'll be cooking a lot of Crockpot dishes from the Seventies. 'What's your favourite food?'

'Beef and Guinness pie,' he says. 'Served with a side of mushy peas.'

'Ooh, now that sounds like something I can get behind. How hard can pastry be?'

'Can't be too hard.'

'I'll attempt it over the weekend and then you can let me know what you think. It'll be a good motivator for me so I don't live on cereal and frozen pizza.' My mother would keel over if she heard me talk like this but I delighted in serving myself a big bowl of Cheerios this morning for breakfast, instead of the green power shake I usually have.

'Sounds good to me.'

'Microwave's in the kitchen,' I say. 'Help yourself.'

'I'll whack the kettle on too?'

'I could murder a cup of tea.'

'Do you mind if I take a quick shower first?'

'Go for it. And for future reference you never need to ask – that's what they're there for.' I smile as he limps away, hoping when he finds the small toiletry pack and big fluffy towels I left in there, that he knows they're for him.

I'm at the dinosaur-aged computer, trying to magic up money, when Harry returns, tears in his rheumy eyes. 'What's wrong?'

'You put all that smelly stuff in there for me?'

I laugh, taking it he means the body products. 'I did. Sorry if you don't want to smell like a strawberry. It was either that or peach.'

'I don't mind smelling like a strawberry.' He grins through tears. 'Aside from Finn, you're the only person I've spoken to in years.'

Years? I take a moment to swallow the lump in my throat. 'Why?'

He shrugs and his lip wobbles ever so slightly. 'I'm invisible to them. They pretend they can't see me, so they don't have to wonder how I got to be living like this. Then they don't have to care, I suppose. Sometimes, I feel like a ghost, hovering on the edges of society, forgotten, put out with the rubbish.'

I debate what to say, what to ask, then figure Harry seems comfortable sharing with me so far. 'Why are you homeless, Harry? Where's your family?'

Harry casts his eyes to the floor and I know whatever his

story is, he's not quite ready to share it with me just yet. 'It's . . . it's still so hard to talk about.'

'I understand. If you ever want to talk, I'm here.'

'Thanks, Elodie. Forgive an old man his tears.' He wanders away, head down, and my heart is heavy at the thought of what Harry's been through, made worse by becoming an outsider in what seems like a tight-knit community. It saddens me that, aside from reporter Finn, no one has made an effort to befriend Harry or offer any assistance. Why?

Chapter 6

Later that day, I start cataloguing our stock. Reluctantly I remove damaged books, those with loose pages and torn covers, and some that are inexplicably water damaged. Does the roof leak? Hard to tell when the lighting in the library is dim at best. The old fluorescent tubes lights are mottled and yellowed with age. But the dimness makes the space warm and comforting so I'm loath to change it. While we don't have a lot of new stock we do have a huge range of classics still in good shape. Some with beautiful hardbound covers with gold lettering. They deserve to be on show in all their glory, so I take them and make a display table. I go to the office and print a sign – *Classics never go out of style!* – and laminate it before returning and putting it front and centre on the table.

Once that's done, I go back to removing damaged books, and I also make a pile of tomes that are out of vogue, Seventies and Eighties style, that haven't aged well and probably won't be borrowed in a hurry. I set them up on a table by the front door with a sign advertising the prices – a fire sale of sorts – and even though it'll only be pocket change, every pound will be put to good use and hopefully these old books will find a happy home and be read again.

I head back and continue to the shelves on the other side and almost bump into Maisie who sits with her feet up on a chair, her head lolling backwards. Is she sleeping?

I prod her shoulder and she snorts as she comes to. 'Whaaat?'

Maisie is really grinding my gears. 'Can you nap on your own time?'

She rubs at her red-rimmed eyes. Has she been crying or is it from being in a deep slumber in the middle of a workday? 'Sorry, I didn't mean to. I was just watching you do things in your strange new way, and it got me thinking about how it was before you came and how much things have changed and I just . . . fell asleep. It's all a bit much some days.'

Is Maisie struggling with the thought of losing her job? Maybe that's what's driving her lack of enthusiasm. Or perhaps she misses her former boss Agnes Bitterweather, who didn't enforce many jobs around the place by the look of it. I try to understand Maisie's motivations but come up blank because those scenarios just don't make sense to me. Shouldn't that be what motivates her? 'Can you make a start sorting out the children's books so we can decorate an area for them ahead of the rhyme time sessions?'

Maisie narrows her eyes. 'You're doing things so differently to how they've always been done. Even the way you catalogue books is strange. Where did you work before?' She's not going to let this go. And I don't know if it's because I've caught her skiving off or if she's truly suspicious of me.

'I've worked all over the place and I'm changing things because the old ways didn't work. That's not me having a go at the way Agnes did things, not at all. I can see from an accounts perspective she tried lots of things to make this place solvent.

That's why we really have to shine – really make a splash to remind the locals the library is here and can be built up again into whatever they need it to be. A refuge for some, community for others, a place to lock out the world for a while with a book in hand. We're not here simply to lend books; it's so much more than that.' I soften my tone, trying to appeal to her. 'We've only got until October 21st to submit the paperwork for more funding. That's not even three months away, Maisie. I really, really need your help to make this happen. And before we get to that stage, we have to get five hundred and—'

'October 21st is a Friday,' a little voice says, interrupting me. Probably a good thing in case Maisie digs in, asking about where I've come from, which would be akin to Mars in her eyes.

I turn to the voice. 'Good guess,' I say to the golden-haired boy with a cherubic face.

'It's not a guess.'

'Oh?' I say, confused.

'Ask me another date. Go on.' He motions with his hand for me to get on with it.

'Umm,' I say, taken aback. With his bright blue-eyed gaze, he stares just past me, as if looking over my shoulder. 'OK, what about November 10th?'

'That's a Thursday.'

I cock my head and take my mobile from my pocket and check both dates. Friday and Thursday. 'Could be a lucky guess,' I say. 'What about the following year? January 9th.'

He grins and stands on tiptoes, rocking back and forth. 'Easy, Monday.'

We zigzag from years ago to years ahead and he gets every day correct. 'Huh. What's your name?'

'Alfie.'

He grins, as if he knows how impressed I am with his extraordinary skills. 'You're a little bit clever, Alfie. Have you got a photographic memory or something?'

He shakes his head. 'I can calendar count. My mum says it's my superpower, which makes up for the fact I have no filter. Your hair looks all wrong on you. You'd look better with yellow hair.'

His frankness provokes a stunned laugh. He's right – I do look a lot better with my natural blonde hair. The dark brunette washes me out, but I can't tell him that. 'I'll take that under consideration,' I say.

With a shrug, he says, 'It's your life.' He turns to Maisie. 'Why're you back to buying the cheap biscuits again? They're full of sugar and my mum says *a minute on the lips a lifetime on the hips*, and I want to be straight up and down when I'm older, not a barrel like my *deadbeat dad* who always ate the cheap biscuits before he *ran off with his floozy*.'

I'm stunned silent as laughter threatens to burst out. I'm guessing little Alfie is copying verbatim what he's heard his mum say when she hasn't realised he's in earshot. I bet she has her hands full trying to explain him away when he throws her under the bus like that in his own sweet style.

Maisie grins, she actually grins, and it lights up her pretty face. 'Sorry, Alfie. I haven't had a lot of spare time, is all. Things have been a bit . . . all over the place. I promise I'll bring in better biscuits next week, OK?'

'*Next week!*' he says, incensed.

I bite back laughter. He's a lovely, animated little boy, full of pluck.

'You're very forthright for a boy of . . . ?' I ask.

'Eleven and I'm autistic,' he says with a grin.

'Aha, another superpower,' I say. 'Why aren't you in school today?'

'Mum home-schools me, because there's been too many . . .' he makes air quotes '. . . *incidents* at school. You know mainstream, those kids can be *brutal*. My mum says they *just don't appreciate how special I am*. And the teachers, they try but they don't understand that the kids act one way in front of them and another way when I'm on the playground by myself. Probably because they're old and forget what it's like to be a kid. But that's not the only problem! Once on an excursion my teacher, Miss Macey, told us to keep our eyes peeled for the museum, but how would peeling our eyes help us see? And isn't that a bit *drastic*?

'I told my mum and she said it's just an expression but Mum wasn't there, was she? I couldn't trust Miss Macey after that – and she's always going on about the eye contact thing, too. "Look at me when you're addressing me, Alfie!" Yeah, because she wants to peel my eyes! Mum didn't like it when I told the teaching assistant that she said he had *small-man syndrome*. She said I was to keep that private.'

He throws his hands up as if he's bamboozled by the rules. 'There was a lot of that at school and the kids *bullied me* but Mum says it's only because they're jealous but it didn't seem like they were jealous, it just seemed like they were mean. My mum can be feisty though and she said *enough was enough* and I was not to be treated in that way anymore, so when I left I told the mean kids that Mum reckons *they've got bad manners and have been raised wrong and that's why they're so nasty*. They didn't like that. Mum said it's a truth bomb. I don't even want to get into that – how *can* it be a bomb?

'Before I left for good I told Miss Macey that her eyebrows were like two caterpillars fighting it out and that I found it very distracting. And then Mum said *it helps to think before you speak* and *some things are better left unsaid*, but that makes no sense whatsoever. Mum always says things that make no sense and I tell her so, but she reckons I'm too literal. Can you be too literal though? And if so, why?'

I try and process it all. 'There's a lot to unpack there, Alfie. But it sounds like you're enjoying being home-schooled and if that means you get to come to the library a lot then we need to figure out what kinds of books you like reading so we can order some in for you. What do you think about that?'

Alfie taps his chin as he considers it. 'New books would be helpful. I like sharks. Or basically any apex predator. Do you know that . . .' and he goes off on a tangent about every shark species he knows, which seems to be a lot. As he speaks his words gather momentum and soon my head pounds as I try to process it all and find the space to reply.

'OK, sharks, got it. I can make a start with that information. Anything else you'd like us to do to help with your schooling?'

'Well, one thing that would make a huge difference is if you managed to lose the boiled cabbage odour that hangs around the history section. I don't know what it is, but it's pungent and I *hate* searching for books there. I have a highly developed sense of smell but Mum doesn't listen to a word I say and makes me search for them anyway and the whole time I just want to gag. Can you fix that?'

I laugh. 'I have noticed it myself.' The scent is hard to

pinpoint but I'm presuming it's something foul that's soaked into the carpet at some point back in 1987. 'I'll see about having the carpets steam cleaned. Would that help?' My first week's pay looks like it's going to be spent already and I only have a slight wobble when I remember I have things like rent and bills to contend with now too. But who can resist this pint-sized polymath?

He rocks back and forth, as if considering my offer. 'It would but tell them not to use those fake flowery-smelling cleaners. I hate that smell. It's like they're just trying to mask the boiled cabbage with roses and no one is fooled by that.'

I take my pad from my pocket and make a note, so I don't let down our littlest library member. 'OK, I'll ask for them to use only neutral products. How's that?' Pint-sized Alfie has managed to steal my heart even though he makes my head spin at the speed of his words.

'That should be OK. But make sure you keep an eye on them. My *deadbeat dad* was a tradesman and according to my mum *a bit slippery*, which doesn't make sense since he has all this hair even on his *back* but be warned, is all.'

'I won't let them out of my sight. If you go look on my desk there's a biscuit tin there, but I don't know if they're up to your standards. You'll have to let me know.'

He sighs. 'Let's hope they're halfway decent. Maisie usually brings me the ones I like in exchange for leaving her alone. She doesn't like hearing about sharks for some strange reason. For an assistant librarian her knowledge about apex predators is terrible.'

Before I can say anything Maisie dashes off. 'I'll bring them tomorrow, promise!'

I grin. So there's a bit of life in Maisie yet. A woman approaches. She smiles sweetly but looks as if she could use a good night's sleep. 'Hi,' she says searching my face as if for clues on what we've been discussing. 'I'm Alfie's Mum, Jo.'

'Hi, Jo, lovely to meet you. Alfie's been telling me all about his love of sharks.'

She makes a face to imply she knows it was a long conversation. 'He's very passionate about them.'

'I can tell. We're going to order some new books in for him so he can further his studies.'

'Really? That's brilliant. Alfie will love that.'

I wave her away, just wishing I had the funds to buy every shark book ever made for the little fella. 'Is there anything else we can assist with for his schooling?'

'We're fine. It's just that . . .' Her voice peters off and she studies her nails as if she's questioning whether to speak up.

Alfie steps in. 'Everyone in town is talking about the library and the possible changes. It's all over social media too, which I'm not allowed to use because *it will rot my brain*, but Mum is allowed to for some reason – how is that fair? Mum's worried that if the library becomes a big noisy place what with the campaign to save it, I won't want to come here anymore. I don't like big noisy places. And sometimes Mum leaves me here while she runs errands because she works split shifts at the petrol station and she's *as tired as a person ever was*.'

'Alfie, that was a private conversation between you and I,' she admonishes him but it's full of love as if she's just repeating an oft-said phrase knowing Alfie will continue to air their private conversations.

'Oh, sorry.'

It sounds like this mamma is juggling a lot of balls to keep their little family going. 'I understand, and it's a tricky one as we do hope to get more people through the doors to save the library.' But this is Alfie's safe space too and we need him to be able to concentrate on his schooling and not feel overwhelmed by others. 'What about if Alfie had a dedicated space he could use? If it's too loud he can go into one of the glass-fronted cubicles, shut the door and Maisie and I could keep an eye on him? He could set it up like his own personal schoolroom and that way he wouldn't have to cart all his things here every day.'

'That would work,' Alfie says. 'I can use my noise-cancelling headphones. Show me this cubicle, so I can check out what it smells like. You might need to get the carpet cleaned in there too.'

'Alfie!' his mum says with a laugh.

'What have I done this time?' he says, blankly.

'Follow me, young man, and take your pick of the cubicles.'

Ten minutes later, Alfie's picked the cubicle next to our office and asks us to move the desk under the window so that he can still be part of the goings-on of the library but in the quiet of his own little sanctuary. 'I can live with this smell,' he declares.

'He's great,' I say to Jo as we watch him lay out his pencils neatly in an orderly row.

'Yeah,' she says and leans her head against the doorframe. 'He's such a lovely kid, but he's so lonely. I don't know if home schooling is the right move or not. Am I making it worse by removing him from that school? This is our *third* move. We can't keep going from town to town in the hopes it'll get better. But the kids, Elodie.' She shakes her head at the memory. 'They were so cruel. They mimicked him stimming, made fun of the way he talks and so many horrible things. When I approached the parents for a quiet word they didn't want a bar of it. How can he thrive in that sort of environment? How can he grow up confident when they try and push him down like that?'

It's tricky to know what to say when her words are laced with hurt for her little boy. I imagine how powerless she must have felt when being met with a brick wall from parents who should know better and care more. 'Urgh, Jo, those parents need to take a good hard look at themselves. I can see how hard it's been for you both. Removing him from that situation seems like the right move to me.' Alfie happily completes a workbook, neatly filling out each question before reading the next. 'Look at him now. He's a funny, confident, amazing little storyteller.'

'If only people could see what you see, Elodie. He's desperate for some friends but the last one he made told him to drop his iPad because the cover was indestructible, and Alfie believed him so he did it. It smashed and they all laughed at him. He was so afraid to tell me because he knew how long it took for me to save for it. How could they do that to him?'

'So you're super hesitant about him becoming close to any other kids, which is totally understandable. Surely there's a way we can introduce him to some nice kids here at the library who share the same interests as him.'

Friends. It's something the library could provide. After all, it's a meeting place. A place to discuss big ideas, like apex predators and their environment. 'Let's put our thinking caps on and see how we can make that happen for Alfie, eh?'

'You really are a miracle worker, aren't you?'

I grin. 'Well so far I've only talked the talk, let's see if I can walk the walk.' And God help me, I will move heaven and earth to make sure this family gets what they need.

Maisie calls out for me. As I turn to go Alfie gives me one last piece of advice. 'I'm not an expert on make-up. I don't know how you can stand the feel of goop on your face but think about wearing that pink stuff on your cheeks. The dark hair washes you out.'

Laughter bursts out of me again. He's such a prescient little boy and I love his lack of filter; if only everyone was so honest in such an innocent way. 'I promise I will.'

Jo just shakes her head and gives me a what-can-you-say grin.

Chapter 7

Dusk falls on Friday and I'm exhausted in the best way. I lock up and say goodbye to Harry, leaving him with a bag of goodies including fruit and drinks for the weekend before I meander slowly home. It's a warm night and I'm happy the weather is nice so Harry will be able to keep dry and hopefully sleep less fitfully with only a soft breeze blowing through.

I catalogue the week as I walk. While I've been learning on the go, I've adapted quickly and done the best I can with the resources at hand, but even better than that is I've enjoyed every second of this new bookish life. Doing things my way, to promote the love of reading – is there anything better? The workdays are so strikingly different to Astor, and while I'm still very new I fantasise about making a life here for good. It's something to dream about. Aside from having no money to sink into the library, the only other issue is Maisie and her distinct surliness.

I'm not quite sure how to handle an employee who outright disregards everything I say. Back at Astor, a person like that wouldn't last five minutes. The NDAs and employment contracts would put paid to any potential problems arising from their removal. But I don't want to be like that. I want to inspire her, make her fall in love with librarianship again, but is that even possible? I sense there's more to Maisie than she lets on. Sometimes I catch her with the saddest look on her face, staring off into the distance, lost in the ether. It's hard to know how to broach it with her prickly nature, or even if it's my place – which being a work environment it definitely isn't – but so far everyone in Willow Grove seems to blur those lines. If only I knew if I could with Maisie. Does she need someone to confide in? Hard to tell . . .

Memberships are slowly climbing: 470 to go as per the last tally before lock-up. Word is spreading but we're still an impossibly long way off our goal. Finding my feet slows efforts down, but I'm hopeful the following week will be even better as I gain confidence in my job and how to go about it. There's been no real buzz, and I know from my experience at Astor, if I want people to visit the library, I have to make a splash. A lot of noise. Something to pull people from their lives with a budget that may as well be zero. But how? It's definitely doable, I just need to drum up an idea that's out of this world.

My little thatched-roof cottage comes into view, which always provokes a smile and a warm cosy feeling. Inside, I throw my keys and handbag on the hall table and then myself in the overstuffed chair by the window, wishing I had time to press my nose in a book.

Nerves are fluttering at the impending date with Finn. The welcoming committee of *one*. If any other guy had suggested such a thing, I'd have run a mile, but Finn's different somehow. There's something downright wholesome about the man. Maybe it was that he put me at ease, and it felt more like an invitation to get to know one another with the hopes of becoming what – friends? So then is it officially a date? It certainly came across that way under the guise of a tour of Willow Grove, which I'm itching to see in more detail. There hasn't been time, except for a quick supermarket shop and a walk here and there some evenings.

My love life has been sporadic to say the least (if you don't count all the fictional men I've been infatuated with). I'm not into the rich playboys that are everywhere in London. They're all too vapid and shallow. Work colleagues were out too, because I never trusted their motivations. The dating pool invariably shrinks when you second-guess every man you meet. Being an unknown here in Willow Grove allows me to let my guard down a bit – because no one knows I'm an Astor, they can't be angling for anything in that regard – and it's the most liberating feeling. *That's* probably why I'm excited about the date with Finn, and not just because he's a bit of all right.

There's no time to ruminate. I throw myself in the shower and then dress casually in jeans and a tee. I briefly debate about whether to put on make-up or go natural. In my former life, I was always made up for work or events, so I decide to go bare-faced tonight, except I take Alfie's advice on board and dust a bit of blusher on my cheeks. It's such a freedom, and I delight in these small wins in being able to choose and not have that choice dissected. I throw my hair into a loose ponytail and spritz on some perfume. Looking at my reflection is a revelation, because staring back at me is a woman who looks happy, with bright sparkling eyes that speak of the anticipation of what's to come.

There's a knock at the door, so I take a deep breath and tell myself to relax. It's simply a casual date with a gorgeous man and a chance to get to know him better. He will be a useful resource for the library and I hope we can work well together for both of our sakes.

I open the door and there he stands, also wearing jeans and a tee. He's every girl's dream with his mop of dark hair, and soulful eyes. 'Hey, Finn,' I say, waving him into the small foyer. The cottage came furnished, which helped since I haven't had time to think of anything other than the library, but I'm looking forward to putting my own personal touch on the place. So far, all I've done is fill up the bookshelves with some favourites from home.

Inside, Finn gives me a peck on the cheek like a gentleman and it's hard to ignore the fact that he smells downright luscious. He brandishes a bunch of wild roses from behind his back. So, he's a romantic too? It doesn't end there; he also gives me a book: Matt Haig's *The Midnight Library*. If this isn't the way to woo a bookworm, I don't know what is.

'I hope you haven't read it yet.'

I read the blurb on the back cover, already knowing it's a book I'm going to devour in one sitting. A book about a librarian – tick! 'Thank you, Finn. I haven't read it, but it looks like the perfect book for me. It was very sweet of you. Come in, while I find a vase for these beauties.' I'm touched beyond words and only wish I had a gift for him. I'm beyond out of touch with the dating world.

We head to the kitchen. I can't find a vase so I settle for a jar, fill it up and set the flowers free. 'The welcoming committee are doing an outstanding job so far, I must say.'

A blush creeps up his cheeks. Huh. I didn't think he'd be the blushing sort. I've met a lot of reporters in my life, and if I'm to tar them all with one brush the word I'd use to describe them is *confident*. *Egotistical* is another. Yet Finn isn't like that. Maybe it's growing up in a smaller town, so he's never developed the ruthless part of his personality like so many men in London.

'Glad to hear it.' He grins. 'Are you ready to be *wowed* by the town of Willow Grove?'

'Am I ever.' So far this man is doing everything right but I silently warn myself not to get swept up in him. *I can't.* Nothing about my stay here is certain yet.

I grab my things and we walk into the balmy summer night and wander towards town proper. Finn points out who lives where and what they do. If I need a plumber or a painter, I'll know which door to knock on. 'Willow Grove is a decent-sized town but has more of a small village vibe, so as you can imagine everyone knows everything and it's impossible to hide a secret, which is great for me – being the town reporter – but not so good if you're trying to keep your life private.'

I'm counting on some of these residents joining the library, and I only hope there's enough people here and in the neighbouring towns in order to make it happen. 'What do you usually report on? I can't see this place being a hotbed of crime.'

'Oh the usual,' he says, sweeping his hair back from his face. He has the most striking chiselled jawline that conjures a hero on the cover of a romance novel. I don't think I've ever noticed a man's jawline before. What's happening to me! 'Like who won the best Victoria sponge at the bake-off. Then there's the annual model train symposium – tensions are always high for that. The twenty or so model railway enthusiasts are extremely competitive and set up their stations as if they're about to board real passengers. It's quite the coup for Willow Grove – it draws a huge crowd. Then there's the knitting circle. They sell their creations and donate the money to various charities. I interview them all and eat a lot of that Victoria sponge I was telling you about. It never stops. There's bingo, bird watching, the gardening club. There's the ruins of an old castle – that's always ripe for a good story come Halloween or when someone of note takes wedding pictures there. Not to mention the various animal refuges, and events with them throughout the year. I'm telling you, you have to keep your finger on the pulse in these parts. If you blink, you'll miss all the fun.'

'So you're a social commentator too?' I manage to say and focus on looking forward, instead of at Finn. There's a distinct wobbliness to my legs, which I can only put down to being in his presence. This whole being free of the Astor name has a lot to answer for. It's sending me downright batty.

He gives a light shrug. 'I'm . . . everything. I like to think I stand up for the underdog, but there's not a lot *to* stand up for here.'

I bite my lip and debate whether to disagree. I'm still new here. I really don't know what happens behind closed doors, but Harry and Alfie spring to mind as two really special people who've been cast aside and could do with someone speaking up for them. 'Are you sure about that?'

'Why, what do you know?' He mimes taking a pad from his pocket and writing notes as if it's a hot story. 'Oh . . . Careful.' Finn grabs my arm and pulls me sideways around a puddle.

'Thanks.' I bet he's the old-school romantic type.

He waves me away. 'Sorry to interrupt – puddles are downright ankle-breaking around here. What were you saying?'

I dig my hands into my pockets and formulate my answer.

'Well, it's just that I've met a couple of people here who look like they could really use a friend or two. From what I can see they haven't been given a fair go. I sort of expected the opposite in a tight-knit community like Willow Grove.'

He frowns, the light gone from his eyes. 'Harry, you mean?'

'Yes, Harry and a little boy called Alfie. I can only guess about Harry's history but I was shocked when Maisie took offence at me letting "Homeless Harry" into the library.' I cringe using the moniker but it needs to be told. 'And she warned me that I'd lose memberships over such a thing. I felt like I was in some kind of twilight zone.'

Finn shakes his head, his dark hair turning silver in the filmy dusk. 'Homeless Harry – such an awful way to describe someone, but for what it's worth I expect the name's stuck over the years for most of the locals in Willow Grove and they don't even realise how offensive it sounds. I don't know too much about him or how he came to be homeless but I do know he was married and had children once upon a time. Makes you wonder where they are and why he's living this way. I've tried to link him in with organisations who can offer support but he wants no part of it.'

Finn lift his palms as if to say it's out of his hands. 'But perhaps I didn't try hard enough. It pains me to think he feels like an outsider and I gave up on him so quickly. I just got the feeling he wanted to be left alone and I didn't want to overstep the mark.' The way he explains it shows me that this man has a heart that it seems some of the people in town lack.

'Yes, it's hard to know exactly what to do in that situation. I wasn't sure how much to pry either. Harry mentioned that you were the only person he's talked to in years.'

'I'm the *only* one?' Finn's face registers shock.

I nod. 'He says people pretend he's not there, and that he feels like he's invisible. You have to wonder what sort of psychological damage that does to a person. Feeling as though they're so worthless that they're not even worth the time of day to say hello to. Maybe there are people in town who would say hello and help if they knew his story, but Harry's confidence is already at an all-time low so he hides out, stays among the shadows. The previous librarian didn't help by banning him from the library.'

He grimaces. 'I knew he had problems with Agnes Bitterweather – she wasn't exactly understanding of his plight, but then again, she wasn't really understanding of anyone. Old-school in her ways. Archaic, even. I guess once the library started sinking and she couldn't save it she just gave up, and dare I say it, became quite *bitter* and Harry probably copped the brunt of it.' He shakes his head and dips his head as if he's disappointed with himself. 'I had no idea he felt so unseen, so invisible. I *presumed* that's what he wanted, to be left alone.'

Perhaps the residents of Willow Grove aren't as heartless as I'm imagining; maybe like Finn they thought that Harry wanted to be left to his own devices, his presence ignored so as to not make a big deal about his situation and potentially make him feel vulnerable. 'That makes sense,' I say. 'But it's not the case it seems. Harry feels ostracised. I'm hoping I can find out more about him, and see what he wants, what he needs. He's been spending more time in the library, but it's all baby steps. He hasn't opened up about himself, as much as he has about the locals in town, and let me tell you, for someone who doesn't have conversations with many people, he certainly sees and knows a lot.'

'I bet! And what about Alfie? I haven't come across him.' We come to a crossroad and Finn grabs my hand as we cross. We stop briefly to wait for a car, and then he lets my hand go. He's quite the protective sort, it seems. It makes me wonder if Finn has a child, the way he looks out for me in an almost subconscious way as though he's had a lot of practice crossing roads with a small child in hand. Maybe that caring side just comes naturally to him . . . still my palm pulses from his touch – am I truly going mad?

I try and focus on the conversation and what I'm trying to explain. 'Alfie's an eleven-year-old boy who has all these superpowers but doesn't attend mainstream school because of the bullying he's been subjected to. He's the funniest little lad. He's got absolutely no filter and blurts out exactly what he thinks. At the moment he's using the library as a schoolroom but we don't have up-to-date books for him. His mum Jo is run ragged trying to provide for them *and* be his teacher. Jo says he's lonely and he needs some friends . . .'

'Sounds like a great kid.' Finn ponders it for a moment. 'There must be a local group he can join in the hopes of making friends? If there's one thing Willow Grove has, it's an abundance of social clubs.'

That gets me thinking. Why don't we try and offer that kind of thing at the library, so Jo doesn't need to fit anything else into her busy schedule?

'The library could definitely host some sort of pre-teen social club. Maybe a Minecraft group or what's that other game they're all into at the moment . . . ? Where you have to guess who the imposter is?'

'Among Us? Pretty sure that fad has passed already.'

'Already? Fickle kids!' We laugh.

Finn turns to me, excitement sparkling in his eyes as if he's buoyed by the thought of what could be at the library if only we tried. 'Minecraft is a great idea. It's used to teach coding at some schools, so it could also be pitched as educational.'

That same buoyancy races through me. The library has so much *potential* as long as we don't run out of time and resources. It really could be the hub this town needs if it all comes together the way I imagine it can. 'I'll talk to Alfie's mum, Jo, and see what she's comfortable with. In the meantime, I'm going to make his little library cubicle the best I can.' I've ordered times tables, periodic charts and human biology posters he can tack up, and a few interesting shark diagrams. 'What boy of eleven do you know who manages without a friend their own age? I'm just wondering why another family haven't come along and invited him on bike rides, or offered to take him out for pizza, you know? Jo said this is the third school they've tried and that she doesn't want to keep moving him from town to town and rightly so. Why should *they* have to move?'

Finn shrugs. 'I'm a blow-in here too, I've been here for years now but it took the town a while to warm to me. I'm originally from a county over but you'd think it was outer space the way they looked through me. It's an old town; generations have grown up together and they're cliquey. Sometimes, it feels like we've regressed a hundred years. So, maybe it's that. No excuse, but that's how it is with new people.'

It makes me wonder what's in store for me. Another blow-in, one who isn't exactly who she says she is. Yikes. 'Can we help bring them kicking and screaming into the twenty-first century?' I ask with a sheepish grin.

'It would take a miracle, but I believe in magic.'

Finn is someone special with his genuine demeanour. We continue down the high street and he shows me all the points of interest in town: the local church, and then the bowls club, where they're hosting a social night for members. I introduce myself and ask to stick up some flyers about the library. Finn's right about how they treat newcomers; they give me a disinterested nod and resume their conversations.

We visit the rowdy corner pub where locals sit nursing frothy beers. I say hello to as many people as I can including the publican and I ask permission to tape posters to the front of their windows. Here everyone seems accommodating enough and the man agrees I can advertise here whenever I like as long as I promise to stop by for a drink sometime so they can get to know me and my plans for the library. I do love a small-town pub; they're the best place to go to find out the ins and outs of a place.

Back outside the sky is awash with swirls of magenta and lilac. 'Last stop before dinner on the insider's tour of Willow Grove is none other than the swanky office of the *Chronicle*, where yours truly bleeds over his laptop in order to produce cutting-edge news for the masses.' He waves up at the office space, which is above the pub and looks like the size of a bedsit. 'I like to call myself a roving reporter, so space isn't a priority.' I love his self-deprecating sense of humour and the way he isn't hung up on material things. It's obvious he loves his job and his life in Willow Grove.

I grin at him. 'You can't report what you can't see. I bet that's a good vantage point to watch the world go by on the high street.'

'Can't beat it. I get my best stories from that perch. Although, I'm sure your story is going to beat them all. Who can compare with a ravishing librarian who is new to town?'

I gulp. Little does he know I won't be part of any story for his paper. At least not photographically. 'So where to now?' I subject change subtle as anything.

He gives me an odd look, sensing what? That I didn't respond to being called ravishing? I'm sure he meant it in jest anyway. 'We're off to Chez Jacques, a little bistro that's owned by a local couple. They do British/French fare and win awards for their dishes but they're *very* humble about it. Like for instance if you look closely, you might see the *teeny* tiny sign in their window announcing their latest win?'

He points to a bistro up the street, at least I assume it's a restaurant. It's hard to focus because of the garish neon yellow signage on their window that reads: NUMBER ONE AGAIN. DON'T BOTHER GOING ANYWHERE ELSE.

'I'm lost for words. Humble is an *understatement*. I'm partially blind in one eye now.'

Finn laughs. 'Likewise. Helps to blink away the neon. I hope you're hungry.'

'Starving.' And I am. This cooking malarkey was fun at first but after a week of early starts and long days the lustre soon wears off. If it wasn't for Harry, I'd have given up by now and been living off buttered toast.

We're greeted by a waitress who fawns over Finn. 'Here he is, the man who put us on the map!'

'He did?' I ask with a smile.

The exuberant waitress nods, her curls bouncing. 'He did a story about us after we took our first prize in French/British culinary awards for our famous hazelnut dacquoise. Before we knew it we were being inundated by celebrities and the like.' She moves closer and whispers, 'Keep this to yourself, but that's the only reason you have a table tonight with a last-minute reservation. We're booked solid for months, you see, but we can't let our superstar reporter go unfed, now can we?'

'No, you most certainly can't. I can't write if I'm hungry,' Finn says, laughing off her praise. 'Mary here is married to Jacques the chef who hails from France. Theirs is one of those love stories where they . . .'

Mary slaps him playfully on the arm. 'Oh shush you. You know very well we met on a Contiki tour.'

Finn pretends to be shocked. 'Well it must have been a very romantic Contiki tour.'

'Let's just say his accent didn't hurt one little bit.' Mary's boisterous and bubbly and I like her already. It seems like she's the what-you-see-is-what-you-get type, a trait I find enormously comforting in people because you never have to guess their motivations. 'Coming through,' she bellows, waving us to join her as she zigzags through tables. 'VIP guest, coming through!' We're seated at a table by the window. The signage manages to bathe us in a jaundiced yellow light. I'm sure it makes me look decidedly ill, but we're in the *most* happening of places in Willow Grove so I can't complain. 'I'll bring the fancy wine, since this looks like a date.'

With that she springs away, and I exhale. 'What a welcome,' I say, blushing as patrons stare at us. I presume wondering exactly who the VIPs are. 'So what's her husband Jacques like? Mary doesn't quite have the poise of the French but she has a certain *je ne sais quoi* that I bet attracts people to her like a magnet.'

'Yeah, she's popular in town and has a big social circle.' Finn leans closer. 'Jacques is her polar opposite.'

I smile. 'I can see how that would be necessary.' Mary has an energy about her that probably needs a steady sort.

'For sure. If I was into stereotypes, I'd say he's your typical French chef. Brooding, quiet and wears a perpetual scowl. They make a fine pair. Mary brings out the best in him, and when he's not working he's been known to smile *and* laugh, at the same time.'

'Wonders will never cease! I feel like I've been living under a rock. All these different personalities are quite the breath of fresh air.' Where I've come from, people aren't as open, as honest. You see a façade, their camera-ready faces, their public personalities. And then you have others on their best behaviour because of the Astor name. It's all so phony, it's enough to make me scream. Here, people are *real*. They don't pretend to be what they're not.

'You say that now, but just wait. Soon, you'll be one of them and sick to death of hearing the same old stories exaggerated every Friday at the pub.'

Sounds like bliss to me. But before I can say anything a woman who wears a smart suit wanders over, waving to Finn. She's heavily made up and has bright burgundy-coloured hair and looks to be around fifty or so. 'Hey, Finn!' she says. 'I've been hoping to run into you! I read your article about the crochet group, but when I rang to join they said they were full.' While her voice is upbeat, there's hurt in her eyes. Finn's phone flashes with a text message as the name *Katy* appears. He gives it a cursory glance but doesn't pick it up. Then the name Lia appears. Finn doesn't react.

'Lovely to see you, Sofia,' he says. 'Who told you the crochet group was full?'

Sofia scrunches up her nose. 'Charlotte, of course.'

Finn rolls his eyes. Just who is Charlotte?

Sofia shakes her head and continues, 'She said they weren't taking new memberships at this time, but I thought the whole point of your article was that they were actively searching for new members so they could expand and find a bigger space to hold the meetings?'

'Erm . . .' Finn scrubs his face and struggles with a response. It seems that the members of the crochet group have purposely blocked this woman from joining, but why? As Finn grapples with what to say, I jump in to save the awkward silence.

'Hi, Sofia, I'm Elodie. The library needs more members as a matter of haste. Have you ever thought about joining? I'm the new librarian, and I'd love you to come and visit.'

Sofia turns to me and gives me a warm smile. 'Nice to meet you, Elodie.' She bends down to my level and gives me a hug as if we've known each other for longer than a few minutes and I find it affectionate in a maternal way. 'I've never thought about joining the library. I'm more looking for some social interaction. After being in this town for five years, I'd really, *really* like to make some female friends. Finn's great and all but sometimes you just need the support of women, you know?' Five years in Willow Grove and she hasn't made a female friend? Just what is going on here?

'You could bring your crochet things and use one of the cubicles there and maybe we could advertise for other like-minded souls?' I scramble to think of a way to get her to join and offer her something that will help. I need 470 more members and every single new sign-up counts. Besides, I get the feeling Sofia could really use a supportive atmosphere.

'Well, you see my passion is cooking, but I thought joining the crochet group would help me make some local friends. It's not the first time I've been rebuffed when I've gone to join in.' Why don't they include her? Finn's phone beeps again and I eye it: *Miranda*. He gives it a cursory glance.

I struggle to think of how I can help Sofia. There must be a way. 'There's always a possibility you could run some cooking classes at the library. Perhaps we need to meet up and have a bit of a brainstorm.'

Her eyes light up. 'Really? That would be just fabulous! What about lunch at my place tomorrow. Are you free?'

'Sure, say twelve?'

'Twelve it is! I best head off home and start making some notes about the menu. Enjoy your meal. The gratin dauphinois is exquisite.' Sofia hugs us in turn and scurries off to the counter to pay.

Finn smiles as his phone starts ringing again: *Frankie*.

Does he have a coterie of women waiting on the sidelines? I cast my mind back to the gifts he surprised me with and wonder if he's got a shelf of relevant books that he gives to each woman. I'd pegged Finn as a steady sort, but maybe that's what he wants me to think. 'You're very popular with the ladies' today. Aren't you going to answer that?'

He flicks it on silent. 'Trust me I'm not as popular as you think. It's my pet hate when people answer their phones at a meal. Maybe I'm a little old-school, but there's a time and place for calls and dinner with a beautiful woman is not one of them. Plus, I know what they want and it's not going to happen.'

I wait him out to explain.

'They want the inside scoop,' he says with a shrug. 'And if I answer now, I'll never hear the end of it. I'll turn it off. I should have already done that. Sorry, Elodie.'

'It's fine by me.' Finn does seem old-school in a lot of respects. The kind of guy who'd open your car door or invite you for a candlelight dinner. I'm intrigued about Sofia and why Finn was struck silent about the whole matter. 'It seemed like you didn't want to hurt Sofia's feelings and tell her the truth. Who is Crochet Charlotte and why doesn't she let Sofia join in?'

Finn pulls a face. 'Urgh, was it that obvious?'

'I don't think Sofia noticed.'

Mary comes back and plonks a bottle of red wine down but is called away again before we can thank her.

Finn pours us a generous glass and lets out a sigh. 'Sofia's ex-husband turned out to be a bit of a con man. He came in and splashed cash around, made all these promises. Managed to use his influence to get a treasury position on the town council and then started siphoning off funds. Next minute he was gone and so was the council's money.'

Whoa. 'But Sofia wasn't part of it?'

Finn shakes his head. 'No, she had no idea what he was up to. In fact, she repaid the council out of her own pocket. He was as slimy as they come, but he had this way about him, this charisma that drew people to him like flies. Locals are embarrassed they trusted him, put him in a position of power without doing their due diligence. Unfortunately, Sofia is left to bear the brunt of it all.'

I cock my head. 'How's that fair?' I'm upset for her. She paid the money back even though she didn't have to. Her poor excuse for a husband left her to deal with the fallout and they still don't let her in? By the sounds of it she had been conned just the same as they were.

'It's not. But I'd hazard a guess that it's a self-preservation thing on their part. Word is, there's a quite a number of people who were duped by him and Charlotte is one of them. In fact, I'm certain Charlotte was instrumental in getting him voted in as treasurer.'

I frown. 'So she's bullying Sofia because of her poor own judgement? That's not fair on Sofia.'

'No, it's not. And sadly, she's not the only one. I really don't know how to help Sofia. That's why I got so tongue-tied. She's been through enough, so how do you tell her it's because Charlotte got caught up in the hype of her ex-husband? It'll just make her feel worse. I get the feeling Charlotte leads the pack and has warned others off befriending Sofia too.'

Willow Grove isn't as pretty behind closed doors, not even close. 'Finn, I'm starting to regret I ever stepped foot on Willow Grove soil. Please tell me there's something redeeming about someone?' I say only half joking.

He gives me a soft smile. 'I promise you, it's not as bad as it seems. Everything is heightened because you've stumbled on these people all at once. There's a woman here who knits jumpers for rescue dogs. And there's a seventy-year-old man who pushes his daughter's wheelchair in marathons because she always wanted to be a runner. There's a couple who adopt children and had to extend their house because even as the children grew into early adulthood they never left, so they keep adding on to their house to fit them all in. There's a mystery elf, who delivers presents to the children's ward at the hospital every year. Trust me, there's a lot of good here too.'

'That's so sweet. I'll have to get used to the fact that everyone's lives are entwined.'

Mary rushes back over. 'Sorry for the delay, lovelies. It's bedlam in here!' She hands us each a leather-bound menu.

'I'm happy to try whatever you recommend,' I say.

'Me too,' says Finn. 'As long as it's not escargot.'

'Where's the fun in that!' I tease.

'One date and she's already trying to make me eat slugs. Do with me what you will.'

Mary waggles a brow and says, 'Leave it with me, treasures. I promise you'll be impressed.' She shoots a glance outside and frowns. 'Oh no Pilferer Pete is lurking. I better shoo him off before he makes away with my pot plants.'

Quick as a flash, my estimations of Mary sink. *Pilferer Pete.* Really? What chance do these people have when they're judged like this?

Finn shrugs but his cheeks colour as if he's embarrassed. 'Poor guy can't catch a break.'

'Sounds like it.' I don't want to keep whining either but sheesh. 'What's with the insulting names?'

'Bad habits, and long memories or something like that.' Silence falls and I struggle to make conversation. Something is seriously wrong in Willow Grove and I can't stand to live here and be privy to it without speaking up for those who are discussed in such a way, behind their backs no less.

Finn must read my mood and changes tack. 'If you're still amenable I'd really like to interview you about your plans to save the library, everyone is curious about the new librarian and I'm sure it'll help secure more memberships . . .'

Suddenly I have the *most* incredible idea! My synapses fire and I have a moment of such clarity as this vision of what could be takes place in my mind. Images of Harry, Alfie, Sofia spring to mind and how they just want to be noticed, fit in, form friendships. I'd hazard a guess that this mysterious Pete is just the same. A fuzzy idea takes shape. I don't have money to buy books, but I could still provide stories . . .

The idea is unconventional, but it *could* work for those special people. First, I'd have to get their permission and work out just how to go about it. It would be an . . . experiment of sorts. I realise I've been sitting there open-mouthed and silent for too long so I hurry to reply, 'I'd love to, Finn. Can you leave it with me for another few days – I've got an *amazing* idea but I want to pitch it just right.' The hair on my arms stand on end and I have this overwhelming feeling that if I get this right, it just might save the library.

Now I can see there's a *reason* I met these people in the first week of my stay at Willow Grove, of that I'm sure. There's one intriguing character after another. A whole host of untold stories that are ripe for the plucking if my plan comes to fruition. There's not enough money in the coffers to buy much new stock so . . .

If I can't lend books, then I'll lend people!

What if members heard their unique tales first-hand, instead of down the grapevine? Everyone has a story, and sometimes you have to read between the lines. They just need a chance to have their stories heard. To be listened to. To be *seen*. There's a lot to think about but the idea grabs hold and doesn't let go.

Chapter 8

I'm spritzing on some citrusy perfume, almost ready to leave for lunch at Sofia's, when my mobile rings. It's been such a dream having it ring so sporadically, so very different to when I was an Astor and it beeped and buzzed night and day. I follow the noise and find the phone on my bedside table.

'Teddy!' I say, happy to hear his voice. 'How are you? I've missed you like crazy.' It strikes me I've barely given my poor brother a second thought as I've been so caught up here but hearing him down the end of the phone line makes my heart squeeze. I do miss him.

'I'm good, good. You sound happy.'

'I am, Teddy. Blissfully happy. So far I've been on a date with a handsome reporter, and I'm about to have lunch with a local woman called Sofia. I've come up with an audacious plan to save the library . . .'

'And it's only been a week! Imagine what you can do in a year.'

'Right? So how are you, dear brother?'

There's a pause – as if he's weighing up how much to tell me. I hurry to reassure him. 'It's OK, Teddy.' I might be miles away but I know things in London will never change and by default I'm still part of it all. 'You can tell me.'

He sighs and I picture my roguish brother, scrubbing a hand down his face like he does when he doesn't have a quick fix for things concerning me. 'I don't want to ruin your vibe but Mum is laying it on thick. Questioning me as to your whereabouts and when you'll be back. She's told Astor staff you're on an assignment, researching all the ways people commit to a life detox. It's quite brilliant really, but she wants you back.'

I let out a long groan. 'I know, but the best thing for me to do is stay distant so she knows I mean business. If I talk to her, she'll end up convincing me and I really can't leave now I've made this promise. It's been a real adventure already and I'm loving every minute. If I speak to Mum, that shine will soon wear off.'

'Why go on a regular trip when you could go on a guilt trip?'

'Exactly,' I laugh. 'What about you, Teddy? Any luck in being taken back into the fold?'

'They won't even discuss it. They'll only discuss you.'

It's always been this way, ever since Teddy made those mistakes. I thank my lucky stars that we're so close and that what could be seen as abject favouritism hasn't put a wedge between us as siblings. If anything, it's brought us closer. 'Don't take no for an answer, Teddy. I know you've got the skills to run Astor, but they're never going to believe it unless you step up and *show* them.'

'But how? They won't even give me security clearance. I had to bribe Barry the other day just to sneak up to your office.'

Even though he can't see me I waggle a brow. 'Well. I do have a very particular set of skills and with the click of the fingers I can get you security clearance and anything else you need.'

'Is that so? I didn't know you had it in you to bend the rules, Elodie.'

'Only for you, Teddy. Plus Barry owes me a favour or two since I once saved his job . . .'

Barry is head of security at Astor and takes his job seriously. He's got a soft spot for me after I once saved him from being fired by taking the blame for an incident that got out of hand when one of his staff failed to react in time. He's never forgotten it and always reminds me he will be there for me in return if I ever need it.

'So, make that magic happen, sister, and we'll see what I can do.'

'Just waltz in there with all the confidence in the world and take my place. Mum isn't going to kick you out and lose face in front of them all. But then you've really got to wow them. I don't know how, but I'm sure you'll figure it out.'

'What's the worst that can happen?'

'I know you can do it, Teddy.'

'Thanks, sis.'

'Is everything else OK? You don't seem like yourself.' His voice isn't as upbeat and teasing as usual.

'You didn't see it?'

'See what?'

He lets out a long sigh. 'Louise all over the news with her co-star, sunning it up in Spain even after I warned her about the guy! She's not like other women and for the life of me I just can't forget about her, even though I'm trying to make myself. Urgh, those tabloid pictures are burned into my brain.'

'Aww, Teddy. You know what the press is like – you know better than anyone. How do you know it's legit? I highly doubt they were just hanging out at the end of a long week. It'll be a PR stunt, put together to raise the profile of the movie they're shooting and tamp down his bad-boy reputation. We work with PR firms at Astor and set up these "candid" shots for a story all the time.' It goes against everything I believe in, but it's par for the course in media. Usually, these so-called paparazzi shots are scheduled ahead of time, and done as a marketing ploy so the movie gets publicity. It helps highlight the 'chemistry' two leads have, when it's all a complete set-up.

'Could be, but Louise doesn't strike me as someone who'd go along with that sort of thing.'

'It would be out of her hands and she probably hates it even more than you do. Don't give up hope.'

When we hang up, I shoot Barry a message without giving too much away and call in the favour, asking him to grant Teddy security clearance and tell him to say I ordered it if he gets questioned. Soon enough he replies and assures me it's done. Then I text Louise: *How's the shoot? Things are looking spicy in Spain!*

Before I can blink there's a reply: *Not quite! Co-star as chauvinistic as they come but the powers that be said the pics had to be taken to get ahead of all his bad publicity, as if that's my problem!* ☹ *Tell Teddy I said hi.*

Just as I thought! It happens more than people know.

Urgh, I get it. I'll pass the message on to Teddy. Enjoy that sunshine while you can. ☺

That taken care of I head outside, following the text directions to Sofia's house. I don't have a car, because I've never learned to drive, but I figure it's something I should look into. I could take some long weekend adventures and explore the surrounding areas and go further afield when time permits. It would be another thing to tick off my living-a-real-life list.

The landscape is lush and green with bright blue skies over-head. According to the text message Sofia's house sits beyond a hilly crest, which I huff and puff my way up, delighting in a monarch butterfly who seems to follow my progress. Once I reach the top, I do a double take. In the valley below is what can only be described as an estate. An estate that looks as though it was once royal. I double-check my directions; this is definitely the place. There's stables, and a long rounded driveway, and an imposing castle-style abode sits smack bang in the middle, turrets the whole way around as if sentries once stood guard there.

Sofia lives *here*? I'm not sure why it's such a shock – maybe because Sofia seems so real and genuine, so bubbly and bum-bling that I'd sort of pictured her having a cosy little cottage like mine, hand-making all her meals from scratch on a well-loved Aga. The pieces suddenly click into place – I'm guessing her ex-husband was after her money from the start?

I stumble down the grassy bank and around the curve of the driveway, half expecting liveried servants of yesteryear to be stationed at the grand entrance. The butterfly flutters away, as if its job of leading me here is done.

Out of breath from the long walk, I rap on the imposing double door, wondering just what's on the other side. Soon enough Sofia appears, face lit with a warm smile. 'Elodie!' she says. 'Welcome, come on in. I'm making us a delicious lunch, so I hope you're hungry.'

'Always. Your property is awe-inspiring, Sofia. I didn't expect something so grand when I crested that hill. I love how hidden it is. You'd never know it was here.'

She gives me a sheepish look. 'I love it too. It feels a bit like a fairy tale, this big old castle hidden away, like I'm Rapunzel or something. It was once owned by an Italian family famous for their designer handbags, but the family dynasty turned against one another and eventually they sold most of their properties to bail the company out. Didn't quite work and now their company isn't owned by the next generation.'

'Wow, would I know the brand?'

She whispers it.

'Oooh!' As I look around the entrance hall, I see ornate gold Italian touches. 'What a delicious piece of history!'

'Isn't it? I never got to meet any of the family. It was all handled by boring starch-faced lawyers, but it still makes a good story and I feel like I'm living in a part of their history. Let's go to the kitchen,' she says, and walks swiftly through the glamorous marble-floored hall. 'It's how I stay so fit, walking around all these galleries and up and down the staircases.' The castle, or I suppose it's more an Italian *castello*, is immaculately maintained and filled with antique furniture and fine artwork.

We continue downstairs into a huge marble kitchen. 'This is lovely.' While it's been updated it still has an old-world charm about it, with copper pots hanging above one end of the island bench.

'Thanks, Elodie. I had the kitchen freshened up to suit my tastes. Don't get me wrong, salmon-coloured stone had its time but it was a little too orange for me. I went light and bright to open the space. Take a seat.' I pull out a stool and sit opposite Sofia who bustles around with lots of pots on the go.

I remember the wine I brought and rustle through my hand-bag for it. 'To go with lunch,' I say and hand Sofia a bottle of red.

'A nice vintage,' she says giving it the nod of approval. 'Shall we be fancy and decant it?'

'Sure,' I say, and take the decanter from further down the island. I'm used to this level of detail from my mum who believes the wine always has to open up and breathe like it's a living thing. To be honest, I can never taste any difference and part of me wonders if it's all just part of the theatre of enjoying a nice meal.

I let the wine awaken and watch Sofia bustle around the kitchen, looking like a dab hand as she stirs pots and shuffles pans. A satisfied smile sits upon her face as if she's in her element, her happy place. 'Are you a professional chef?' I ask.

Sofia wipes her hands on her floral apron. 'I wish! Self-taught. What's not to like about cooking up a fabulous menu of dishes, pouring your heart and soul into each one? The worries of the world fade away when I'm in the kitchen, and then I'm rewarded with a delicious meal at the end of that toil. My only issue is, not having enough people to cook for. Finn's been here a few times, but he's always busy. That phone of his never stops, but he's too polite to answer it in company – he has lovely manners but I always feel like I'm pulling him away from his busy life.'

Hmm, his phone constantly rings off the hook like it did at our dinner? For a small-town reporter, I wouldn't think he'd have *that* many calls, especially after hours, but the way he explained it about them wanting the inside scoop led me to believe it was about work. Could it have been about something else? It's a mystery for another day as Sofia continues, 'I'd love to fill the dining room with friends but people around here look at me like I've got two heads.'

'Why though? You're lovely, I can't see why they'd treat you in such a way, Sofia.' I want to hear Sofia's version of events and truly I'm hoping she says things are not as bad as Finn painted them – but part of me wonders if the real story will actually be worse.

I figure the wine is breathing well enough for both of us and a tale like this deserves to be shared over a nice glass of red. I spot the wine glasses in a cabinet and fetch two and pour us a healthy dose.

'Thanks,' Sofia says, taking the proffered glass and a deep sip. 'What a nice drop!' Sofia turns down the heat on her pans and comes back with a tray of appetisers. 'For starters we've got scallop pops, Cornish crab with pink grapefruit mayonnaise and caramelised mushroom tartlets.'

'Sofia, wow.' These delightful morsels would rival most high-end establishments in London, no question, and Sofia acts as blithely as if she's just thrown together a tin of sardines and a plate of crackers. We fill small plates and Sofia settles in beside me.

'Thank you, darling. Eat, eat and I'll tell you my sorry story.'

I start with the Cornish crab, sure I've never tasted anything as sweet in my life.

'You could say I was a late bloomer – didn't marry until my early fifties. There were men, of course, but none that I had a real spark with, an unshakeable knowing until Jacob came along. He proposed on our second date. That should have been a red flag, but at the time it seemed wildly romantic, like the wait was worth it. Jacob was devilishly handsome and charming to boot. He literally took my breath away, and that had never happened to me before.' Yikes, reminds me of the way I feel about Finn, but I stay quiet so Sofia can continue. 'We bought this place and moved in when the modifications were finished. I've always wanted to live where there's a bit of countryside, and this place ticked all the boxes. The town's big enough to have a newspaper, but small enough that there'd be a close-knit community that we could be part of.'

I get the feeling Sofia and I have a lot in common but I don't disrupt her tale.

'Well Jacob just loved it here, went right on into town that very first day and struck up friendships right and left. I was still unpacking and here he comes with some locals to check out the property. He had that way about him, you know?'

I nod.

'I only found out later what stories he was spinning. He told them that he'd worked on Wall Street in his youth before moving to Hong Kong as a venture capitalist. You name it, he'd done it. In reality he'd been an electrician. It's why he was voted in as treasurer, because of his so-called finance background. They saw him as this charming, retired man, living in this big old estate, with that wealth of knowledge going to waste . . . but that all came later. Before that, the bank called me and said one of my accounts was overdrawn, the only account that *he* had access to. I told them it must have been a mistake – it couldn't be empty! I confronted Jacob and he admitted he had an online gambling problem.'

'Oh, Sofia, I'm so sorry. That is awful.'

She shrugs. 'Yes, it was but I thought it was OK, we could get him some help. Work on the addiction, you know? I logged on to my bank and checked the balance, crushed to find the money really was gone. We talked into the night. He had all these excuses. They were so believable! Looking back now, I shudder to think how naïve I was. When Jacob saw me he saw dollar signs. An easy life. Or perhaps a way to relieve me of most of my wealth – who knows.'

'Oh no.'

'It's all family money. My father had a successful boat-building business that expanded over the years and got contracts to build for the navy. I took over the business before selling it. Why work so hard, when I could enjoy the spoils? When Jacob came along shortly after I honestly thought he was a gift from God.'

Did Jacob know about the business sale and target Sofia from day one? I really hope not.

'I thought our marriage was saveable. I told him he'd have to find a job, prove to me that he could take care of himself. Deep down, I thought if he agreed then I'd know he loved me for me, and not for what I could provide. If he wanted to gamble, then he'd have to use his own money. So he comes home one day and announces they've voted him in as treasurer. I was so proud of him! I thought he'd really made an effort to prove to me he could stand on his own two feet. And then not long after, council money went missing. Never in a million years did I imagine he'd siphon funds from the town! I didn't know at that stage all the lies he'd told about his past about being this financial whiz. And that whole gambling malarkey – that was another lie.'

I frown. 'So how did he get found out?'

'From what I can gather, one of the council members was suspicious all along, but it took some time to follow the paper trail and find out where the money went. The outgoing payments looked genuine, so at first the suspicions fell on deaf ears. Soon enough he couldn't account for it all and it quickly came crashing down. The lies caught up with him – they figured out he was never a venture capitalist in Hong Kong, or a Wall Street stockbroker. The jig was up so he left that evening, telling me he had council business out of town and would be away for a few days.' She smacks her forehead. 'I packed him food for the drive! Pressed all his shirts.'

With a shake of the head she continues. 'The next morning some of the council members came knocking and demanded to know where he was. When they told me what he'd done I was mortified. They may as well have carried pitchforks, they were so angry. I never thought he'd do something like that, even after he'd drained one of my accounts. I was *so* blindsided. Love can really distort reality. I just *knew* he wasn't coming back and I'd have to face them all alone.'

'How did you know for sure he wasn't coming back?' Part of me hopes he had a good reason, something, anything to explain such heinous treatment of Sofia and abandoning her to deal with the fallout.

She shakes her head. 'After they left with threats of legal action and whatnot I found a note in his dressing room. He said it was their fault for not having the right systems in place to stop theft, and that none of us would ever find him. I was crushed, as you can imagine. He was a con man all along and I got played. I felt so utterly stupid and so alone.'

'Urgh, Sofia that is the worst but it wasn't your fault. By the sounds of it *everyone* was duped by him. Did the council search for him? Get the police involved?'

'Yes, and they're still searching but I doubt they'll ever find him. He's probably in Mexico or Thailand or somewhere living it up. I insisted on paying back what he stole – the council couldn't survive without it. It affected a lot of places in town, including the library and the recreation centre. Staff were laid off because there were no funds to pay them, and I couldn't have that. I even hired my own private investigator, because I wanted answers. Turns out Jacob has a history of this kind of con. Takes the money and runs. I'm not the first woman and won't be the last.'

'He's so brazen. But he will get caught, these days there's technology everywhere – CCTV, banking records. He can only hide for so long.'

'I really hope so. He's hurt a lot of people. I'm just lucky a lot of my savings aren't liquid so weren't accessible to him. I'm thankful he's gone. All my life people have treated me in a certain way, knowing who my father was, so I've always been guarded about it. But Jacob managed to break down those walls just enough . . .'

We have a lot in common and I wish I could tell Sofia that I understand her completely. Having to always second-guess whether someone likes you for you, or for what they think you can do for them can make a person go mad. There's always that doubt creeping in that they're not genuine. It makes it hard to form proper friendships. It's why I find comfort in books: I never have to doubt those characters.

'Now people in town treat me like an outsider as if I had something to do with the theft. They're mostly embarrassed they trusted him but I wish they'd see I am too. We're the same, all of us. Got swept up in the charisma, the lies he told. It's been the loneliest time.'

'Is that why you started cooking, Sofia? As a comfort?'

She gazes back to me with watery eyes. The last few years have taken their toll on her and I wish I could snap my fingers and make it all go away. 'Yes, when it is just me rattling around this big old castle, I cook, chatting away to myself as if I am a chef on telly . . . Silly really, but that's how I get through each day.'

'Why don't you open a restaurant?'

'It would ruin the fun, I suppose, and I don't need the income. Here, I can do it at my leisure, so it's a pleasurable pursuit. Besides, who'd eat at my restaurant? There's even rumours I've got Jacob buried around here somewhere. Can you imagine?'

'What!' This time we both laugh at such a preposterous notion.

I take another bite of the mushroom tartlet. It's earthy and rich and I know I'm going to be ruined for cooking after eating food of this quality. Maybe she'll teach me her ways? I take a sip of wine to wash it down and ask, 'What about love? Have you sworn off it, or would you try again if the right man came along?' I sense that her heart has been broken so badly that it'll be hard for her believe in a man ever again and that's such a shame for someone who has so much love to give. As I sit here and drink a robust red and delight in her gourmet starters, it saddens me to think she should be sharing this with the love of her life. Someone who repays the love she shares on the plate, by making her a cup of tea in the morning and placing her slippers by her bed just so. Sitting next to her of an evening watching *Great British Bake Off* over bowls of figgy pudding.

'I'd love to find the right man, but as I get older I wonder if I ever will. Trust is such an issue for me as you can well imagine.

Maybe I'm one of the unlucky ones, who knows, but I'd be happy with a companion. Someone to share a meal with. To take a slow evening stroll to chat about inconsequential things. I don't want much, do I?'

'No, Sofia, not at all. And I believe you'll find what you're looking for, but maybe you need to go about finding your people in a different way.' And I have just the tonic for such a thing!

Sitting here is a woman with morals and a big heart who wants nothing more than to cook for friends and shower them in her love for fine food. Some people show their love with words, Sofia shows hers through her menu. 'The locals haven't even given you a chance and that's on them. It really is their loss but I'm sure if we pull back the curtain we'll find the right sort of friends for you.'

'I've tried everything to get a foot in. I joined the knitting club, walking groups, and still I'm never included. It's like I'm on the periphery. Perhaps I'm too loud, or I try too hard and say the wrong thing? It can't only be the memory of Jacob, can it?'

'No, don't start blaming yourself for the way others treat you.'

She sighs, sadly. 'I've been toying with the idea of selling up and moving but I'd hate to lose my castle. It was a dream of mine to own such a piece of history but being here has brought nothing but isolation.'

I reach into my bag and take out a handwritten card and hand it to Sofia. Nerves flutter and I only hope I've made the right call. I *think* I have.

'What's this?' she asks.

'Read it. I know we talked about you doing a cooking demonstration but what about this instead? I know it might sound a little zany at first but I really think it could work. Not only will it help the library but it just might be the solution to your problems too.'

She fumbles for her glasses and pops them on and reads aloud.

'*We'd like you to share your story. You matter. Wouldn't the world be a better place if we didn't judge a book by its cover? #PeopleLibrary #BorrowPeople.*' She stares back at me with wide eyes. 'This is your grand plan to save the library?'

I nod. 'There's no money until we get the grant, and I can't get the grant until we get more members so I have to magic up something that will draw a crowd. This might sound cuckoo, but I feel like this is what drew me here. This was my purpose all along.'

'It doesn't sound cuckoo at all.'

'That's a relief.'

Her eyebrows pull together. 'By sharing my story, you mean about Jacob?'

'You can talk about whatever you're comfortable with. Your childhood, the boat-building business, anything you want. What you've gone through is big, Sofia. I'm sure people will relate to it. Or perhaps the borrower will think about you in a whole new light and be empathetic to your plight, having realised they'd pegged you all wrong from the start.'

She's silent for the longest time before her face breaks into a wide smile. 'It's genius, Elodie.'

We exchange grins. 'I hope so. It just might help break down some of those judgements I keep hearing about around town.'

'There's others like me who don't fit in?'

'Exactly like you, who have so much love and friendship to give but are unfairly gossiped about for whatever reason.'

She wipes away a stray tear. 'I'm in! But I'm telling you now, Elodie, it might not be as easy as you think. People here are set in their ways. They *prefer* gossiping than hearing the real story; at least that's my experience. What if no one comes?'

'Don't you worry about a thing,' I say, voice full of confidence. 'We'll get their attention if I have to scream it from the rooftops. And failing that, I know a reporter who can spread the news.' I give her a wink. 'I bet we'll have a line a mile long wanting to have their thirty minutes listening to you. If there's one thing Willow Grove has in abundance it's inquisitive people.'

'This might just work and I might make some female friends as quick as that.'

'You've already made one,' I say and hold my wine glass up to clink against hers. But part of me feels guilty promising friendship when I'm not exactly who I say I am, knowing that trust is a big thing for Sofia. Would she be upset if she found out who I really was? I'd hate to think she'd tar me with the same brush as her missing husband, Jacob. We're different, right? I'm here for good, not evil. Surely she'd understand?

Chapter 9

By the time Monday rolls around, I'm eager to get my idea off the ground. It could go either way. The locals might not accept it and it could backfire but I have to give it a try. We're not signing up enough new members with our other initiatives so I pray this will work.

The People Library experiment has the potential to save the library and more importantly can bring those lost souls who stand at the periphery back into the fold.

Harry's head appears as I get to the front doors. 'Good morning, Harry!'

'Elodie. You look bright as a button today. The weather must agree with you.'

The sun is out and the day is warm. 'I had a great week-end. And I spent most of last night nose pressed in a book.' Daydreaming about this place between chapters, eager to get in today and make things happen.

'I haven't read a book in years,' Harry muses. 'Not sure I'd have the concentration for it these days.'

Keys in hand, I open the door, face aghast. 'What! Let's remedy that today, Harry. What genre do you like?' I motion him to follow me inside and we go to my desk.

'I used to like spy thrillers, that kind of thing.'

'Say no more. I've got the perfect novel for you.' I dash off to find the well-thumbed, doorstop of a book.

'*I Am Pilgrim*?' he says dubiously.

'You won't be able to put it down, trust me. An epic espionage thriller that will leave your heart racing. Are you a member here, Harry? If not, I can sign you up now and set you on your way with your book and a nice hot breakfast.'

'I'm not a member, no.'

'Let's get that sorted then.'

Harry searches through his things for some ID. It's well out of date but has enough details that I can use. When it comes to his address, I pause, then put in the address of the library. I print him a shiny new laminated library card and hand it over with a grin.

'VIP Harry White, eh?' He grins back.

'You're the only one to have that dubious honour so far, Harry. I just made it up then.'

'I've never been called a VIP before. I could get used to it.' He grins through the woolly mane of his beard.

'Why not? Now even though my Sunday was mostly spent prone, I managed to give the beef and Guinness pie recipe a go. Have to admit the pastry is store-bought – turns out that's a lot harder to make than it looks! I've made you a few smaller-sized pies, so you can leave them in the fridge here and heat them up whenever you're ready.'

He takes the proffered container and pops open the lid. 'These look delicious, Elodie. We'll make a gourmet chef of you yet.'

I laugh. 'I don't know about that; you haven't tasted them

yet.' Or seen the state of my kitchen after attempting such a feat. The clean-up took the better part of an hour and a half. I've learned that making pastry is strictly for professionals and that store-bought is the only sane option. I'll never look at a pie the same way again.

'Well, thank you very much, Elodie. I'm going to be barrel-shaped soon. Anyway, I'll pop to the shower and then I'll get my breakfast sorted and my book started.'

'Let me know what you think of *I Am Pilgrim*.' I know he'll love it if he's into espionage thrillers. I'm not usually a fan of spy books, and I couldn't put it down. 'Oh wait! Before you go . . .' I take another handwritten card from my handbag and hand it to Harry.

'What's this then?' He pats his pockets for his specs and eventually finds them under his jumper and places them on the bridge of his nose. Harry reads the note aloud in a halting voice. *'We'd like you to share your story. You matter. Wouldn't the world be a better place if we didn't judge a book by its cover? #PeopleLibrary #BorrowPeople.'*

'What do you think?' I ask, knowing that Harry might not be as amenable as Sofia who so desperately wants to join in, but I still hope he'll consider it in time. I feel as though Harry has only just come to trust me but asking him to trust in an audience is a whole other level.

'You're the shake-up this town needs,' he says so softly I have to lean closer to catch it.

'Thank you, Harry. Will you consider being part of the People Library? I'm wondering if it'll help to share what you've been through? Maybe it'll stop you feeling invisible because I have an inkling if people knew how you felt about being ignored, they'd act differently.' I bite my lip, hoping I haven't gone too far. I don't want to make Harry feel anything other than respected but deep down I know he wants to be included, *seen*; he just doesn't want to risk being rejected again like he has so many times. 'Part of me thinks the locals act in such a way because they incorrectly assume that's what you want so this could be your chance to set them straight.'

He swallows hard, fighting against emotions that are so clear on his ruddy, etched face. 'Would they really want to hear it from me though? Sometimes I wonder if I'm real, as people step aside, and look anywhere but me.'

'I presume it's misguided politeness on their part, Harry. If you tell them your story, I bet things would change for the better. But it's completely up to you and I want you to make sure you're comfortable about it before you say yes. I know that it's not an easy thing to do, speaking up in front of people about such personal matters.'

Harry glances at the card again, as if willing himself to say yes. 'OK, thanks, Elodie. I'll give it some thought and let you know.' He shuffles off, head down. I hope the book will give him some joy today and ignite his love of reading once more and convince him that every story matters, *his* more than most. Like Sofia, Harry has so much goodness inside him. I'd love for him to be able to look people in the eye and not scurry away like he does now. *He* matters, and I hope the People Library experiment will prove that to him.

Maisie arrives and I check my watch. Twenty minutes late. I let it go so we don't start the week off on a bad note, but it feels like she's pushing the boundaries to see how far they stretch. I want to inspire her today so I know I need to start off on a happy note. 'Good morning, Maisie. Once you're settled in we can go over the plans for the week. I have sugar-glazed doughnuts!' Like any good Brit, she cannot start the workday until she's got a cup of tea in hand and I know her morning process is a slow one.

'Are they gluten-free?'

My face falls. 'Oh, no sorry they're not.' Damn it! I thought we could bond over sugar! 'Let's sit down anyway. There's something I want to run past you.'

'I've got a few things to do first.'

'Oh like what?' I ask.

'Like returning calls, and emails.' She flicks the red of her hair over her shoulder.

'Well, that can wait for a bit.' I'm keen to tell her about the People Library idea and work out how we best tackle it. Might it be just the thing that perks her up and makes her fall in love with her job all over again?

Harry wanders back and goes to the kitchen to heat up his pie. Maisie narrows her eyes and tracks his every move. 'You're still letting *him* in here, strutting around like he owns the place? A word of advice, people don't like it. Everyone thinks you're going to let Pilferer Pete in next. May as well let that thief clear out what stock we've got remaining, since there's no chance we're going to save the library.'

I'm so shocked I can barely form words, but that soon wears off as anger replaces it. 'Pilferer Pete?' I ask, knowing this poor man has this terrible name given to him by locals, but wanting to hear Maisie's reasoning.

She tuts. 'Yeah, the local shoplifter. Comes from a family of bad apples – there's only him left now. Would steal from his own mother, if he could, but then again, he probably learned off her, so . . . ?'

I take a deep breath and weigh up how to handle this. 'Maisie, you can't speak about people that way. It's insulting and it's not professional. If you're not up to the job here, then just say so. What I'm looking for is a staff member who is prepared to give their all to help save this place and not look for excuses to do the opposite.'

She bristles but stays quiet.

'I'm sure we can do this together, Maisie.' I try and think of a way to appeal to her while her face is a closed book. 'I'll have to get used to small-town life . . .' As soon as the words escape I want to snatch them back. Her eyes widen and I know Maisie's caught it.

'I thought you *were* from a small town?'

I let out a sigh as if my patience is thin so she'll back off. 'I am, I meant *this* small town.' She's not quite buying it but she stays quiet. I give her a dazzling smile and remind myself to be more careful. 'Let's get that tea brewing while we have our meeting, eh?'

We spend the next hour making plans for the week, including advertising space for a writer's group, a poetry group and inviting the historical club to use the library for their meetings. I bring up the subject of a cooking demonstration, but I don't mention Sofia's name. The idea is on hold for now anyway but it's something to consider.

The way Sofia cooks is quite theatrical, and I'm sure members would enjoy the show. I can't handle Maisie gossiping about another person in the space of an hour so I stay quiet about who the demonstrator will be for now. Because of her earlier remarks

I hold back on telling her about the People Library experiment too – I'm not sure about Maisie's motivations, and I don't want the news spread around town before I'm ready to share it.

'You can't cook in here, among the books; the place will smell disgusting.'

I pinch the bridge of my nose as a headache forms. 'It *already* smells like boiled cabbage, Maisie, so I'm sure whatever's cooked can only be an improvement. Besides, it would only be a demonstration, using electric hobs so we could hold it in the open part of the library where there's room for spectators. We've got to think outside the box to get enough memberships in a town where not everyone wants to use the library for books. We have to draw them in somehow.' Little Alfie springs to mind – cooking is a practical skill we could incorporate into his home schooling.

'Fine, I'll leave that with you then. I'll get onto advertising the space for these groups and posting on social media. Anything else?' Maisie seems to be enjoying handling the social media side of things, so that's something at least.

Our never-ending to-do list flashes in my mind. 'If you could set up the children's area for our sessions this week that would be fab. And I've got some posters on my desk for Alfie's cubicle if you could show him those when he comes in. He might like them in a particular order, so it's best if we let him decide.'

At the mention of Alfie, she softens. It makes me think Maisie might eventually come around if only she'd give away with that brusque manner of hers.

'Oh, there's the carpet cleaner.' I wave to a guy who is dressed head to toe in an orange jumpsuit. 'Can you let him know what we want? Neutral stuff so it doesn't upset Alfie's time here. Get a quote and find out how long it needs to dry and when he can do it by. That should sort that boiled cabbage smell once and for all!'

Once our meeting wraps, I go to the health section and hunt for some books on the psychology of shoplifting, because as far as I can see without meeting 'Pilferer Pete' he is on the outer edges of society, just like the others. I'm curious to know what drives someone to shoplift, other than economic reasons. I find some books and check them out in my own name.

'Some light reading?' I jump at the voice.

Finn. 'Do you always sneak up like that?' Somehow, he makes the space brighter when he's around. Gone are the drab brown carpets and dull beige desks and all I see is him, as if he's got a giant spotlight above him, showing me the way. It's hard to reconcile this feeling. Is it some kind of love-struck thing? I do feel slightly woozy when he's around and my mind scatters like a thousand marbles. It's quite the predicament not being able to think straight.

'Always use my ninja stealth mode,' he says. 'I'm a nosy reporter, remember?'

I raise a brow. 'I remember. So what can I help you with today, Finn?' I try to keep things professional while my heart beats a rumba, and I pretend we didn't spend the better part of the weekend texting back and forth.

'I've come to join the library, and to ask you if you're ready to be interviewed.'

'Yay! Another member! And I'm *almost* ready. I just need to get permission from the "books" first.' I make air quotes so he knows I don't mean actual books.

'The *books*?'

I give him a secretive smile, but I'm sure he thinks I'm batty because what do air quotes really mean in this situation! 'Yes, the books – it'll all make sense soon, I promise. But for now, let's get you signed up as a member before you change your mind.' I need to chat to Alfie and his mum Jo before I explain to Finn about the People Library experiment.

'I heard there was some sort of sweetener to sign up. I could be wrong . . .' He gives me a look I can only describe as sizzling.

'Oh yeah? What did you hear?' I fold my arms and pretend to be suspicious about this so-called sweetener.

'Something about . . . a long lazy dinner Friday night? I've heard *all* about your cooking prowess from Harry.'

I laugh. 'Well, he's still alive so that's always a good sign, but the cooking thing is kind of new to me, so don't get your hopes up. And this sweetener is only being granted because you're the world-famous reporter who puts places on the map so I'll have to take my chances.'

'Anything for you.'

'Friday night it is.'

'I'll bring the wine.'

'Deal.' We stare at each other for what feels like an eternity and I find myself wishing it was Friday already.

Finn inspires romance for some inexplicable reason, so while I'm feeling love-struck I have another idea I've seen in bookshops before. I find a bunch of popular romance books and wrap them up in butcher paper and tie them with red ribbon. On the front I write a short description about each book without giving too much away. Then I make a sign saying, *Blind Date with a Book*, and go to laminate it. The old-school laminator chugs along at a snail's pace so while that's doing its thing I go outside into the blazing sunshine and pick some wild flowers. Back inside I take the sign and set up another table with the books and a vase for the flowers. Everyone needs a little romance in their lives and sometimes the best place to find it is in a book!

*

Later that afternoon, Alfie arrives and goes to his cubicle, checking that everything is in place. When he sees the posters on his desk he claps his hands across his mouth. 'Wow! These are surprisingly good quality. I'd expected something . . . cheaper-looking, like a photocopy.'

You can't help but smile when Alfie is around. 'Hey, Alfie, good to see you like the new additions.'

'Well except the periodic table – I find that super boring but the shark posters are cool!' A harried Jo comes in, carrying his schoolbooks and library bag.

'Oh, Elodie, these are *lovely*.'

'Maisie can help put them up for Alfie. We thought he might like to decide exactly where they go.'

'That's so sweet of you both. He'll never want to leave.'

'That's our cunning plan.' Alfie lines up his pencils in meticulous height order and arranges his desk to his liking before turning to the blank walls to consider where his posters should go. 'This might take a while . . .' he says, tapping a finger to his chin.

'Take your time, Alfie.' I turn to Jo. 'Can we have a quick chat?'

She raises a brow. 'Oh . . . sure?'

I lead her outside the cubicle so Alfie can't hear. 'Feel free to say no but I wanted to run the idea past you and if you agree then I can ask Alfie.' I go on to explain about the People Library experiment and how library members could 'borrow' Alfie for thirty minutes or so and give him the opportunity to tell his story. Jo patiently listens. Her expression gives nothing away. 'I'm wondering if it would help people understand Alfie better. He'd be in control of what he shares . . .'

Jo interjects. 'Which would be *everything*.'

I grin. 'And then some. You sparked the idea when you said to me: *I wish they'd see what you see*. In this controlled and supervised environment, we know Alfie will be safe and cared for and it gives him the opportunity to call the shots and show people just how extraordinary he is. My hope is that it can lead to more social interactions for him, as you said he's keen to make friends.'

Hesitation flashes across Jo's features. 'I don't know, Elodie. It sounds good in theory but he's been hurt too many times. He might act as if it doesn't bother him, but it does and then I deal with the fallout. The long meltdowns, and the anxiety that never goes away.'

I rub her arm in support. 'I totally understand and I don't want you to feel pressured at all. I'd hate it to go wrong. The very *last* thing I want is to add to Alfie's anxiety.'

She gives me a tired smile. 'You know, I always feel torn when making decisions for him. Am I protecting him too much and holding him back? He can only stay in bubble wrap so long, but because there's just me at home I do what I can to get through every day as best we can with the tools I've got. It's so much harder when every choice is made through a fog of fatigue. Is he missing out on life, on friendships because I'm too scared to let him stay in school, or try new things like the People Library experiment? I know at some point I have to let go; it's just so hard to know when that time is.'

My heart goes out to the exhausted mum who's trying so hard to make her little man's life better but is doubting herself every step of the way. 'You're following your gut, your maternal instinct, and you have to trust in that. Alfie is lucky to have someone like you protecting him and loving him the way you do. I'm sure the worry you feel is normal because of how much you love your little boy. You've made some incredibly hard decisions, but have a look at him, he doesn't look like a boy who is missing out to me. And if we can add a friendship into the mix, all the better.'

We glance at Alfie who's now busy doing his schoolwork, a look of deep concentration on his face. Really, he's so self-sufficient. Jo has done a great job at putting his school curriculum together.

'Thanks, Elodie. Maybe we *should* tell him about the People Library experiment and see what his take is? Maybe that's the first step in me letting the reins go a little.'

I hold up my hands as if in surrender. 'It's totally up to you. But Alfie's a smart cookie and I don't think he'd do something like this if he wasn't comfortable with it. In my humble opinion the kid was born to be on stage; he's a natural storyteller.'

Jo laughs. 'You're right about that. He doesn't mind the limelight, that's for sure. Let's put it to him then.' Worry lines Jo's face and I realise every choice she makes for Alfie comes with that same level of uncertainty. I wish there was some way to assuage her fears, but I know I can't. I only hope that he loves the idea, and more importantly that it actually helps him.

'Hey, Alfie,' I say. 'Sorry to interrupt your schoolwork but I can have a quick chat with you about something?'

'A quick chat is one minute or less. Is it going to be one minute or less?'

I grin. 'Maybe a medium-length chat then.'

'OK. Five to ten minutes should suffice and I won't need to alter my schedule too much as long as you don't go over that.'

He's a planner all right. 'Sounds good.' I give him the card. 'Read it out loud if you want.'

'*We'd like you to share your story. You matter. Wouldn't the world be a better place if we didn't judge a book by its cover? #PeopleLibrary #BorrowPeople.* So, wait. You're saying that I'd be a BOOK?'

'Yes, a human book.' I tell him all about the People Library experiment and he quizzes me until my head spins. Alfie has to know the rules and what's expected of him before he's comfortable agreeing – it's an admirable trait to have.

He glances at his watch. 'OK, so you're promising I can talk about sharks as much as I want and no one will tell me to move on?'

'Yes. That's totally up to you. You're the "book" so you get to make the rules on what your story is about. You can talk about schooling, your life, your superpowers, whatever. Your canny ability to calendar count is very interesting and I don't think many people have heard of such an extraordinary talent, but the floor will be yours.'

'I get to keep it?'

'What?'

'The floor.'

'Oh.' I laugh. 'No, it's an expression.'

'Good because honestly, no one would want this carpet. No one.'

'That's true, but we're working on that and I'm hoping it'll be cleaned before then.' I make a mental note to check what happened with the carpet cleaning quote.

'You're doing this so I make friends, aren't you?'

So much going on in that clever little head of his. 'I hope it'll lead to that and again, that will be totally up to you and if you connect with your "borrower" and if you decide you'd like to go for a bike ride, or pizza or something we could possibly arrange that. We are also looking at setting up a Minecraft coding club here, after school hours, so you could also arrange to meet them for that.'

'Minecraft is my jam. It's an expression.'

'I get it and who *doesn't* like Minecraft?' I grin.

'As for your proposal . . .' He looks to his mum who gives him an almost imperceptible nod, as if to say she's on board with it if he wants to try. 'I'll accept your invitation to be a real-life book as long as my mum is here with me.'

'Of course I'll be there, Alfie. I wouldn't miss it for the world.'

'Time's up, if you'll excuse me,' he says so formally it's hard not to smile.

'I'll leave you with it, and we can chat more later.' Jo gives me a loose hug and I leave to find Maisie to tell her I'll be out for a bit. There's one other person I need to ask; I just need to find him.

Chapter 10

After searching up and down the high street I finally spot Pete through the window of the local supermarket. I watch him for a beat, before deciding to attack this head on. I have no idea if I'm out of line, but I figure there's no time to waste and I can't exactly strike up a friendship with the guy in time for the People Library to start.

Inside, I take a basket, and throw in a packet of chocolate biscuits and a handful of apples as I make my way down the aisle towards him. Pete appears slightly unkempt; his clothes hang off his large frame as if they're a couple of sizes too big. Every few moments he darts a glance over his shoulder, which makes it look very obvious that's he's searching for staff, as if he's about to smuggle something into his jeans pockets. Is that why his clothes are so voluminous? To hide his prizes? I find it strange that no one is watching him, if he's truly the thief they peg him for. Perhaps they search him on the way out? As I get within a step of him, I see him take a bottle of chilli sauce and place it in his pocket. He does it so slowly, it's almost as if he *wants* to be caught. What's that about then?

'Hey,' I say, and give him a friendly smile.

Pete shoots me a challenging look as if waiting for me to call him out.

I place my basket on the edge of the shelf so I can free up one hand. 'I'm Elodie, the new librarian, and I wanted to give you this.' I hand him the same card as the others. 'I *think* I understand you, Pete, and why you do what you do. I'd love you to be involved in the People Library experiment. If you want to join in, my phone number is on the back.' With one last supportive smile, I take my basket and walk to the checkout. Pretending to be engrossed in unloading my groceries I surreptitiously peek at Pete, who wears an expression of bewilderment as he reads the card.

I don't yet know why Pete steals – there's so many reasons aside from economic and I'm still doing my research into it – but I have a feeling it's to do with other people's expectations, rather than a genuine desire to do it. It'll be interesting to find out and I only hope he's agreeable to joining the People Library and opening up about his experiences.

Once I've paid for my goods, I dash back to the library and am hit with a glare from Maisie. I give her a winning smile, drop the biscuits and apples on Alfie's desk before going to the computer to check membership numbers.

We still need 451 members. The number seems so high compared to the amount of effort we've put in. Despite our best intentions there hasn't been the influx I'd hoped for. All hope rests on the People Library experiment. It's the only way I can see us getting ahead while we have little to no funds to play with.

Even our pre-loved book sale isn't working well and I've found plenty more to add to the collection, books that are so out of date I can't fathom why they were never switched out before now. I change the sign and write: *5 books for 5 pounds*. While it's peanuts, even a small bit of cash can be put towards new stock. I take some pictures and send them to Maisie's email and ask her to post on our socials. I take a picture of the '*Blind Date with a Book*' display and ask her to schedule that post for the evening so they're not uploaded all at once.

Once that's done, I get to work, designing posters for the experiment. I need to get Finn involved. I have to tell Maisie about it first, but something holds me back. I still don't know if I can trust her and I don't want the news spread around town and take the shine off the announcement before we're ready.

Forcing a sunny expression, I wave her over and am met with an eyeroll. 'You're selling bundles of books for five lousy pounds now?'

'They haven't been borrowed in a decade or so, Maisie. The price is more than fair.' I pick up one as an example. '*One hundred and one ways to cook eggs in the microwave.* Do you think we should keep this on the shelf?'

'Well, not that one.'

I choose another. '*The Roving Dick Detective.* You've got to wonder what kind of detective doesn't wear trousers but who am I to judge?'

She laughs. 'OK, I see your point.'

'I don't like losing books either, but there's so many here that need to go. Keep an eye out for anyone who wants to buy them, OK? I know it's small change but we can really use it. Let's go to the office. I've got some news.'

'You're leaving so soon?' And just like that the same old Maisie returns and the smile vanishes.

It's my turn to eyeroll. 'Would you like that, Maisie?' She shrugs. We sit at the desk and I take out one of the posters to show her. 'I'm not leaving – sorry to burst your bubble. I'm implementing an initiative called "the People Library experiment". We're going to promote *real* lives. Members can visit the library and "borrow" a person for thirty minutes and hear their stories. We don't have money for new stock until we get the grant, so until then we'll lend people.'

'We'll . . . what?'

'If Alfie, an eleven-year-old can understand the concept, I'm sure you can too, Maisie.'

'But we loan books, not people.'

'Now we do both.'

'And just who is going to agree to share their story? People around here are dull and boring. What makes you think anyone will be interested in hearing about their gardens, or their daily walks to the letterbox? Look, Elodie, I *want* to be excited, I want this place to work but this is just silly. We'll be laughed out of town.'

Worry comes off her in waves but I let it float above me. 'Actually, I've already invited four people to share their lives and they're definitely not dull; they're anything but. And we have to try something, Maisie, or else this place will close forever. We need a miracle at this point – so why not try this? Who cares if some people laugh – at least it means we tried.'

She sighs. 'Who are the people you've chosen?'

'Harry, Sofia, Alfie and Pete.'

Maisie cups her face and groans. '*Homeless Harry and Pilferer Pete*? Oh, it gets worse! Why can't you choose locals that people actually *like*? Do you know anything about Sofia and what she's done?' She doesn't give me a chance to reply, just steamrolls ahead. 'Her husband stole money from the council! Money that was meant for the library. There's no way she wasn't part of that. Have you seen her house? It's a castle for crying out loud that was most likely purchased with stolen money! You'll find that a lot of people are still very angry with Sofia, and including her will only keep them away from the library.'

I take a deep breath. 'Come on, Maisie, have a listen to yourself. Sofia is the innocent party in all this. She was conned by that poor excuse of a man just like the rest of you were.' Maisie clenches her jaw – talk about overwrought. 'Look at your reaction to this. It's the reason we need such an initiative.' To think there's people discussing the fact that Sofia could be part of her husband's theft without ever sitting down and asking for her side of the story just astounds me.

Willow Grove residents need more than the People Library; they need a Doctor Phil intervention!

'This is the worst idea I've ever heard. You should rethink it.' She folds her arms as if the conversation is closed. I hope I haven't made a mistake sharing it with her.

'Just keep it to yourself for now, OK? No one knows about it yet, except the "books" and I'd prefer to keep it that way.' I don't bother showing Maisie the marketing materials for the People Library. 'Forget about that, and let's focus on today.' Maisie stares at me like I've got bananas for brains, so I swallow a sigh and let it go for now. 'We've got the first book club meeting in an hour. Have many registered?'

'Two.'

A book club of two? 'Including us, that's four, and that's enough to start with.'

'I'm not discussing books with the likes of . . .'

'Oh, Maisie, honestly, didn't your mother ever teach you that if you don't have anything nice to say, then don't say it?' I get up and stomp away. It's like head-butting a wall at times. Perhaps I should give her a written warning about her conduct? I'm puzzled why she'd continue to work here if she's going to argue with me every step of the way, not to mention the way she judges people. If only she'd approach these chats with a more professional demeanour, so we could nut out the pros and cons like adults, rather than the petulant child she comes across as. But it falls to me and I vow to do better. There must be a way to get through to Maisie. Surely she wasn't like this with Agnes, who from all accounts was quite domineering? There's no time to ponder it so I get to work, setting up an area for the book club in a quiet corner. Who am I kidding?! Every corner is quiet because people rarely visit the library!

I exhale all the angst. *I can do this and I will do this*. We might not be where I projected we'd be by week two, but that only means there's plenty of room for improvement. At least two brave souls have registered for book club and I thank my lucky stars for that.

It doesn't matter how many of us there are, I'm going to make it the best damn book club that ever was. I take out the collection of books that we have multiples of and which are new in terms of stock at Willow Grove library. Jenny O'Brien's *Silent Cry* is the first in a police procedural/psychological thriller series that I've heard good things about and has been popular among members at the library.

The book club members duly arrive and I make a big fuss over them. Maisie has deigned not to attend but it's probably better anyway, in case she manages to offend them with her curtness. We settle down to chat and despite us being a lonely trio of bibliophiles, we soon warm to one another.

Donald, a big boisterous man of about sixty speaks up. 'I've been meaning to join the library for a long time. But there was never much new stock. Do you think that will be rectified?'

I nod. 'Yes, that's the plan. As soon as we secure more members we can apply for extra funding, so it might take a few more months, but I'm confident we'll get there. What genres do you like?' I try and focus the conversation on what I can control and hope that Donald will return again next month and perhaps with some friends.

Donald rubs his chin and says, 'Historical fiction, true crime, even a soppy romance wouldn't go astray. I do like happy ever afters if I'm honest.'

Janice, our second member, a slim elegantly dressed thirty-something says, 'I love romance too, and cosy crime. But I'm happy to read any genre. I'm delighted that you've taken over, Elodie. I couldn't imagine the library closing down. I used to come here with my mum when I was a toddler and I've been coming ever since. I'll bring Mum to book club next month; she'll enjoy it. Be warned though, she can talk the hind legs off a donkey . . .'

I laugh. 'Your mum sounds like great fun. Definitely bring her along. The more the merrier! And I promise you we're going to do everything in our power to save this place so our book club can continue for years to come . . .'

'We believe in you! Right-oh,' Donald says. 'In the meantime we'll read *Silent Cry* and then come back to discuss next month. Is that how these things work? My wife said something about book clubs being a front for drinking parties. I told her I'm certain that's not the case, not in a library, but she insists that's what they're all about?'

I might just have the two sweetest book club members in the history of book clubs. 'Well, Donald, to be honest, a lot of them are like that. I was a member of one in London once and it was all champagne and gossip. They never even read the book! Now I can handle a glass of bubbles and some chitchat, but I most certainly cannot handle book club members who don't actually like to read. So in saying that, are you happy to continue the book club during the day where we have cake and coffee, or shall we move it to night-time and have cheese and champagne? I promise it won't be a front for a drinking party – it'll be all above board and very demure.'

Donald and Janice exchange a glance and a cheeky smile. 'I like prosecco,' Janice says. 'In moderation, of course.'

'Same with me,' Donald agrees and grins.

'Well, that's settled then. We'll meet next month, same day, at 6 p.m.? Does that work for you both?'

'Works for me, and I can bring my neighbour, Onkah. He loves reading but can't get to a daytime book club,' says Donald.

'And I'll bring my mum. Looks like we're expanding already!'

'I can't wait!' And I really can't.

We chat for another hour about our favourite authors, our automatic buys – Kerry Greenwood for Janice, and Harlen Coben for Donald. We've got enthusiasm, if nothing else!

Chapter 11

I spend Wednesday morning planning the People Library and just how we're to go about marketing it. How to explain to people exactly what it entails. Once I have my pitch in order I call Finn.

Butterflies flutter inside as I dial his number. It's probably because I'm nervous about sharing the idea with him after facing Maisie's lacklustre reception. Finn, of all people, will be able to gauge how the town will take it and if he says they'll hate it, I'll be crushed. But I'm determined to go ahead with it, no matter what. We have no other choice really, so I'll either fall flat on my face, or I won't.

'Let me guess, you're desperate to see me and you can't wait until Friday night,' he says, his voice oozing warmth.

I laugh. 'Am I *that* transparent?'

'I'm right?' he says surprise in his voice. He's really just too sweet for his own good.

'Sort of right. I want to buy you dinner tonight and run my idea past you for the article. I'm sorry for all the mystery leading up to this point but I had to get permission from a few people and make sure it was good to go. Also, I kind of need the article written post haste.'

He lets out a theatrical sigh. 'Only wants me for my mighty pen. Always the way.'

I shut my office door so no one can hear my flirty voice. 'You know what they say, the pen is mightier than the sword.' *What, Ellie?* My flirt game is so rusty it's cringeworthy!

'That was to make us nerds feel better about being nerds.' Maybe Finn doesn't think so, but sheesh. I really need to learn how to do this better. I shake the thought away. I'm here for the People Library!

'Didn't you get the memo?' I ask. 'Nerds are cool now.'

'What a relief.'

He makes me smile just hearing his voice. 'So dinner. How about we meet at the local pizza place?' I struggle to remember the name. 'And you can stuff your face with pepperoni pizza while I wow you with my bright idea.'

'I do love stuffing my face.'

'Then it's a date. Say 7 p.m.?'

'Done. I'll bring my mighty pen.'

I giggle. 'You do that.' In actual fact I've seen Finn take notes and he always uses his iPad but I make a mental note to buy him a novelty sword pen, if there's such a thing!

We say our goodbyes and I get the rest of the day underway. We have our first rhyme time session tomorrow and I only hope we have more than one child attend otherwise it's not going to live up to expectations about being a social event for parents and children. I check the area that Maisie set up and am happy how colourful she's made it with beanbags and knitted poufs that she found in the basement. I look forward to the day we can fill the children's area with brand-new books.

When the day comes to an end, I walk home, shower and

change, ready for dinner with Finn. I give my appearance a cursory once-over and decide that it'll do. I'm sticking with the make-up-free look and casual attire. More importantly I skim through my material, making sure I haven't forgotten anything that Finn might be interested in to use for his article. I place it all in a tote and head off to dinner. One thing I'm loving about Willow Grove life is the ability to walk everywhere without the need for cars or trains. Nothing is too far away, not even Sofia's castle.

When I get to Fuoco Pizzeria, Finn's inside already, a pretty waitress paying him particular attention. I shake my head and smile. That small-town charm works a treat with the ladies and he's got it in spades.

He stands when I get to the table and gives me a loose hug. 'You smell good,' he says and I laugh in surprise.

'Well, shucks. You certainly have a way with words, Finn Ford.'

He blushes. 'Sometimes my mouth runs away and I have a helluva a time catching it. But you do smell good, almost edible like candy floss.'

A jolt of electricity runs through me. 'I aim to please.'

The pretty waitress completely ignores me. I don't take offence. She's blinded by Finn's dazzling smile and who can blame her? As she perches on the edge of table, Finn jiggles in his seat, as though he's uncomfortable with the attention while she chats away about her day and the fact the coming weekend is *wide open* with no plans. Zero. None. When he manages to get a word in he says, 'Ah, erm, Donatella, this is Elodie, the new librarian. Elodie, this is Donatella. Her parents own Fuoco, but Donatella is the brains behind the rebranding.'

'Oh?' I say. 'It looks great. What was it like before?' It must be a recent thing because the scent of fresh paint lingers faintly in the air.

Donatella rolls her eyes as if the memory pains her. 'Well, it was called Tony's Pizzeria for about a million years. Like so, meh, right? My papa is old-school and still thinks he's in the hills of Sicily most days, but I managed to convince him to rebrand and renovate, though I must admit it took me a while to convince him. But I did eventually. The trick is never giving up. When you want something, you go for it.' She waggles her brows at Finn and lets out a flirtatious giggle. 'And so Fuoco was born.' Finn is beetroot red and looks like he wishes the floor would swallow him up. He's so wholesome, he can't even deal with a saucy Sicilian like Donatella.

I try to help him by getting her attention. 'And fuoco means fire in Italian?'

'Sí. I like things *hot*!' Another giggle in Finn's direction.

I crush my lips together so I don't laugh at her over-the-top performance for Finn's benefit. I don't blame the girl though – she's doing her level best to get his attention but he's busy studying his lap as if he's worried Donatella is about to throw herself in it. Which I'm convinced there's a chance she might.

Flirtations aside, Fuoco has a chic Mediterranean vibe, as if we've been suddenly transported to a contemporary eatery in Europe. 'How did the big change go with the locals?' I'm keen to know how this traditional town reacts to such a thing, because this is what I'm planning to do with the library. Make changes that might divide them.

She gesticulates as she says, 'Oh, you'd have thought I'd turned it into a tattoo parlour or something, the way they went on about the renovations. They warned me I was losing the Italian charm, and once it was gone I'd never be able to get it back. But seriously, Elodie—' she finally turns in my direction and Finn's shoulders relax '—the place *needed* an overhaul. The once-red vinyl booths were outdated, faded to orange and ripped. They needed to go not only because they were an assault on the eyes, but because they were ancient and impossible to clean. We reordered the space so we could fit smaller tables, so couples could also have an intimate dinner, rather than the long banquet tables we had in the middle before. Times have changed. No one eats with twenty family members anymore. Sure, we'll have parties every now and then but most of our reservations are for couples or families of four. These improvements were so overdue but the locals have shown their disapproval by not eating here anymore.'

'You're kidding?' My jaw drops. Why wouldn't a business owner be able to make updates without worrying that they're going to offend locals and lose their patronage? It doesn't make any sense.

'Change is so alien to most here. Talk about stuck in the past. So not only have I made these changes against their wishes but I've also broken my papa's heart. I promised him things would improve but it turns out I've made a grave error. He warned me not to do it, but I really believed in myself and the vision.' Just like that, her earlier verve evaporates and the light in her eyes dulls.

Part of me deflates. This doesn't bode well for the library changes either. Are people really stuck that far in the past here, or is it that there just haven't been enough changes for them to embrace? Whatever the reason, I feel sympathetic towards

Donatella's plight. She only wanted the best for the family business and it's backfired on her. A sudden idea lands. 'Finn, you *have* to put Fuoco on the map like you did with Chez Jacques!'

Donatella's eyes widen and she claps her hands together. 'Could you, Finn?'

'I could try?' Finn makes an awkward face as though he doesn't really believe in himself.

Donatella's confidence returns. 'I'd make it worth your while,' she purrs. She actually *purrs* and this time my laughter gets the better of me.

I give him a reassuring smile. 'You can do it, Finn! You're great at promoting businesses you care about. Look what you did for Mary and Jacques. You could easily do the same for Donatella, and she'd be a dream to photograph . . .' My Astor background comes into play, and in my mind's eye I picture the layout of such an article with the fire licking the top of the oven as Donatella brandishes a piping-hot, freshly made pizza and stares sultrily at the camera.

Finn scrunches up his nose. For a reporter he doesn't handle the spotlight of a lusty Italian goddess very well. 'Sure, sure, I can do a restaurant review. Perhaps Elodie and I can come back in a professional capacity and we'll get photographs of the dishes for the paper?'

'*Sí, sí!* I'll make sure we have everything perfect.'

How else can we help until then? For a place situated on the high street, it's sad to see there's more staff than customers, especially on hump day when I know the working week tends to catch up to people and they look for ways to relax, including getting take-away or eating out. So far, there hasn't even been any food couriers in to pick up orders. Maybe I'm used to London where practically every establishment has drivers waiting to take orders all over the city.

Could Donatella be a future 'book' too? She's definitely got the pizazz for it and from what I can gather she's got an interesting background. Perhaps if she sees the experiment herself she might be intrigued. While we have the perfect four 'books' to begin with, I need to be thinking long term in case this initiative does take off. 'Donatella, we're hosting a big event at the library soon in the hopes of attracting new members. Would Fuoco consider catering it for us? I'm working with a budget, so it doesn't need to be fancy, just good honest Italian food.'

She gives me a wide smile. '*Sí!* We could provide antipasto platters . . . a grazing table like we have in summers in Italy.'

'Sounds delicious.'

'Let me show you! Are you happy for me to select tonight's dishes so you can try them all?'

'More than happy.'

Donatella shrieks and rushes off to the kitchen. Now my only problem is, finding the funds for catering, but as long as the rent on my cottage is paid, I can use the remainder of my salary that week. There must be more items around the library I can sell to help make ends meet. The old computers wouldn't fetch much, besides we need them until there are funds for newer models. There must be superfluous things that can fetch a few extra pounds. I haven't checked out the basement yet, so I make a mental note to investigate. I've put it off so far because it's dark and dingy and creeps me right out.

'You have a way with people,' Finn says surveying me. 'Some women might have been offended the way she had her back to you. But it didn't bother you in the slightest, did it? And then you managed to turn it all around. How do you do that?'

'Ah, how can I be mad when she's got a crush on you? I'm sure she's one of many. In fact, I quite enjoyed watching you squirm. It must be hard to be the hottest ticket in town.'

He throws his head back and laughs. 'That's a *slight* exaggeration.'

I cock my head. 'Really? Your phone buzzes off the hook with women's names popping up like fireworks, yet you don't answer. Every woman we meet, no matter their age, swoons in your presence yet you don't react. In fact, you look like you want to disappear.'

Finn plays with his napkin. 'Well, I wouldn't go that far. I'm still a novelty here, despite living in Willow Grove for ages now, so it boils down to that. If I lived anywhere else, I wouldn't get a second glance.'

I find that hard to believe. For all our catch-ups, I know virtually nothing about Finn. I know where his office is and that's about it. 'Why did you choose to move to Willow Grove?'

'You're a bookworm, Elodie. Surely you felt the same when you walked into town and it looked like a scene from a fairy tale. It just felt right; it felt like magic could happen in a town like this. A fresh start, a new beginning, and taking a chance on what might be.'

'I did feel the same, actually – I used to go to Hamersley boarding school when I was a child. We had monthly excursions to Willow Grove and that's when I fell in love with the idea of being a librarian. Before Agnes took over, there was a lovely librarian who made me believe in the magic of books and that has never waned.'

His eyebrows knit. 'You went to boarding school?'

That must seem strange to Finn so I'm quick to downplay it. 'Yes, my parents went to boarding school there and were convinced it shaped children into the right kind of people – that's what they believe at any rate. I believe we were more like an assembly line of robots, until lights out when all hell broke loose.' I laugh. 'While we were away my parents worked hard on their professional lives. They can be kind of aloof, at times.'

'Huh, it seems written in the stars. You boarded so close and you'd been to the library as a child – thankfully not under Agnes's reign or you may not have wanted to be a librarian. I've heard about Hamersley and some of the bigger scandals. Like when they drained the lake nearby as a prank. And the statue of poor old Queen Liz who lost her head.'

I giggle, remembering all the silly little things that went on to help pass the time. 'There was a lot of that, especially at the boys' school.' I don't say my brother was one of the main culprits and my parents paid a fair bit of restitution so he didn't get expelled. 'What about you? Do you have family here?'

'My siblings were close by for a bit but now they've moved on, scattered like so many marbles. Anyway, I'm the reporter here. Shouldn't I be quizzing *you*?'

'I haven't even got down to the gritty questions yet and you're turning the tables on me already?' I say, feeling relaxed in Finn's company.

He laughs, displaying those pearly whites of his. 'You've kept me hanging for ages about this big idea of yours, and I'm *desperate* to know just what you've cooked up to save Willow Grove library. Put a man out of his misery, please?'

Donatella comes back with a bottle of chianti and pours us

two glasses. She darts back to the counter and returns with a plate of *tagliere di salumi*. There's all sorts of thinly sliced cured meats, cheeses, olives and pickled vegetables. 'Wow,' I say, eyeing the lusciously presented platter. 'This looks delicious, and absolutely perfect for the library event. Members can graze as they listen . . .' It strikes me just how many amazingly talented people there are in Willow Grove. If only they'd connect! Sofia for one would love this place. I make a mental note to invite her to dinner here.

'*Grazie, grazie*, Elodie. I would love to help at your event. Now eat, eat because there's a lot more coming. Arancini, focaccia . . . many other things!'

'This is exactly what I want for the event.' The antipasto is a feast for the eyes with all the different colours and it smells delicious peppered with the scent of garlic and rosemary.

Donatella thanks us again and heads to the front door to welcome a table of two inside.

'If this tastes as good as it looks I can't understand why this place isn't packed every night of the week,' I say, filling my plate with delicious morsels.

'Wait until you try it; it's even better than it looks and their wood-fired pizzas will transport you straight to Italy. Don't even get me started on how good the stuffed porchetta is. But let's not get distracted. You were saying . . . ?'

I grin through a mouthful of thinly sliced prosciutto which thankfully melts in my mouth. I hold a finger up while I finish. 'Right, so I had this idea called the People Library experiment . . .' I go on in detail about the plan to Finn, who stops eating and starts making notes on his iPad. As I continue his grin grows wider and I know he thinks it's a great idea – or maybe just that it will make a popular article? Either way, he seems entranced by the idea, which is a massive relief.

'Elodie, this is gold. *Seriously*. Let me write up the article. You can approve it if you want. Get some photos of you and the "books" ahead of the first event . . .'

I almost choke on an olive. 'No, no, *I* don't want to be part of it. I want it to be all about the "books" and library itself. Really, Finn, we only get one chance to get their attention and get them through the doors so I'd rather focus on that than boring them with the fact I'm new to town.'

Finn stops typing and stares at me. 'But everyone is curious about you and it *will* help draw a crowd.'

I nod as if I agree, and dab at my mouth with a napkin while I formulate an answer that's believable. If I showed my face in the paper and my parents found out, they'd be furious that I didn't tell them the real reason I left. More so, that they've lied to their staff about my whereabouts. It wouldn't look good for anyone. 'The People Library experiment has the potential to be huge. That's worth promoting more than the fact there's a new librarian. The library itself needs to stand on its own two feet, rather than be centred around one person. And I'm hopeful that we might be able to find new members from far and wide because we're offering something unique. Let's not muddy the waters, eh?'

He considers it. 'OK, that makes sense. It *could* be massive. Most people would love to take the credit and have their face splashed all over the paper but not you.'

'It's not about me, it's about the "books" and that's why it's so special.'

'I see your point. Where did you come up with the idea?'

'The library is dangerously in the red. There's no money for new books, so I figured if I couldn't lend new books, I'd have to lend people! But really, Finn, it's about so much more than that. It's about not judging a book by its cover as I've seen so many people in Willow Grove do. It's about prying those pages open and reading between the lines. I can use cliché after cliché to explain it, but what I'm hoping is that it changes the way people treat others. Instead of gossiping behind their backs and calling them awful names maybe they'll reach out to them instead, offer a helping hand. I'm hoping they'll relate to their plight in some way – *there but for the grace of God, go I* sort of thing.'

His eyes are wide with excitement, as if he's trying to take it all in at once. 'I have to get this article right. Make sure I sum it up in such a way so that they're intrigued and *have* to know more because this has such a huge potential that it could change lives.' He blows out a breath. 'I'm going to put everything I have into it.'

I let go of all the worry. Finn gets it! 'I know you'll do an expert job, like you always do.' Finn's articles are different from most, in that he writes with more feeling, making a person want to join his crusade, as it were. Like the article that led me here – it had been written in such a way that I could envision a town with no books and had to act. I'm hoping whatever he writes for the People Library is a call to arms as well. 'You're a bit of a superstar, Finn, and I know whatever you write will convince the masses to see what all the fuss is about.'

'Superstar, that's me.' He shakes his head as if he's anything but. 'So let's aim to publish next week, or the week after? Does that give you enough time?'

'As soon as you're ready. I've organised as much as I can; now it'll be all down to my special human books. For their sakes, I hope this goes the way I want it to.'

'It's an experiment, that's for sure. And all experiments need tweaks, so we'll adjust if needed. Perhaps the article will be a serial, so people can follow along and those who don't come to the first couple, might come after and we'll keep those numbers ticking over.'

'That's a great idea. I'm going to make a real event of it. A real party atmosphere, as if we're celebrating. I get the feeling—' I look around the empty restaurant '—they don't like change much in Willow Grove.'

He takes a slug of wine. 'But they do like gossip.'

'True.'

'Where have you come from, Elodie, to dream so big like this?' He gazes at me like I'm something special. It's enough to make my heart race, because when I look at him I see a man who I could fall in love with. A man I trust implicitly because he has no idea who I really am and he likes me on my own merits. Will this lead to something more? Part of me is desperate for it to happen; the other part is telling me to slow down, to wait. Would Finn care if I admitted I was Ellie Astor? Lost Ellie Astor who in this bumbling backwards way is trying to find the path right for her? It's hard to tell.

I toy with the stem of my wineglass. 'Dreaming big is all I know, and up until recently, I never had the chance to act on those dreams. If I can save the library, that will give me the confidence that anything's possible. That I can pursue my passions and design my very own future. Anyway, it's you I'm interested in.' I have to divert the conversation away from me, as the more wine I drink, the more I want to open up to Finn.

'You're a reporter for the *Chronicle*, and you moved here a few years ago and that's all I know about you. Would *you* make a good "book"?'

He waves me away. 'It'd be like reading the telephone book, monotonous and sleep-inducing. There's not much to tell. Time has marched on and nothing much has changed in my life, except the dreary weather.'

'Are you single?' He's never outright said so and I think about all those unanswered phone calls. 'Or been married, divorced, anything juicy?'

He packs his iPad away. 'Single as they come. There's not been a lot of time for romantic pursuits with family commitments, that sort of thing. My life is slower now, so I'm hoping that can change. What about you, got any ex-husbands stashed away?'

I bite my lip to tame laughter. I haven't even had a relationship go the distance, let alone get to the point of matrimony. 'I've had a *lot* of romantic attachments, some sizzling bad boys, some home-grown heroes, cowboys, billionaire businessmen – you name it, I've loved them all . . .'

He waggles a brow. 'Book boyfriends?'

'This is how I know you're a keeper, Finn. That you even know the term *book boyfriends* says a lot.' He's a reader too and that is a definite plus for me. 'Are you happy here? Was this where you always wanted to be?'

He considers it. There's more to his story, but what? I never seem to get past the surface level with him. Probably because I'm not sharing much either, but I have a reason, so he must have one too.

'I had these big dreams once,' he says looking just past me, 'of being an investigative reporter, but it'll stay just that – a dream. Why leave all this behind?' Finn points to the high street where the trees sway in the wind and the odd shopper or two walk by, heads down against the breeze. 'I'm happy in Willow Grove.'

I smile back at him, but I question why he hasn't tried to find work as an investigative reporter, if that is where his heart lies. Surely it's as easy as applying for that job. I know, I've lived that life and had to vet many of our staff at Astor news. If I owned up to who I really am, I could help get Finn the job of his dreams, but if he really wanted that, wouldn't he have tried himself? Finn doesn't come across as unambitious to me. Is it a confidence thing? Probably not – he presents as self-assured and in control, albeit without the cockiness and ego that so many men in the news business wear so proudly. I bet he's too good to fight to the death over a breaking story. 'So why didn't you follow your dream?'

'Life got in the way, I suppose. But I'm grateful for what I have and the way things ended up. Did you always dream of being a librarian in a small town, or did you have your sights set on something else?'

I pile my plate with olives while I figure out what to say. 'I worked in publishing for a bit, at a large company, but it wasn't what I thought it would be. Being chained to a chair in a boardroom didn't suit me. It was less about the beauty of books and more about business. Saying that, it was a good learning curve; it's made me aware that I want to be on the ground level, helping in the community, being part of initiatives that make a difference. I want to bring books and programs to those less fortunate, so they have the same chances as everyone else. But I'm still working out how to achieve that. In my previous job,

I didn't really feel like what I did mattered. I wasn't helping anyone except the company – and that's fine if you're the type who cares about a big salary and the bottom line, but that doesn't inspire me at all. It's a sort of hollow road.

'When I saw your article for the library, it felt like my whole purpose came into focus, so I have you to thank for that. The power of words, of books, and what reading means to people can't be diminished. We can't allow libraries to close, because if so where does it end?' My light-bulb moment, really I'm still pinching myself that I'm here.

'I love that, Elodie. You're here for the right reasons. That's why I wrote that article and I used whatever contacts I could find – which wasn't many – to share it far and wide. In the end I used most of my yearly marketing budget on paid Facebook ads to spread the word. I feel exactly the same about libraries closing. Such a daunting thought. My biggest fear was that we wouldn't find a librarian. Who'd take on such a task with the odds stacked against them? And then in you walked, our miracle maker.'

'Let's not get ahead of ourselves.' I let out a nervous laugh. 'We can only hope everyone embraces the People Library experiment.'

'How can they not? I myself can't wait to hear Harry's story.'

'Me too. Let's hope he doesn't get stage fright.' Harry hasn't actually confirmed he'll be part of it yet. It's on my list to follow up ahead of Finn's article but something tells me Harry will do it, even if his voice shakes and his knees knock. There's a quiet resolve to Harry, as if he's ready to open up no matter what it costs him.

'I'm sure he'll surprise you. Surprise all of us. But you

understand you'll probably have some locals who oppose the idea when the article publishes, right?' He grimaces as if the thought pains him.

I nod, knowing from experience nothing good comes easy. 'I'm expecting it. But won't that make a great talking point?'

'You're good at this, taking risks, fighting for what's right.'

'Either good or wildly naïve.' One or the other!

'I'm going with good. Now since this was purely a business meeting, I'd like to confirm we're still on for Friday night dinner?'

I grin. 'You're a brave man, actively pursuing a home-cooked meal by me.'

'I'm prepared to risk it.'

'Get the article done first, just in case.' We laugh. If I can't live authentically here where can I? I cross my fingers that the experiment will work, and get us closer to those magic numbers so we can file the funding paperwork. I have so many ideas to get people back to the library but it all comes down to having the finances and time to invest in them. If I save the library, then it'll be a sure-fire sign that I can let down the last part of my guard with Finn and see what blossoms.

Chapter 12

Later that week, I'm dusting a cobweb off my arm. I shudder as I gingerly walk around the basement using my phone light to guide me. So far I've unearthed boxes of old encyclopacdias. I dig through them, happy to find that they're full sets. I drag the boxes close to the stairs to carry up once I'm done. They're sure to sell for a decent chunk of money as they've become popular for collectors now they're no longer in print.

Off to one side, I find some dusty old library catalogue drawers. I open them, excited to see cards written in cursive with the names of the books and the old borrowers. These will fetch a pretty penny! Mum recently purchased one for her home library and paid a significant amount for it. I give them a wipe-down with my sleeve and take some photos so I can list them for sale. There's boxes of old-style Christmas decorations, a raggedy old tree and some knotty lights. I spend a bit more time hunting around but only find junk, broken stools, burst beanbags. When I trip over a plastic skeleton, I squeal in fright, and hop, skip and jump out of the bowels of the basement. Leaving the encyclopaedias abandoned for another day. Perhaps a day where Finn visits and I can send that big, brave man down instead.

I head back up, taking the stairs two at a time, before seeing the light and letting out a gasp. I'm alive! After patting myself down to remove the dust from 1967, I take a deep breath and vow never to go down there again unless it's with an electrician who can sort the lighting out.

Once my pulse returns to regular programming, I go to my computer to search for other library card catalogues for comparison prices. They sell from anywhere between a thousand pounds apiece up to tens of thousands for those with a more French flair. These ones are a plainer, more commercial style, so I presume will be at the lower price point. Still, if they sell, it'll be a win for us. We could buy some new stock, for a start. Pay for the carpet cleaner whose quote was a little higher than I expected, so Alfie can handle the history section. Pay for the catering.

Teddy's name flashes up on my mobile and I catch Maisie glance at it. I make a mental note to change his name just in case. I hurry into a cubicle and shut the door. 'Hey, how are you?'

'Oh you know, feet up on some poor pleb's desk, in charge of the masses.'

'You're in! And get your feet off my desk this instant, you monster!'

'Why, you want it back?'

I smile. 'Never! So fill me in, what's going on there. Are they OK with you taking my spot?'

'Worked like a charm. I fronted up and by the looks of it, just in the nick of time. I haven't quite seen Mother look so *harried* before. She's been attending all your events, and methinks she's starting to realise just how tiresome they can be when you've also got to front up for work the next day.'

I run a hand through my hair, dragging the silvery filament of more cobwebs. 'Teddy, I'm so thrilled for you but a bit sad for Mum. Although, it's good she can finally see that I'm not complaining for the sake of hearing my own voice. She might finally understand what I've been up against. Not that I didn't mention it to her four thousand times or anything.'

'Right? It's slowly dawning on her, not that she'll admit to it. She's popping vitamins like they're lollies. I've put my hand up to take your place as the face of Astor, but got a stern no. Poor Mother will eventually wear herself out and will give in. I'm biding my time and trying hard to win her over. Everyone is still asking how you're doing, so they've said you're investigating the wellness industry and rumour has it Astor is about to branch into that too. It's quite amusing really. Part of me thinks we really *are* going to launch some health and wellbeing centre.'

'Does everyone *really* believe that?'

He chortles, big and loud. 'Of course! Mum is talking up ashrams and how we should all focus on living a more enlightened existence. Can you imagine? Everyone just nods and agrees, because she is the *least* Zen person we all know but no one is brave enough to mention that. She has taken up yoga, says she needs it for the stress relief, so who knows what might happen. Maybe we bloody will get into that industry – stranger things have happened.'

'So Mum hasn't mentioned me coming back?' The guilt creeps back in at the thought of my mother being run ragged. Why can't she just let Teddy take my role and be done with it?

'Only every three minutes or so. That's why I'm calling.'

My heart sinks. 'What is it?'

'Mum has been here from sunrise to sunset. Her eyes are

popping out of her head most days, it's a bit of a shock seeing her look less than poised so I wanted your take on it. Reckon there's a real chance she'll trust me, or do you think she'll run herself into the ground because "surrender" isn't in her vocabulary?'

I sigh. She's sixty-something and follows a punishing schedule, made worse if she's also doing the events that I usually do. But Teddy is right: she won't surrender, not without a fight. 'Surely, you're proving to her you've got the nous. What else does she want?'

He expels a heavy breath. 'Well, that's just the thing. I'm sorry to tell you this over the phone, Elodie, but Dad isn't well. He's been in and out of hospital with his heart again. They've managed to keep it out of the press so far. They've accepted that you're probably not coming back for a bit, but personally, part of me wishes you would. It's not that the wheels are falling off, but it feels like they're a little loose. All of a sudden things have changed here and I've tried everything in my toolbox to make it work. To make Mother see. If she doesn't hand me some of the load, I can't do much without you.'

'I'm proud of you for reaching out to me. Together we can formulate a plan, surely?'

'You're the one who stays the course, and it all feels a little up in the air. Mother really needs to administer to Dad but she won't take her eye off things at Astor, and it's to their detriment. We forget that they're not spring chickens anymore. I don't think she can keep this pace up for long, and Dad really needs to recuperate without all the worry. I guess I just want you to tell me to keep pushing, it'll all be OK. I really wanted to do this on my own merits, without having to beg for your help, but without her trusting me, there's little I *can* do.'

'Whoa, this is a lot to process.' I knew I'd never be able to stay long term at Willow Grove. That same old guilt returns – that and not being able to say no to my family, especially when Dad is unwell. I can't leave them in the lurch. 'I need more time, Teddy. I can't leave this position after I've given my word. I *can* try and get the funding in ahead of the October deadline but that will mean I need the membership numbers ahead of time, and so far, that's proving difficult. Do you think they can wait until October at least and I can help you out by phone as much as I can?' The last thing I want to do is have taken this job and then leave them floundering with no librarian and no hope of meeting the deadline. Regret claws at me. I should have made boundaries when I first started at Astor; *hell*, I should never have started there. And with my dad growing frailer I know I'll never forgive myself if I don't go home and help. I feel a sense of suffocation just thinking of it all.

'Just do your best, sis.' He tries to make his voice sound upbeat but it's not convincing. 'If things get worse, I'll let you know. Any pointers on how to handle Mother? How to convince her that she's making life more difficult than it needs to be?'

I consider it. Mother is not your average woman and you can't make demands and expect her to take you seriously. You have to approach things in a certain way. 'You have to appeal to her in a business sense. Talk about KPIs, profit margins, and how you feel you can boost them but you need to take on certain aspects to make that happen. The *Eyrie* documentary was a hit in the box office. Start small, mention that you'd like to be involved in the film side. Mother prefers print, so this could be your way in. Mention your affiliation with Louise.

As a narrator she hit the mark in a big way. Show Mother that you know the ins and outs of that project and that you want to tackle the next one. It's slated to be about a group of ice climbers. Research the hell out of the project and go wow her with what you know and how you plan to take it to dizzying heights. If you can convince her you can handle that, then it won't be long before she trusts you can handle it all.' I send a prayer up to the universe to make it so.

'OK, wow that's great advice, Elodie. I'll do that. And to be honest, the film side is where I want to be, and not just because of Louise – before you come to that incorrect conclusion. Maybe I should reach out to Lou and mention that I'm keen to work with her?'

'Yes! Do that. Get her onside professionally, and then she'll see that you're taking life a lot more seriously these days too.'

'She sent me some pics of Spain . . .'

I laugh, the tension clearing. 'Things are getting serious!'

'Slowly but surely. Louise is special and is going to be the mother of my children one day, so I'm happy to take things slow. By this time next year, I'm hopeful we might have progressed to talking on the phone.'

'You can't rush these things.'

'What about you? How's it going with that guy you went out with?'

How will Finn fit into my life if I have to leave? If I have to tell him I'm really Ellie Astor and not some bumbling librarian who wants to change the world by helping everyone access books. 'It's going well. Slowly too. It's sort of hard to open up to him because of who I am, and is there any point if I have to leave?' The thought is a depressing one. I try to hold on to hope that Teddy will pull a rabbit out of the hat and manage to turn things around but I'm not convinced he even believes he can do it anymore – and that's saying a lot. My brother is usually supremely confident, so to hear that worry in his voice, well, it doesn't bode well for my future at Willow Grove.

Teddy lets out a sigh. 'Yeah, right, that is tough. I mean, maybe we can swing it so you *can* stay in Willow Grove, but it's going to be difficult unless Mother stops trying to be everything here.' He lets out a frustrated sigh, which is so unlike Teddy who is usually upbeat even in the bad times.

'Look, I'll give them a call at some point. I need to speak to Dad. I can't bear to think of him so ill.'

All I know is Mother will try to convince me to come back and then this will all have been for nothing. I need to stand my ground and finish what I started at least. I'll be sorry to lose all my new friends.

Will they forgive me if I up and leave? Sofia already has trust issues and I've promised her friendship. Who will make Harry feel welcome and bring him nice home-cooked, nourishing meals? And what about little Alfie with his no-filter approach to life – and his need to be taken under the wide protective wings of people other than his mum.

Then there's Finn. Beautiful, laid-back Finn who would surely be hurt that I'm not who I say I am despite my best intentions. Would they feel cheated? Will Finn wonder what else I was hiding? I know I would.

'Dad's doing OK. He simply needs to rest but you know what he's like. Thinks the world will stop spinning if he takes time off being Mum's shadow.'

I take a deep centring breath. 'He loves her so much.' I'd always thought of Dad as Mum's faithful sidekick but being away has given me the space to realise that's how he shows his love for her. By supporting her in business as that's her love language. That's her baby – so he's right there nurturing her as she nurtures it. 'Buy me some time, Teddy?'

'I'll try. I really will. Tomorrow is another day!'

We say our goodbyes and when I end the call and open the door, Maisie springs away, guilt plastered all over her face. How much did she hear? 'Can I help you, Maisie?' I ask, trying to keep my voice steady as I gauge her expression, hoping it will tell me how much she knows.

'I added some more cushions to the children's area as per your wishes, if you want to have a look? And I've pinned up bunting across the ceiling to make it appear a little more festive too.'

Maisie doesn't appear to be her usual haughty self. Maybe she didn't hear a thing. My thoughts are so scrambled it's hard to know what to think. One thing that stands out is that Maisie seems more enthusiastic when it comes to children's initiatives in the library. While she's still adamant she doesn't want to read aloud to them, she seems to enjoy organising that section and making it look the part. Perhaps, if the funding does come through, I can put Maisie in charge of the design. Give her some extra responsibility there and see how she handles it. She can set up a kids' craft session, a children's book club . . . the possibilities are endless. If only Teddy can sway Mother.

I check my watch. Rhyme time was supposed to start ten minutes ago. 'We better hurry – they'll be waiting.'

Maisie shakes her head sadly. 'None have arrived, Elodie. Not one.' She shrinks in on herself as if she's truly upset.

'Really? Why? You've done such an amazing job with that area, Maisie. I'm so sorry that it hasn't panned out.' It's all too much. Why don't they come? Is it me? Maybe I'm not the person for the job after all? Have I made a huge mistake thinking I could save this place when in fact I'm damaging any chance Willow Grove library had?

*

'Good morning, Mum, it's me.'

'Ellie! It's lovely to hear from you. Where are you?'

There's no point hiding it anymore. I don't have the energy for it and maybe if she knows I'm gainfully employed she'll be more understanding. One can only hope! 'I'm in Willow Grove. I'm working at a library here.'

I'm met with silence and then finally: 'You left Astor to work at a *library*?'

I close my eyes briefly. 'It's not that much of a surprise, is it? I did study librarianship for a reason, Mum. You know I've always wanted to follow that path.'

'But Astor offers you so much more. Why . . . ? I will *never* understand you, Ellie.'

I let out a laugh, we're polar opposites and yet she's still trying to change me, mould me into a version of her. 'Teddy called. He said things are a bit hectic at Astor. He's concerned you're taking on a lot of extra work and the pressure is intense. And now Dad has been back in hospital? How bad is it?'

'You really did choose a terrible time to leave, darling,' she admonishes me. 'Your father is OK, but his corporate days are numbered. The cardiologist seems to think that stress is the culprit so has advised him to consider retirement. Can you *imagine*?' Her voice rises.

'Imagine retirement?' I frown.

'Yes retirement, what else! It's ridiculous. What's one supposed to do? Sit around all day and watch Netflix? That's just not the Astor way.'

I roll my eyes. Everything always circles back to Astor. 'Have you ever thought that Dad might *like* retirement? He might like to watch TV all day and take an afternoon nap. Or go on a cruise around the Caribbean. Eat creamy camembert in Paris? Climb the steps of Machu Picchu.'

She scoffs. 'Machu Picchu! They're called the *Steps of Death* for a reason, Ellie! When you retire, you're basically throwing your hands up to the universe and saying: "Take me, Death, I'm ready." He can't retire, he's mid-sixties for crying out loud. His doctor is a buffoon.'

'Oh, Mum! That's not true at all! Why wouldn't you want to enjoy this season of your life together? It's not like I'm suggesting you should retire too but you could definitely ease back a little. Take some time to travel. You and Dad have achieved great things but you've never enjoyed life outside of work. What about lying in on Sundays and eating buttery croissants in a hotel in Paris. Walking the Camino in Spain. Swimming in the Aegean Sea at sunset. Won't you regret that you didn't take this time, under doctor's orders, to spend with Dad? You said you were all set on handing me the reins of Astor, yet it appears that was never the case.'

'How can I, Ellie? You're nowhere to be found. I can't leave

Astor in Teddy's hands; even if I trusted him, he's still got so much to learn. It's a billion-dollar business. One can't just walk away on a whim.'

Deep down I knew she was never going to hand Astor over to me. She'll die on her throne. And I find it so desperately heart-breaking – not because I want to take over, but because she doesn't know anything outside of working. It's such a limited life. More money than Rupert Murdoch and no time to enjoy it. 'Teddy is a fast learner. He *can* be trusted. It's what he wants, and it's what needs to happen if you want the future of Astor to be secure. Without him, all you've worked for will eventually fizzle away.' I could never let that happen, but I hope the threat is enough to galvanise her.

'No, darling, that's just not true. We need *you* back, Ellie – you're the way of the future, the face of Astor. So when will that be? You're right – things have been hectic without you, and I can't keep up. Your father needs me too. This is a family business and that's all there is to it.'

My heart squeezes. 'What about what *I* want though?'

'You were born for better things, Ellie. When will you see that?'

Has Mother ever listened to me? Ever wondered what makes me tick? 'I've made a commitment to save Willow Grove library . . .'

She cuts me off. 'How much money do you need? I'll buy the bloody thing if I have to, even though it makes no financial sense.'

I heave a long sigh. 'You're missing the point like you so often do. Look, I'll come back as soon as I can but that's all dependent on keeping the promise I made here. I'm an Astor after all and we keep our promises.' That will get to her – it's an oft-said phrase from my childhood when Mum sent us from one activity to the next when all we wanted to do was be kids. 'And I'll only return on the condition that you train Teddy to take over, and not me.'

'You always were whimsical. I'll hold the fort, but don't keep me waiting long.'

Did she agree, or step around it, like she so expertly does?

I end the call and I feel more confused than ever about what to do. My phone pings again. An antique dealer wants to buy the library catalogue drawers! Finally, some funds!

Chapter 13

The interminable week ends on a low note. Yet another initiative, the writers' group, failed to yield any members. Not one person showed up. I'd have thought there'd have been a few scribblers in town, but if there are, they don't want to share their stories with a group. We still need 438 memberships, we've barely made a dent in the numbers at all. Short of dressing up as a book and walking up and down the high street, I don't know what else to do. Everything hinges on the People Library experiment and if that fails then we will fail. It's enough to make me queasy.

I trudge to the supermarket to get groceries for dinner with Finn, but my heart isn't in it. Failure washes over me and it's hard to shrug it off. I don't want to let down the people of Willow Grove and lose their library but it feels inevitable, somehow.

Inside, I distractedly place all manner of vegetables in my basket, having no real plan. Maybe we'll have frozen pizza, and I'll drink my body weight in wine instead. I go to the freezer section and grab a few pizzas, thinking it's sacrilege compared to Fuoco's delicious wood-fired creations. I shake my head – I will not give up. I put the pizzas back and pull myself together. If I want to save this bloody library, then wallowing in self-pity isn't going to damn well help.

I decide to make a proper home-style roast with all the trimmings and only hope it'll cook in time. Just how long *does* a roast take? Well, we'll soon find out. When I get to the fridge section, there's a tap on my shoulder. I turn to find myself face to face with Pete, who is wearing a similar outfit as before, wildly big on his large frame.

'Pete, lovely to see you.'

'Did you mean what you said?' His eyes are pools of sadness and I'd challenge anyone to stare into them and not be moved.

'I meant every word, Pete. I understand that things aren't always as they seem.' It was the way he acted as if he wanted to be caught that got me. There was no sneaking about; it was quite the opposite.

Pete gives me a quick nod. 'Then I'd like to be a human book. I'd like that very much.' He attempts a smile. It's wobbly, as if he hasn't had much practice.

'Really?' I say with a grin. Out of all of the 'books' I didn't hold much hope Pete would join in because we hadn't really connected, he didn't know my reasoning and obviously just has blind faith in me. I have to make this work.

'Really.'

'I'm so pleased, Pete.' He's managed to turn my despair around and I jump up to his burly height and give him a friendly hug, which provokes a shocked expression on his features. 'This is wonderful, wonderful news! If you're free I'd love to invite you for an informal meeting on Monday morning at the library with the other "books". Finn and a photographer will be there to take pictures and interview you all ahead of the start date the week after.' I haven't exactly squared this with Finn yet, so I hope he's amenable.

'Sure, Monday is good.'

'Great. We can chat in more detail then about what being a human book means but it's simple really, you'll just share whatever you feel comfortable with and we'll go from there.'

'Do you think people will care about what I have to say?' The million-dollar question, which I'm also quite keen to know the answer to.

'The *right* people will care and that's a start.'

'OK,' he says with a shrug. 'Well, I better be off. Have a good weekend, Elodie.'

'You too, Pete.' I go to the checkout and pay for my things, walking home with a spring in my step to start preparing dinner for Finn.

*

'Something smells good,' Finn says, and hands me a bottle of wine as he crosses the threshold.

'Thank you. It's roast beef.' I called Sofia and got some pointers so I feel quietly confident that I'm not going to poison the man but only time will tell.

'My favourite.'

'Before I forget . . .' I mention my encounter with Pete, including the plan to meet him on Monday morning accompanied by Finn and the *Chronicle* photographer. 'And I've texted Sofia and Jo who are happy to join. I only have to confirm with Harry, who I'll see when I get to work. I don't have time to dilly-dally anymore. I've got one chance to push this so I need to go all guns blazing.'

'Sure, I'll speak to my photographer but consider it done.' He grins.

'You're the photographer, aren't you?'

He laughs. 'How did you guess?'

'You're a one-man band but you're too humble to take the praise for single-handedly running the whole paper.'

'Shucks, there you go with the compliments again.'

'Calling it like I see it!'

We go through to the cosy little kitchen. The rustic space is warm and inviting, the kind of place you feel comfortable making a mess. It's not precious and sterile like my kitchen back in London. I've never felt so at home like I have here. Finn's presence only enhances the mood. He looks at ease, his athletic frame propped up against the wooden island, looking like a hot bachelor in his knit jumper and jeans. 'A glass of red?' he asks as he pours two glasses and hands one over.

Just as I'm about to compliment the wine, his phone pings and the name Katy flashes up again. 'Do you need to tend to business?' I ask, arching a brow.

He shakes his head. 'It's not business; it can wait.'

I'm reminded of lunch with Sofia where she also mentioned his phone ran hot but his good manners prevented him from answering it. Is it good manners, or is it leaving some poor woman pining for him?

The phone pings again, and this time a picture flashes into view of a woman who I presume is Katy wearing a bright red dress.

I'm not one to beat around the bush, so I bring it up. 'Who is Katy?'

'Sorry, I hate being rude but if I don't reply she'll bombard me with texts all night. Usually, I have a hard-and-fast rule never to answer my phone when I'm socialising. It's one of my pet peeves when your friend is only half there, the other half in cyber space.' I know this about him, but he sure does get a lot of texts of an evening.

'Go for it.'

With nimble fingers he texts a reply and within a moment another photo appears, this time she's in a blue dress. He sighs. And texts again. I can't help but peek over his shoulder. *I like the blue. Take a jacket. Charge your phone. And make sure you've got enough money for a cab, OK? Don't stay out too late. Love you.*

Love you?

Before I can jump to conclusions Finn holds his phone up and shows me the two photographs. 'What would have you chosen, red or blue?'

I frown, not sure where this is going but decide to play along. Finn doesn't strike me as malicious, so I don't think he'd be rubbing my face in the fact he's dating another woman. And are we dating? It hasn't exactly been confirmed.

I study the two dresses. The red is short and tight, and the blue is long and flowy. 'Red.'

'No way! It's too short.'

'For what?'

'For my baby sister.'

There is a God! 'So that's why you chose the blue?'

'That's exactly why. She's just started university and is out on her own for the first time. It worries me endlessly.' Is this why he said before he's suddenly got more free time? His baby sister has flown the nest?

'You sound like her parent, not her brother.'

He nods. 'She complains about that constantly. She's the baby, but there's three more just like her. They message me a thousand times a day, giving me a heart attack about every little thing. I'm too protective, they say, but surely there's no such thing.'

Frankie, Miranda, Katy and Lia. All those texts were from his sisters.

I grin. Finn's background finally makes sense. All those messages, all those veiled references to him being too busy to follow his own dreams. He must have had a hand in raising them, or else they're a really tight-knit family. 'Where are they all?'

He pulls a face as if it pains him to think of it. 'Out in the big wide world, too far away for me to feel comfortable. Katy is at uni in Sussex. Frankie is in London taking over the world of fashion. Miranda is a nanny in Kent and Lia is on a gap year that's lasted *four* so far. She flits from country to country and wakes me up at all hours because she can never remember the difference in time zones. She's in Mexico now – the worry has sparked a few grey hairs.' He points at the hair at his temple, which remains stubbornly black. 'They're all amazing, strong women but sometimes I wish they'd be amazing and strong right here in Willow Grove so I know they're safe, you know?'

When Finn speaks of his sisters his face lights up. He resembles a proud dad, as he swipes through his phone showing me photos of each of them. It's sweet he's so close to them and this shows me just what kind of man he really is. There's a lot more to Finn than meets the eye. 'Do you have any siblings?' he asks.

I hesitate for a fraction of a second. 'Yes, I have a brother, erm. T, we call him T. He's a handful but I love him to bits. He's a late bloomer but he's coming into his own now at the pointy end of his twenties.' I don't tell Finn that Teddy's sudden blooming is one of the things helping to keep me in Willow Grove and the fact that this is tenuous at best. There's the faint smell of garlic in the air, which reminds me to go to the oven to shake the pan of roast vegetables. Sofia says the shaking is necessary so they cook evenly. I trust her implicitly and am happy to see the potatoes are crisping nicely on all sides.

Dinner is a jovial affair and my sides hurt from laughing. Afterwards, Finn suggests we take a walk along the river to counter our full bellies and red wine lethargy. I leave the dishes in a pile by the sink and make sure I've switched everything off.

Outside the fresh evening breeze stings my face, but it wakes me up from the food coma I've slipped into. 'You're full of surprises, Finn.'

'Me?'

'Yeah, the way you look after your sisters is admirable.'

His eyes crinkle as he smiles. 'They're great people, and that's all you can ask for.'

Again, it strikes me that he speaks more like a father than a brother. Whatever the reason, they seem as close as can be and I like that in a man, who puts his family at the top of his priorities.

I'm about to quiz him about his role in their lives just as we get to a lookout point and are rewarded with the stunning vista of the moonlight shimmering on the river. Finn stands so close to me I swear he can hear the sound of my heart beating. His family is forgotten as we gaze into each other's eyes. It's a heady moment. I can feel myself flushing from the wine, the company and his proximity. It's as natural as anything when I turn my face up to his and he kisses me so gently it feels as though the world shimmies and shakes underfoot.

Chapter 14

When I get to the library early Monday morning, the nerves are already fluttering but they ratchet up a notch when I don't see Harry anywhere. There's no sign of his mop of grey hair or any of his possessions. The area where he sleeps is pristine, as if it's been swept.

Has he decided not to participate in the People Library experiment article? I only hope that if he has, he's somewhere safe. Maybe this was a bad idea – I don't want to disrupt Harry's life for my own benefit and make him feel pressured to hide. What if this is all a mistake?

I open the library doors and feel anxiety roil in my gut. There's nothing else to do but switch on the lights and get the library ready for the day. Finn is coming to take photographs and the human books are attending an informal meeting. It won't be the same without Harry, but I understand how easy it would be to have a change of heart.

I run the hoover over the carpets, holding my breath when I get to the boiled cabbage section. The carpet cleaners are coming at the end of the day, thanks to the proceeds from the sale of the catalogue drawers. They've promised to use neutral products so I can't wait for Alfie to wander the history section and find it smells like absolutely nothing! Although, to be honest, after a while, you kind of get used to the fact there are certain areas here that you have to walk a little faster through.

As I'm packing the vacuum away, Sofia arrives, and calls out to me. 'There you are!' She surveys me. 'Elodie, darling, have you eaten? You look downright pale.'

Hearing her voice and her motherly concern warms me to my core and takes the edge off the worry I feel about Harry. 'Good morning, Sofia,' I say. She's holding a tinfoil-wrapped platter.

'You haven't eaten, have you?' She stares into my eyes as if she can tell without me having to speak.

'No, I ah . . . I wasn't hungry this morning.' If I'm this nervous for an informal catch-up about the People Library experiment, how am I going to be on the day itself? And what about the human books? They're the ones who'll be in the spotlight, baring their souls, not me. It's the build-up of worry about this failing. I don't want my human books to suffer and I don't want the library to close. What if I stuff it up on all fronts? It's also the calls from home. Teddy isn't making any leeway with Mother. The clock is ticking and it feels more like a time bomb – like I'm one step closer to being forced back to Astor. Still, I'm here now so I have to make every moment count.

'You have to eat, darling,' Sofia says. 'Keep up your strength. I'm nervous too, even though today is just us "books" having a chat and our pictures taken. I've made breakfast baps, and I know it might not sound fancy but I made the bread rolls fresh this morning and they're still warm out of the oven.'

'You made the bread rolls?' I love that for Sofia everything centres around food. Having a bad day? Eat this pie. Anxiety crushing you? Eat this chocolate cake. She has a dish for every mood.

'They're sourdough too.' Sofia shrugs, as if to say, *What like it's hard?* 'And I've added a dollop of tomato kasundi in them. I follow this amazing Indian chef on Instagram and all his recipes are delicious.'

'Well, I better try one since you've gone to all this effort,' I say, even though the idea of eating doesn't sit well with the churning of my stomach. I don't want to disappoint Sofia, who must have woken with the birds to get this all done in time.

'What is it? It's not only nerves is it?' Sofia asks, squinting at me. 'You sound almost robotic.'

I give her a watery smile. How perceptive she is. I bet she felt every slight thrown her way in this town because she's the empathetic type who picks up on emotional cues. 'Harry isn't here. What if I've made him uncomfortable in his own safe space by asking him to join the People Library? What if he's moved somewhere not as sheltered, all so he can avoid me? What if he's out in the elements and gets sick? What if . . .' Harry hadn't officially confirmed he'd participate in the experiment but I wanted him to be part of it, even if that meant just standing on the sidelines.

Sofia's expression softens and she says, 'Don't look now, but there's a couple of people at the door and I'm fairly certain one of them is Harry.'

I turn and standing there are Pete and Harry who are shifting on their feet and looking for all the world like they'd rather be anywhere else. Alfie and Jo soon arrive and Alfie blurts out, 'Well don't just stand there, lads! The door is open.'

As always Alfie manages to break the ice and they walk in and wander over to us. Harry nearly breaks my heart when I see he's showered, shaved and wearing a suit. It's threadbare and a little too short for his long legs, but he looks just the part.

'Harry, look how suave you are!'

He blushes behind his beard, which has been trimmed right back, the straggles are gone. 'Thanks, Elodie. I wanted to at least try.'

Where did Harry go shopping and how did he brave such a thing? As soon as I see Finn walk in, camera strung around his neck, I piece it together. Of course he'd have helped facilitate such an expedition and it's confirmed when Harry waves to him and says, 'Finn here helped me pick out the suit. It's not new, but it's new enough for me.'

'Sustainable fashion is all the rage now, Harry, and so much better for the planet. I like how forward-thinking you are.'

His face lights up. 'Well there you go. Who knew, eh?'

'I hope everyone's hungry,' Sofia says. 'I made breakfast baps.'

We pull up chairs and eat. Everyone compliments Sofia on her astounding skills as a home cook. I pop the kettle on and make tea and before long it seems that everyone's nerves have dissipated and there's much laughter among the chatter about just what's in store for our four human books.

When Maisie finally deigns to arrive, we're just packing up the plates. She's an hour late today. I cannot understand her motivations. It's as though she wants to be fired. I'm in such an ebullient mood, I decide to leave it for now and bring it up with her privately later. She storms right past us all, nary a hello, and shuts herself in the office.

'No manners,' says Sofia shaking her head. 'A travesty in this day and age.' I'm only thankful Sofia doesn't know what Maisie has said about *her*, and the rumours she's helped spread about the lonely lady in front of me.

'Right,' Finn says, standing up. 'If everyone is happy to proceed with the photographs, I thought we could have a few among the bookshelves, the four of our human books standing together, then a group shot with Elodie, and one of each of you alone. How does that sound?'

I frown. Not good. Not good at all. Haven't I discussed this at length with Finn? 'Good, good, but as we agreed before, I don't want to make this about me. I want it to be purely about the experiment. About the human books and them only.' I'm met with surprised faces. Is it that they want me beside them as an ally? As a support?

I try another tack. 'You four are the most amazing people I've met and trust me, I've met a lot of amazing people. I want everyone to see what I see. I want them to look into your eyes and face you head on and understand that their judgement of you is a direct reflection of the things they lack in their own lives. For this to work, it's not only up to you brave people baring your souls, but the "readers" have to bare theirs too. They have to look internally at themselves, their prejudice, their own motivations and do a bit of a moral stocktake, if you will. I'm not going to lie, it's not going to be easy and there's a good chance it might not work, but what if it does? What if you take the chance and open up and it changes the way they think? It will be hard, but it will be worth it. I have no part in that, except to support you from the sidelines.'

When my words peter out there's not a dry eye in the house,

including Maisie, who stands just on the edge of the group. Wonders will never cease – it's a good omen of things to come.

'OK-K-K,' Finn says, double blinking. 'Elodie is right. *So* right.'

Little Alfie walks towards me and leans his head on my upper arm. It's his version of a hug and I'm touched to the core. 'We could change the world,' he says softly.

'We have to try, right?'

He nods solemnly.

Harry plays with the lapels of his suit, which reminds me of watching my father do the same when I announced I was leaving. If only my parents could see these beautiful people and do something with their extreme wealth, to share it, rather than accumulate it, like a never-ending game of Monopoly. When Harry speaks, his voice is gravelly. 'I'm tired of being avoided, and maybe I just need to be more open. Maybe I need to explain I don't want them to look the other way.'

Pete nods. 'I'm the same. They said I was a bad apple, so I act like a bad apple. It's almost because it's expected of me and in this strange way I'll disappoint them if I try to live a normal life. But I don't want to steal; I don't want to hover on the outside anymore. I have dreams, you know. Big dreams. But who would take me seriously and where would I even start?'

'What are your dreams, Pete?' Sofia asks.

He drops his gaze to the floor as if he's not confident enough to make eye contact. 'It's probably silly.'

'Dreams are never silly,' she says encouragingly. 'My dream was to cook for people I love, and I'm slowly getting there.' She glances at me and smiles. 'I made my very first gal pal the other day, five years after moving here. And I've got a feeling I'm about to widen my friendship circle right now with you lovely lot. So trust me when I say, dreams are really worth fighting for.'

Pete lifts his gaze. 'Thank you. It's going to take some time to believe, you know? I'm sorry I've never spoken to you before today.'

She nods as if she knows exactly what he's talking about. 'Would you like to come to dinner at my place? All of you are welcome. I'd love to spoil you all with a wonderful meal in return for great conversation. We could meet after the first People Library and discuss how it went?'

Urgh, my heart.

'That would be cool,' Alfie says. 'You have the castle with the dead body buried there, right? Your husband, wasn't it? The lady with the hair on her chin at the shoe shop said you murdered him because he stole some money and you buried him in the stables.'

Sofia laughs. 'Allegedly.'

They all laugh, knowing the gossip, but knowing it's exactly that: gossip. Except Alfie who probably thinks it's real. 'Her name was Janet,' he says, flinging her straight under the bus. 'But Mum says, *Janet just likes to flap her jaws*, which is terrifying when you picture that.' He shudders.

'Alfie!' Jo says and giggles.

'Well,' I say, trying to hide my own grin, 'your mum is right, and you can't believe everything you hear, Alfie. That's exactly why we're doing this.'

'So there's no dead body?' He scrunches his nose in disappointment.

'No dead body,' Sofia says with a grin. 'But there's plenty of home-made ice cream.'

'I'm available,' he says. 'Mum?'

'We'd love to visit.'

'I'd love to as well,' says Pete who still stays schtum about his dreams.

'If I can grab a lift, I'd love to come too,' says Harry. 'The old legs can't wander far these days.'

'I can take you,' Finn says. And just like that we have the first stirrings of friendship. I can't wipe the smile from my face. Even if the People Library experiment doesn't work, this is surely worth it?

'Thanks, Finn.'

'No problem. Right, let's get these photos done, eh?'

They head towards the shelves and band together, laughing and joking before gathering themselves for the shots. There's a sparkle in their eyes, as if magic has happened . . .

Chapter 15

Don't just borrow a book, borrow a human

The Chronicle by Finn Ford
Wednesday August 24th.

Efforts to save Willow Grove library have ramped up with new librarian Elodie Halifax at the helm. The new initiative, the People Library experiment, is set to start Monday 29th of August. Ms Halifax says of the experiment, 'We're offering human "books" to our members. You can borrow a "book" for thirty-minute sessions and hear their real-life stories. All we ask is that you don't judge a book by its cover.'

So far there are four human books on offer and Ms Halifax hopes to add to these numbers as the experiment continues. The idea behind it is that it will draw members to the library, locals who want more than physical books who are willing to look past their own judgements and open up their hearts to other local residents who are bravely sharing their stories. To book your slot you

must be a member. You can find the information here:
www.willowgrovelibrary/memberships

Continued page 2 with profiles of the human books on offer.

I flick to page two and see the bright, expectant faces of our human books. Harry is so handsome with his winning smile. Sofia holds a wooden spoon in the air as if she's about to bake up a storm. Little Alfie grins, displaying his crooked teeth, and it's enough to make me want to jump into the pages and squeeze him. Pete's picture gives me pause – his head hangs low as if even a picture might judge him. It hurts to see those feeling translated so readily on his face. Whatever Pete's been through, it's done a lot of damage and I only hope the experiment doesn't add to that.

Finn's written a profile about each of them, just enough to tempt readers, without giving too much away. If this doesn't strike a chord in Willow Grove residents, nothing will. The *Chronicle* is out in town already and the article is about to go live online too. Finn has shared it with his media contacts so I'm hoping it goes far and wide. I don't use my own networks because I want to do this authentically and I don't want the Astor name anywhere near this.

Now, we need to pray that memberships increase at a rapid rate. I print posters for the People Library, and pack them into my bag and take a roll of tape while I get ready to head into town.

'Maisie?' I find her in the office, staring blankly at the computer screen. 'Can you take care of things until I get back?'

'And do what exactly?'

I hold in a sigh. 'Check in on Alfie, let him know the carpets have been freshly cleaned and he can hit the history section without holding his nose. Approach anyone who comes in to join and explain about our first People Library event. Shelve returned books, you know, the usual.'

'OK.'

Leaning my head on the doorjamb, I consider her for a moment. She's definitely softened a little since I arrived but she's still not working as a team player. 'Maisie, please do be friendly with anyone who comes in, yeah?' I'm loath to leave but I really want to spread the word around town to tie in with the newspaper article.

'I'm always friendly.'

I head outside in the filmy sunshine. First stop, the pub. It's early yet, but the lunch crowd won't be too far away and if they want to gossip then let it be about the human books and just what we've got cooking up.

My phone rings so I find some shade outside and answer it. 'Teddy, how are you?'

'Good, good. Well not so good. Dad is back in the office and I really think he should be at home. He's trying to keep up with Mum still and it's all a bit of a mess.'

I find a spot to sit as my earlier energy leaves in a whoosh. 'The People Library experiment has just been announced so I need a bit more time.'

'Okay . . . I'll try. But what do I do about Dad?'

What story will Dad believe? 'Right – get David, Dad's driver, and pull him aside. Explain the situation: that you need Dad to be resting but he won't listen. Get David to drive Dad home and tell him that he's got a confidential conference call from Dubai about the airline magazine bid. He prefers his top secret business meetings to take place at home, well away from prying eyes and ears. Once he's safely resting at home I'll call him and see if I can convince him that his health is more important than Astor.'

I flail at the thought of going back to that empty existence, that faux life. Red carpets and ribbons. The thought of leaving my four precious human books behind hurts more than I expected. And Finn. The guy stares at me as if I'm magical, as if I'm all his dreams come true and it's only the beginning. But really, they're leaving me no choice – I don't want my dad to have a heart attack at his desk. As aloof as my dad can be, I love him to bits. He's a different generation, one that was taught not to show feelings, not to declare love. He shows me in other ways. I just need to get the library over the line and then I can go home and help Teddy, even though I really don't want to. Some sacrifices are bigger than others . . .

'OK, I'll do that now.'

Still, I'm annoyed this can't be fixed with two other Astors at the helm and a whole team of people behind them. Part of me feels like Mother is taking me hostage by not stepping in to help Dad. 'Why is Mum not insisting he goes home? This is just crazy.'

'I'm sure she's doing it because she knows I'll call you.'

'That woman!' Would she really put Dad's health below the business? I'm sure even she is not that callous. There must be more to this. 'I'll call you later.'

I take a moment to compose myself and continue walking to the pub, seriously contemplating a quick alcoholic beverage to calm the erratic beating of my heart.

I go inside and find the publican, Trevor, cleaning the lines. 'Here she is, the woman of the moment.'

'Me?' I ask, my mind half lost still with Teddy's call.

'Your People Library idea has grown wings and taken flight already.'

'*That fast?*' I check my watch. The paper's been out for a couple of hours, and it's only just been shared online.

'Things move quick here – you should know that by now.'

I shoot him a toothy smile. I really need to get my head straight and focus on this today of all days. But my mind feels woolly as I worry about my dad. 'You're right, I *should* know that by now. If it's OK, I'd still like to hang these posters in your window.'

He wipes down the bar and says, 'Go for it, love. I for one am going to join the library so I can hear ol' Harry's story. I know a bit of it, being of the same ilk, ancient as I am, but I've always wondered why he ended up the way he has. I'd sort of forgotten about him, to be honest. He used to prop up the bar once upon a time and then he stopped coming and I never stumble on him in town anymore. Seeing his picture online today gave me a start, it did, remembering the Harry of old, nursing his pint and having a laugh with me.'

It gives me hope to hear he's going to join! More so because he knows Harry and wants to hear more. It feels supportive, the way he talks, as if he's lost an old friend and has the chance to meet again. 'I'm so pleased to hear it. I'm sure Harry would love to see a friendly face when he shares his story.'

'Too right. My wife and I'll be down directly once the lunchtime staff clock on so we can get our memberships sorted and reserve a time with the human books. She wants to meet the little lad Alfie. Never heard about that calendar counting malarkey before, so she's keen to learn what that's all about. Quite clever the way his mind must work. Goes to show you never really know about people, you only *think* you know.'

My pulse races. 'Yes, *yes*. That's exactly it.'

I can only hope there's hundreds more like Trevor who are open to the idea.

'Get those posters up, love, and I'll make sure I point them out to our patrons too.'

When I leave the pub, I'm buzzing but I have to call my dad and make sure he's OK before I let myself sink into excitement about the library. I find a perch under the shade of a birch tree.

'Darling, I've missed you so!'

His voice is upbeat – strange as he's usually so reserved. 'Hey, Dad. I heard you had a bit of a scare.'

'Oh that. It was nothing.'

I stifle a sigh. 'It wasn't nothing. You're supposed to be recuperating at home and yet here I am getting calls about you strutting around Astor, ignoring medical advice. Why, Dad? Do you seriously not care about your health?'

'I feel fine, honestly. I've lost a bit of weight, what with all the medications so I might look a bit different but I truly feel better than I have in years. Let's be honest, I needed to lose a bit. Trust me, I wouldn't be at work if I felt like I couldn't handle it.'

'That's just the thing, I don't trust you. You'd be at work to support Mum, no matter what. And that makes me feel guilty that I should be there for Mum so you can be at home where you're *supposed* to be.'

'So a library, eh? I can see you there, you know.' He sidesteps my concern just like that.

'Mum told you?'

'Of course, there are no secrets between us. Even when I'm ill. Listen, Ellie, I know you feel like you should come home and we'd love you to. Especially your mother – she's running around like a chicken with its head cut off. But this latest ticker trouble really cemented a few things for me, and one of them is how we haven't really listened to what you and Teddy want to do with your lives. This latest spell has opened my eyes. Teddy has come on in leaps and bounds, and you're finally following your dreams. Maybe this is the way it was always meant to be.'

What is going on? My father never speaks like this. 'Really?' Maybe things aren't as bad as Teddy is making out? Maybe I can stay in Willow Grove. 'But what about Mum? She can't keep up this pace.'

'Teddy has a plan. He's going to take over a lot more of the events. If that happens, then we'll be OK.'

I blow out a breath. 'OK, so you're saying I don't need to come home right now?'

'No, darling. Stay where you are. You're doing important work by trying to save a library, and it's work that you're clearly passionate about.'

'Thanks, Dad. I'm really enjoying it. I finally feel like I'm living the life I was meant to.'

'I'm proud of you. Look I've got a conference call with—'

'No, you don't. That was a ruse to get you home. My idea, before you go blaming anyone else. Please promise me you'll spend some time resting? Even if it's only a few hours every day?'

He chortles. 'I thought it was odd as we lost that deal last week. Lost it to Mogul Media, of all places. Your mother wasn't too chuffed, I can tell you.'

It makes sense now, why the wheels are falling off. If Mum lost the Dubai deal to her competitors, it'll only make her work longer hours in an effort to correct it. She really must be pushing herself to her limits. 'Mother really needs to learn the art of assigning responsibility. She has teams in place for this very thing and yet she doesn't use them to her advantage.'

'I know, I know. She's learning the hard way. It's only that she's a little flustered these days without you here doing the promotions. I've tried to tell her Teddy is a great fit. The camera loves him. As long as we can keep him on track, he'll be fine. But she won't hear a bar of it.'

It's always about how we look to others. How we photograph. It's just so mind-bending – so shallow. What about how Teddy can handle pressure? How he can make a surly advertising executive turn to putty in his hands? How he can lead a team and inspire them?

Dad needs to spend time in a stress-free environment, which means I need to return, or demand that Teddy is given more responsibilities at Astor. Surely I get a say in my own life. The problem is, my father's health is at risk and would I ever forgive myself if I held out here and he had a catastrophic heart attack?

There's nothing left to do, except get the posters up and hope that we get memberships far more quickly so I can go home and assess for myself. My jaunt takes hours, because I'm stopped by locals who quiz me about the People Library. It really has grown wings and taken flight like Trevor from the pub suggested it would.

I hurry back inside the library and am rewarded with a queue of people waiting to sign up.

'Maisie, you should have called me!'

'There was no time!' She gives me a glazed look as if she's been so busy part of her has checked out, turned robot to get it all done.

Maisie continues entering new member names into the database so I grab my personal laptop and sign in, motioning to people to make two lines. I hope they don't get frustrated with waiting and leave!

I almost kiss the ground when Sofia wanders in, yet another platter in hand. She gives me a wink that says, *Leave this to me*. 'Hello, folks, can I tempt you with a chocolate truffle at all?' She goes up and down the queue chatting away, as if she's in her element. It seems she's the woman of the hour as people gush about her biography in the newspaper. The tide is turning for Sofia! Didn't she want to bake for friends? And now she has the attention of the room and it's not even the event yet! I overhear the odd question about just what her story will include and what exactly she's going to divulge. They want the nitty gritty, that's for sure.

Sofia simply says, 'You'll have to "borrow" me to find out, lovelies,' and continues down the line.

After a hectic couple of hours, we get them all signed up and I calculate how many we still need to be able to submit the paperwork for funding.

We need a further 384 members! Is this even doable? It still seems so very far away. But I remind myself, it's the first big rush. There'll be plenty of people who haven't had time to read the paper or look online. Surely there'll be a second wave. We have to be patient and keep spreading the word.

Mid-afternoon, Maisie is busy packing away fallen books and straightening up shelves. I wander over and pick up books from the floor and hand them to her. 'Hey, you did such an amazing job today.' Once I returned to help her sign people up, she relaxed into it. She smiled, she joked, she looked like she was *enjoying* work. It was lovely to see the other side of Maisie. I wish it was like that every day.

'Well, yeah, there wasn't much else I could do, otherwise they'd never leave.' And just like that the shutters come down again. It rings false, for some reason. As if she's playing a part. I *know* she enjoyed today – it was written all over her features.

'Is there any reason why you're acting this way, Maisie? Is it something I've done?'

She gives me the side-eye as if weighing up what to say. 'It's just *you*, Elodie. The way you strut in here like you're better than everyone. You try to change things like you own the place. Newsflash, you don't. You're just an employee the same as me.'

Her words wind me, as if she's struck a physical blow. Have I walked in here acting superior? It's not my style at all but I'm mortified to think I've come across that way. Is it because this job is more than just nine to five for me?

When I leave work at the end of the day, I don't switch off. I work from home, and even when I'm supposed to be relaxing I'm dreaming of ways we can help more people as soon as the funding comes through. Perhaps, it's the work ethic I learned at Astor leaving me in good stead for this new challenge. For me, this isn't just a job, it's the possibility of a whole new life and pursuing a passion that's been dormant for so long. 'I'm sorry if I made you feel that way, Maisie. That wasn't my intention at all. In fact, it's quite the opposite. I'm trying to change things at the library only because the old ways haven't worked. I know I'm an employee just the same as you but one of us has to be in charge, and that's me. If we don't commit wholeheartedly, we won't save this place. So many people will lose the one place they can go that doesn't ask anything of them. And what about Alfie?' I throw my hands into the air. 'What else can I say, except I hope we can come to some agreement about how things are to be done and potentially save *both* our jobs.'

'Look, this is just a job for me. I come here simply to earn money. It's not my life. I don't go home and dream about the place. I leave here and I don't give it a second thought. If the library closes, it closes, I'll find another job soon enough.' Her face reddens. I sense that Maisie is holding back the truth, but what? And why?

I frown. 'Surely you don't mean that, Maisie. Most book lovers I know live and breathe literature. You wouldn't have studied to become a librarian if you didn't enjoy this kind of job.'

She shakes her head. 'I'm clocking off. I've got a headache.'

There's more to Maisie. Her hostility is like a shield, but just what is she protecting herself from? Is it me? I've been more than reasonable with her but she clearly doesn't want to open up. Most bosses would have fired her by now but I know that like the antagonist of any good book she's redeemable. Everyone is.

I decide to push the point. 'Maisie, I don't want to overstep the mark, but I've noticed that you seem a little down lately. Sometimes I see you with glassy eyes, as if you've been crying. I hope I'm not the reason for that, and if so, can we talk about it?' I recall she had red-rimmed eyes when I thought she'd been half asleep but was she really upset and trying to hide it from me?

Her bottom lip trembles and it's all I can do not to embrace her in a hug. I get the feeling Maisie isn't a hugger and definitely wouldn't accept one from me. 'It's not just you, Elodie.' She rifles in her pocket and produces a tissue. 'There's other stuff going on that's made things hard of late. It makes all the saving the library job angst insignificant.'

I gesture for her to sit on an armchair and I take one opposite. 'I'm sorry to hear that things have been hard for you and I understand when there's stuff going on at home that it makes work seem like another burden. Trust me, I *really* do understand. I'm here if you want to share, that's all. And I'd like to help if I can.'

She dabs at her nose with the tissue, holding herself tight like she's trying to keep it together. 'My . . . my gran died a couple of months ago. It's been really tough. She was more like my mum, you know?' Maisie lets out a bitter laugh. 'Mum works in the city so Gran mostly raised me. I feel so lost without her. Like my world has turned grey. When I go home to our cottage, it's so quiet. There's no smell of dinner cooking. No sound of her quiz shows in the background. It's just so utterly *still* without her. I used to think there weren't enough hours after work to get everything done; now it feels interminable. The evenings drag on as I sit there alone wondering how I'm supposed to go on. Then I've had you to deal with, with your Ted-Talk-style meetings and your obsession with membership numbers and it all seems so pointless. We might save the library, but I still won't have my gran.'

And with that she bursts into noisy tears. I wrap my arms around her and hold her while she cries. Poor Maisie! I've been judging her this whole time, while spouting off about everyone else doing the same thing to Harry, Alfie,

Sofia and Pete. It strikes me that I've acted the same way as everyone else. Why didn't I try harder to get to the bottom of Maisie's attitude?

'I'm so sorry, Maisie. I wish that I'd done more for you, been there when you needed it. And I'm sorry about the Ted-Talk-style of meetings – that's quite amusing in a way. I can do better if you give me a chance. I know it all seems so hollow right now, but we can take it one day at a time.

'Can I go home early? I really do have a pounding headache.'

I give her a warm smile. Today has been so hectic, no wonder she's not feeling well, and to have a broken heart all the while. 'Of course. If you need some time off, I understand. Grief is such a process and you have to wade through it at your own pace.' If only I'd have known. 'There's bereavement leave – if you need to take it just let me know.'

She sniffles. 'But then you'll be here all alone.'

'I'll manage.'

With a wrinkled tissue, she dabs at her eyes. 'No, it's OK. It's harder at home. Everywhere I look I'm reminded of Gran. Today, I just need to go lie in a dark room and close my eyes for a bit. I'll be OK tomorrow.'

'If you're sure? Please reach out if you change your mind. I want you to know that I'll support you however you need it.'

Not long after, I close up and head on home, dreaming about a very big glass of red wine and wondering how I missed Maisie's grief, when it's now so clearly written all over her features.

It reminds me of my dad and his flailing health, and I give him another call.

'Hey, Dad, how are you feeling now?'

'Grand, just grand. The expansion plan for Paddington has been approved so now we're full steam ahead on that to try and get it opened before Christmas. I'm not sure we'll get there, but you know your mother, she wants to capitalise on the Christmas market.'

'So you haven't managed to stay home?'

'And do what? Wear my slippers and dressing gown like an old man? Never! Truly, Ellie, I'm fine. Fit as a fiddle. I was inspired after your call this morning. I know we need to make changes and Teddy is the key to that. If anything, I've taken a bit of the load off your mother's shoulders by convincing her to let him take on a few other projects she had her sights set on.'

'Really?'

'She wasn't happy about it, but she had no choice. How are things going there? How exactly are you planning to save that old place?'

I tell my father in detail what I've been up against and my plans for the library.

'You'll make a success of it yet.'

'I still feel like I need to come home.' Seeing the devastation on Maisie's face brings it home how I'd feel if I lost my father while I followed my own dreams at Willow Grove.

'Give it a bit more time. If we can't get on top again, then I will let you know. I know your mother wants you back right this second, but let's just see if Teddy can handle things first. Let's at least give him the chance to try.'

'OK, I will. I can't leave until I've got 357 more members anyway.'

'Get it done, Ellie. I know you can do it.'

We chat for another hour, and it strikes me these phone conversations are the first time my father has really opened up to me. Whatever is going on with him, it's changed him for the better. He's never been interested in my life outside of Astor, not in the usual way parents are. It's nice to have this with him, and I only hope it doesn't mean there's anything serious going on.

Chapter 16

The next evening, I follow Sofia's lengthy handwritten recipe for beef bourguignon. I'm planning to wow Harry with it for lunch tomorrow, but I've used too much flour to coat the beef. It sticks hard to the pot like glue no matter how much butter I use to try and soften it. Just as I'm about to phone Sofia and ask if its fixable there's a knock at the door.

I wipe my hands on a tea towel and go to investigate. Through the peephole I see Finn standing there, hands deep in his pockets.

'Hello, stranger,' I say as I open the door feeling a flutter of excitement at the unexpected visit. We haven't seen each other as much as I'd like because part of me still isn't sure if I can make a life here when my family need me.

'Hello, you.' His gaze drops to my front, which is covered in white flour. 'Cooking?'

'You could call it that or burning would be another way to describe it. Come in. Would you like to stay for dinner?'

'Sounds, erm, lovely. Love a well-charred meal.'

I give him a nudge with my hip. 'I'm sure it's salvageable. It's all about the low and slow method . . . or something.'

He laughs. 'I'm sorry I've come empty-handed.'

'It's OK, I've got plenty so I can drink my feelings away when my cooking fails. What would you like, red or white?'

'Whatever you're having.'

'Make yourself comfortable in the living room and I'll be right back.'

I hurry back to the kitchen and take the pan off the stove, the thick floury mess worse than when I left it. I give it another stir, hoping that a swizzle will miraculously fix it, but it congeals into a rubbery mess. I admit defeat and pop the pan on the sink to cool. I'm on tiptoes reaching for the wine glasses when I hear my phone beep.

'Elodie, you've got a text. From someone called Teddy. Is that T, the brother you mentioned?'

Damn mobile phones flashing messages for the world to see! I only hope it doesn't say anything about Astor.

'Oh?' I say, rushing to the living room, sure that Finn can hear the thrumming of my heart. I flick open the message. 'Yes, it's T! I'll reply later. Bad news – the dinner is a science experiment gone wrong. How about we go to the pub instead?' A bit of noise is just the distraction I need after the week I've had.

'Sure, let's go.'

At the pub, there's a rowdy crowd and they welcome us as we walk past. Trevor greets us at the bar. 'Elodie, the talk of the town. I've heard nothing else since Finn's article ran. Seems we've got two camps: those who agree with it and those who don't.'

I raise a brow. 'So there's a chance fifty per cent of the population might sign up? I'll take that as a win.'

He grins, displaying tobacco-stained teeth. 'I like your enthusiasm. What can I get you, folks?'

Finn runs a hand through his hair and says, 'We're here for a meal, but a bottle of your finest red wouldn't go astray. We'll shuffle to the dining room out back, eh Elodie?'

'Sounds good to me.'

'House red it is! Dot will bring that round in a mo with some menus.'

I laugh at the grand selection of wines on offer. It's a charming small-town pub and Trevor has been nothing but kind to me. It has a cosy atmosphere and is full to the brim with patrons.

We sit down at a table around the back of the pub. It's quieter but still thick with the yeasty scent of beer that you find in old places like this. Like the library, the ruby red carpet has probably been here since the dawn of time, soaking up spills and secrets, but that's what makes it so special.

Dot brings our bottle of house red over and pours. 'So you're the one who's all set to change this town?' Sarcasm is heavy in her voice. Yikes. Dot must be in the against camp.

'Change the town – hmm. Maybe, I guess? Why not give it a go, I say? Are you a member of the library, Dot?'

'Not for me. There's never time to do anything other than work. When I'm off the last place you'd find me is there. I'd rather watch telly, to be honest.' She puts the screw cap in a pocket on her waist apron.

'Fair call. You must be run off your feet in here most days. I understand wanting to switch off and relax when you get home. Me personally, I find comfort in reading. It's where I go to escape the bedlam of busy days. But each to their own. Are you intrigued about the People Library experiment?'

She scoffs. 'No, because I don't understand why you've chosen to highlight *those* people. It doesn't make sense. They're like celebrities now – reaping all these rewards when they're not good, honest people.'

I tamp down frustration and remind myself this is *why* change is needed in Willow Grove. 'But you haven't heard their stories yet, so how can you know that for sure?'

She huffs as if I'm testing her patience. 'I know enough, 'cept I don't know about that little boy. What I do know is that Harry's a mess. Sofia brought a thief into town. And Pete's always been a bad apple. Just be careful, OK? They might have fooled you with their hard-luck stories, but they haven't fooled the rest of us. It's going to end in tears – mark my words.'

I try to consider if from Dot's point of view. I try *not* to judge her, but it's difficult. Surely everyone deserves a second chance? The possibility of a new beginning. 'I can't see how it will end in tears, unless the library did actually close its doors for good. Then I would cry bucketloads.'

'But you're not from here, are you, *love*.' She shakes her head. 'These things run deep. People have long memories.'

Finn goes to protest but I hold a hand up as if to say I've got this. 'That's just the thing. What exactly are they remembering? Are they instead reacting to tall tales they've heard spread about, which have gathered momentum and in turn made these people feel like they don't matter? Have you ever thought about that, Dot?' From her shuttered features I can tell I'm not getting through to her.

Her mouth opens and closes like a pufferfish. 'Enjoy your wine.'

'She didn't get my point.'

Finn says, 'You handled that brilliantly. There are some closed minds in this town. Imagine if you opened a few of those up . . . all while saving the library. You're going to come up against a lot more people like Dot, but they're usually all talk, and isn't that what you're trying to change?'

We cheers to that. After dinner we meander down the high street hand in hand. It feels natural and I don't overthink it. 'That's my humble abode.' Finn points to a cottage that is almost identical to mine, including a thatched roof.

'I want to see inside. See where the man who puts people on the map lives.'

He makes a show of holding his heart as if in pain. 'With no pre-warning? No time to make it look like I'm a very neat, orderly person who has their life together?'

I grab his hand and pull him towards the cottage. 'Exactly! I want to see how you live with *no* pre-warning.'

'This goes against my better judgement, but OK.'

He finds his key and I trail in behind him while he flicks on the light switch.

'If I'd have closed my eyes and pictured your place this is exactly what I'd have imagined,' I say. The living room is full of stuffed-to-the-brim bookshelves. A wrinkled leather sofa sits in the middle, with only a throw rug for company. How many times has Finn fallen asleep there reading a book or working on a story?

We go through to the kitchen where a big dining table resembles a work desk. It's covered with paperwork, old newspapers and magazines. 'You can't trust an orderly writer. Isn't that the saying?' He grins.

'Something like that.' His cottage is warm and inviting and I feel at home, like I do in my own. There's no fancy artwork, no priceless objets d'art. Instead there are framed photographs of his sisters from when they were little girls in pigtails, to their school and university graduations. Finn stands to their left like a proud father celebrating their accomplishments. 'These are great,' I say. 'Where are your parents?' I study each photograph and can't spot them.

'My parents?' he says and then looks at the collection of his sisters' accomplishments. 'There was no relationship with my father – he breezed in and out of my life. And my mum died a few years ago.' So that's why he's been there for the girls. But I look at these school pictures when the girls were young and his mum isn't in those either.

At the mention of his mum Finn's face falls. Is it too soon to pry? It doesn't seem like he wants to open up so I let it slip away.

The mood has turned sombre so I wrap my arms around Finn and kiss him full on the lips. The man has the ability to make me literally swoon. Who knew that was possible? I hold him tightly and we kiss all our worries away . . .

Chapter 17

The day of the People Library experiment arrives and with it a fresh downpour of summer rain, making the air thick with humidity. I stay under the top sheet unwilling to leave bed just yet. The weekend replays like a movie reel, and I let the pictures float past so I can enjoy them once more. Staying at Finn's place had been a revelation and just thinking of him sends a flurry of goose bumps along my skin.

I'm falling head over heels for the guy – can I stop myself now from getting in too deep? It's too late. I feel it in my heart. He's everything I've ever wanted in a man. He makes me feel like I matter, that every word that falls from my lips is worth listening to. But more than that, it's the person *he* is that I'm drawn to. Would our relationship have the same dynamic if he knew I was Ellie Astor, not Elodie Halifax? Which version of me is real? I feel torn down the middle when I think of my life in London and my life here. Add Finn into the mix and I'm at a loss about my place all over again. It's the fact that I can't fully commit to Finn, not knowing if I can stay long term. But my body, mind and soul want to. I want to fully immerse myself in a relationship with this man who has set my heart on fire, but can I? What if he feels I deceived him no matter what my intentions were?

There's no time to ponder it all. Today is the very first session of the People Library, with Harry sharing his story. We plan to hold four events, where each 'book' gets the spotlight for one day. Once those sessions are done, all four 'books' will be available on the same day. This way, their first day is special. We'll also be able to make sure they're comfortable before getting ahead of ourselves in terms of allowing members to reserve them in the future.

After a shower I dress and head to work with a handful of posters I had made specially for the experiment.

At the library, Sofia greets me at the door. 'Good morning!' she says, her arm linked through Harry's, for moral support. Harry is dressed in his threadbare suit but looks for all the world like he's walking to his execution. Green around the gills is an understatement. Should we have started the People Library with Sofia who is a lot more confident?

'Good morning!' I say brightly. 'You OK, Harry?'

Sofia rubs his arm. 'A small crisis of confidence, that's all. Nothing a good breakfast and strong cup of tea won't fix, eh, Harry?'

'I don't think I can eat, sorry.' He swallows as if trying to hold down a wave of nausea.

''Course you can eat,' she says. 'It'll settle your stomach.'

I paste on a smile while internally I fret. If Harry backs out it won't look good but that's not my main concern. It's that I know he'll regret it later. 'Let's get you settled, Harry, and you can tell us what's worrying you.'

Inside I flick on the lights and put the People Library posters on the desk to hang later.

Sofia wanders off to sort Harry's breakfast and get the tea things ready.

'Sorry, Elodie. I thought I could do this, but now the day has arrived, I'm not sure I can.'

My stomach drops. I should have factored in nerves and had a backup plan. It's understandable the human books are going to feel a range of emotions about sharing their private lives and might want to abort mission. There's already a long list of members who've 'reserved' a spot with Harry but I don't tell him that. I don't want to add to his worry.

I motion for him to take a seat and give him a comforting pat on the shoulder. 'I totally understand, Harry. This is a daunting experience, no two ways about it. If you really don't feel comfortable doing it, I won't push you. This experiment is only going to work if our "books" are at ease and I would hate you to go up there and feel like you'd made a mistake agreeing to this.'

He rubs at his freshly shaven face. 'What if they think I'm a horrible person? That I made bad choices and I deserve to be where I am?'

I'm sure I can feel my heart shatter at the thought. *Poor Harry!* It always comes back to that fear of judgement. This is what we *need* to change. 'You're afraid they'll judge you unkindly?'

'Why wouldn't they?' His voice is hoarse like he's been crying. I'm in two minds whether this is a good option for Harry or the very worst idea ever. It's so hard to know because he's first cab off the rank.

I still don't know Harry's story, so it's hard to assure him they won't look down on him. But this is exactly why we're doing this. To open up a dialogue, to allow people the space to see their actions have a direct effect on others. 'All we can hope for, Harry, is that members will sit back and listen to your tale and see you're just like the rest of us. Fallible. It's harder to judge someone when you're sitting there face to face with a person who is opening up their life and heart to you, sharing their innermost thoughts and feelings. Regrets. Mistakes. None of us are perfect, Harry – that's really important to remember. The person sitting across from you has their very own story too, and they've *also* made mistakes. We *all* have.'

Harry's lips wobble. Have I made things worse? 'Here comes Sofia now,' he says with a deep sigh as she carries a tray with a teapot and a plate of scones.

'I'll get the cups,' I say and head back into the kitchen. When I return Harry is tucking into a scone laden with jam and cream. Sofia sits beside him with a triumphant smile on her face. 'Harry's little wobble is over,' she says. 'He's ready to shine a light on his life, and I for one am very proud of him. I feel daunted by the prospect myself but we'll all be here for each other.'

Harry nods, wiping crumbs from his mouth with a tissue. 'What you said, Elodie, about none of us being perfect, that struck a chord. If I don't speak up now, I never will. As hard as it is, I'm going to do it to the best of my ability. People judge me on sight. I'd rather they judge me once they know my life and what I've lived through . . .'

My heart expands with love for him. It takes great courage to tread this path and I'm proud of him for it. 'Oh, Harry, thank you! If you're *sure* you're comfortable going ahead with it? None of us will think less of you if you don't go ahead.'

'I'm sure.'

I let out a squeal, which catches even me by surprise. I'm wound up tight and I expect that's going to be the case until this is over. 'I'll be right beside you.'

'I won't be far away either,' Sofia says.

Donatella and her father arrive, so I wave them in. 'Sofia, would you mind helping Donatella with the catering?'

'Ooh I'd love to! This is the Italian goddess you were telling me about? She's rebranded her father's pizzeria, Harry. We'll have to go there for dinner, eh? What do you say? You look like a risotto man to me.'

'Well, I do have this fancy new suit.'

I grin as Sofia wanders over to Donatella and introduces herself.

*

The time for Harry's first 'reading' approaches as I buzz about making last-minute checks that everything is set up and ready. Maisie is signing up new members, so I want to make sure she's OK. Outside, a queue forms and I smile to myself. Everyone wants to be part of this, even though it's a members-only event. 'You OK here?' I ask her. Things have been calmer since our chat. She even texted me a couple of funny cat memes over the weekend.

'I'm good. If I look frazzled then that's your cue to come and help.'

'OK, define how frazzled looks on you?'

'Like my head is about to bust wide open.'

'OK, got it. I'll do one last check and be back to help.'

Half an hour later I check the membership numbers and am thrilled to see we only need 245 more! Over halfway there and there's still a queue of people so I stand beside Maisie and we get through them as fast as possible.

When we've caught up I welcome everyone to the seating area. They stop and stare at the huge sign strung above.

What do you see when you look at me?

'Welcome to the People Library,' I say and hand out information cards. 'Today is an introduction to what you have in store over the coming months. Today we have Harry as our very first human book. If you'd like to reserve a spot with him, please find Maisie who'll gladly take your details. Don't worry if you don't get a spot today; Harry will be back. And we are also offering upcoming reservations with Alfie, Pete and Sofia.'

In front of the seating area is another sign that reads:

Welcome to Willow Grove library. Feel free to peruse the books on offer today. However, there's a catch – our books are humans, ready and willing to share their real-life stories. Choose the 'book' that most intrigues you. But before you do, we ask you to make us a promise. please don't judge a book by its cover. Everyone's story is special as you'll soon see if you read between the lines.

You may recognise the 'books' on offer today. You may even think you've already heard their stories, but we encourage you to leave judgement at the door, because you don't know their story, not really. So what are you waiting for? Choose your book, pull up a chair and read in a whole new way . . .

The air is electric with anticipation and I only hope Harry is doing OK behind the scenes. Sofia's got him sequestered in a cubicle giving him another pep talk.

Finn wanders in. The sight of him in a snug grey suit momentarily makes my legs buckle. He looks like a *GQ* cover model pretending to be a reporter. How did I get to be so lucky? When he sees me his face breaks into a smile. 'There you are,' he says as if he's spent his whole life looking for me. 'Ready for this?'

I knit my fingers together. 'More than ready. Harry had a bit of a crisis of confidence this morning, but he's pulled it together.'

Finn makes a face. 'Poor guy. It has to be intimidating, especially being first and with all these *people*.' He glances around the library, which is jam-packed with bodies who are mostly pretending to peruse the books, but actually tracking my every move as if not wanting to miss a thing. 'Where did they *come* from?'

'I don't care as long as they've joined up!'

He grins. 'How are the numbers going?'

I shrug. 'Not sure now, it was 245 when I last checked but we signed up more after that and by the looks there's more waiting now so let's hope they're all signing up. Are you going to take photographs?'

He nods. 'I'll do the next instalment in the serial about the People Library experiment and hopefully get you some more bodies in here for Alfie's.'

'You're a star.'

'It's been said before,' he jokes.

I go to kiss his cheek and then pull back. The last thing we need is gossip about us, instead of the experiment. 'Go and do what you need to and I'll be lurking around getting the best shots and interviewing people about their reactions.'

'Thanks, Finn!'

I find Harry and Sofia. 'It's go time,' I say, blowing out a breath.

Harry's whole demeanour has changed. With his shoulders pulled back and a firm smile in place, he appears confident and in control. 'You look like a million bucks, Harry.'

'I feel like it too. It's not often a person gets the chance to be in the spotlight, so here goes, eh?'

'Good luck!' I say, leading him to the seating area. 'And remember this is your story and it's up to you what you'd like to share. If at any time you need to stop, then just signal to me.'

'I'm all good, Elodie. Don't you worry about a thing.'

My gut roils for my friend but I give him a supportive smile. It's such a brave step he's taking, and I'm not sure I could do the same in his shoes.

I find Harry's 'reader' and set them up away from prying eyes and ears, but I'm sure people will sneak as close as they can to hear at any rate.

'Jamie, this is your human book: Harry. I hope you'll enjoy hearing his story . . .'

*

HARRY

'They call me Homeless Harry. They think I don't know that but I do. I am homeless, I guess. But it wasn't always like that. I used to have it all. A wife, daughters, a steady job. A cottage with a garden big enough to grow vegetables. You could say I was living the dream. There wasn't a lot of money, but there was enough. The girls never went without, and my wife stayed home and cared for us all, making the budget stretch with her simple meat and three veg meals. We used to take trips on Sundays, going out in the car, a basket of ham sandwiches and a flask of tea. We'd go to parks and the girls would run around, getting grass stains on their dresses, to my wife's dismay. Looking back, I wish I could bottle those memories and forget what came after. But that's not how life works, is it?

'I was a train driver. Loved my job, until I didn't. These days you have a term for what happened to me, but back then I hadn't heard of it. PTSD, you know it?'

Jamie nods her head, her features sombre.

'A young lad jumped in front of my train one day and there was no time to react. It happened so fast. I can still see his face, the panic in his eyes on impact. The regret. He knew at that moment he had made a grave error in jumping but it was too late. God, his death plagued me. I played the *If Only* games until my head swam. If only I was running late, he might have changed his mind. If only I'd seen him sooner. If only, if only, if only. That's when I took to the drink. It started off slowly, one or two after work. The money had to stretch to accommodate it, but my wife made allowances. She could see the brightness in my eyes dim. The thirst grew. At the weekends I drank to forget, so I couldn't see him, see those eyes of his, pools of terror. I drank and drank so I couldn't see him anymore. Though he still managed to sneak into my dreams, which became nightmares.

'Back at work, my hands shook and my heart raced. What if it happened again? I tried to drive but my vision would blur. The only thing that helped was a stiff drink. Then and only then could I loosen my shoulders from around my ears and drive. I hated every second of it. And I started to make mistakes. Small things at first and more when the drink took hold. I could have killed someone, driving drunk like that – the irony is not lost on me.

'Like my wife, the boss made allowances. But that's just the thing: when people forgive bad behaviour you think you've got away with it, so you push those boundaries again and again. And that's what I did. I missed an entire Christmas with my girls because I went to the pub on Christmas Eve and didn't come home. Woke up on someone's sofa, I swear I'd never met. And on it went. Everyone tiptoed around me and I resented it. But I should have seen that for a reflection of the love it was. They were too good for the likes of me. I stopped giving my wife my pay cheque. I stopped going home at all. In retrospect, I don't know how I expected they'd survive. I don't think I cared. By that stage I only cared about the drink. But that didn't matter because soon I didn't have a job to go to. Got laid off once the boss figured out I was drinking on the job. My life imploded, fell down around me like a house of cards.

'One day, after I'd been gone for months, sleeping rough by the railway tracks, I hobbled home to find another family there. Sitting at the dining table, laughing and joking, just like we used to. My heart shattered that day. Here was this new family sitting where we used to, my own family gone, disappeared because of my actions. I'm sure I could have found them, could have cleaned up my act, and got back on the straight and narrow. But I didn't. I took to the streets, driven by shame, fuelled by anger. How could I face my family after the choices I'd made? And where were they?

'I moved around before I found a sanctuary by the front door of the library. It's quiet at night, semi sheltered from the wind. I don't drink these days, can't stand the smell of it. My body can't handle it. It tastes like the poison it is – and maybe that's a punishment for what I've done. I can't find oblivion at the other end of a bottle now. I can't dull the hurt when it comes. I have to face it head on and let it play out.

'My family are in my heart every day. So is the lad who chose my train and I puzzle over why he decided on such a path to end his life. One thing I know for sure is, he must've been suffering a pain so great that he thought he had no other choice, and I understand that. I've been there myself. As the end of my life approaches, I'm beginning to make amends with myself. You can only beat yourself up so long, you know? I'll never forgive myself for the hurt I caused my family, the way I abandoned them, but I try and make peace with it. The thing about the regret is, it's always just a step behind you, just like your shadow. If you stumble, it catches you and you relive that pain over and over again.'

'You've never heard from your family since then?' Jamie asks, her eyes bright with tears.

Harry shakes his head sadly. 'I never did. My wife had a brother in London, so I presume she went to him. I only hope her family wrapped them in love and provided for them, in a way I never could. I dream of my girls. I picture them now, mothers themselves perhaps, or working abroad, living exciting lives in a big city. I miss them, every single day. My wife too. Did she remarry? I hope she found a wonderful man, a teetotaller, who opened her heart once more and helped her learn to love again.'

'You should find them, Harry.'

He bites down on his lip to stem his own tears. After a heart-breaking pause he says, 'I don't think I deserve it. I'd hate them to see me like this.'

'Don't you think it should be up to them to decide?' Jamie says gently.

He waits a beat. 'How could they be anything other than disappointed? They're probably full of anger. I abandoned them.'

Jamie has fire in her eyes when she says, 'Harry, the story you've just told me is heartbreaking but it's not like you went on a murdering spree. You turned to alcohol to medicate yourself after suffering a traumatic incident at work. You used it as a coping mechanism because for a while, it did help. It blurred the edges; it helped you get through each dark and suffocating night. It went too far, and became an addiction. The addiction controlled you, not the other way around. I'm sure they can understand that. They'd be grown women by now, and I'm sure they could find it in their hearts to forgive you.'

My own eyes shine with tears. God, what a story. I want so much to embrace Harry and tell him he's a good man, but I stay quiet and off to the side while internally I feel a whole gamut of emotions.

Harry takes a moment to consider it all. 'I thought they might come looking for me, but they never have.'

'How do you know that for sure?'

He raises his palms in the air. 'I don't. I was a ghost in Willow Grove. Until Elodie arrived the only person who ever spoke to me was Finn. He's a well-meaning guy but he kept trying to link me in with places who help homeless people and I didn't want that. Then Elodie arrived, this whirlwind who set out to make all these changes. She made me believe that anything was possible. That people might have been ignoring me out of politeness, not because they wanted to veer away from the scruffy homeless guy who stuffs newspapers up his sleeves to keep warm. It made me wonder how many of us have such little confidence that we begin to believe what others say about us. I told myself I didn't matter and locals ignored me because I deserved it. Now I'm trying to reset my thinking. I'm trying to love myself again. But it's going to be a long road . . .'

Finn slings an arm around me and I turn and rest my head on his chest, not caring who sees. Harry's story has touched my soul. It takes a lot of courage to do such a thing, but what moves me most is that he recognises that in order to change, to have any sort of fulfilling life, he has to love himself first. Has to forgive himself.

'God, Finn,' I whisper. 'This doesn't happen often but I have no words.' We step out of the cubicle so we don't disturb Harry.

'You know you're going to save the library, right?'

'*Harry* is single-handedly going to do that. Finn, you should have heard it. I've never listened to anything like it before. Harry shared it all. He's seen the worst of what life has to offer and here he is, sharing it so bravely.'

'He is one amazing fellow. Let's hope this is the start of Harry gaining some confidence back and a having a second chance at life.'

'Yes, yes, it's the start of a new season in his life, no matter what he chooses to do. Are we still celebrating tonight? Didn't Sofia say . . .'

'Canapés at my place tonight,' Sofia says as she leaves the cubicle. 'Harry did such a marvellous job!'

'Great!' Harry has more members lined up to borrow him but part of me worries that it'll take too much of an emotional toll.

Jamie gives him a big hug and holds on tight. 'Thank you for sharing your story with me, Harry. You matter – I want you to know that. You matter to *me*. And I hope we can catch up again outside of here. While I didn't know much about you, I did know you slept by the library and not once did I think of asking you how you were, or if I could sit with you for a few minutes. This is going to make me think twice about being absent when I could be present. You've opened up my eyes, Harry. And I wish you peace.' She taps his heart. 'Peace and good things to come.'

After their goodbyes I approach him.

'Harry, *thank you* for sharing your story. You've blown me away. I'm so damn proud of you.'

He smiles and it lights up his ruddy face. 'It's liberating – I can't tell you how much. It's like a weight has been lifted off my shoulders and I can't wait for the next "reader".'

'That's great to hear! But do let me know if you start to find them tiring. We need to look after our human books, and make sure you don't overexert yourself, OK?'

'Sure, I'll let you know.'

'Sofia is doing canapés at her place tonight to celebrate.'

'I'm going to be round the way she keeps feeding me.'

'Aren't we all.' I laugh.

At the end of the day I check our membership numbers to find we have 205 to go. If we have another busy day like we did for Harry, we'll get a step closer. I only hope the novelty doesn't wear off before we get there.

Chapter 18

By the time the Friday night arrives, I'm ready to fall into a deep slumber and sleep for a week. The air is chilly as an autumnal breeze rattles the windows in the cottage. A draught creeps in, whistling as if introducing the new season. I'm about to throw myself into a warm bubble bath when Finn arrives on the doorstep brandishing champagne and flowers. All we've done is toast to the success of the People Library and used any excuse to eat in Sofia's kitchen.

'I know, I know,' Finn says reading my expression. 'My jeans are getting tight from all these catch-ups, but I figured it's Friday and we've got all weekend to drink fizzy water in the hopes of rejuvenation.'

'In that case . . .' I say and let him in, not caring one iota that I'm in flannel PJs and fluffy socks. 'You're overdressed.'

'I wish I'd known we were having a pyjama party.'

'It's Friday – what else would we be doing?' The blissful feeling of not having to don a gown and heels for an Astor event still hasn't waned and I don't think it ever will.

'Right.' He grins.

I go to the kitchen and grab two champagne glasses and meet him on the sofa. We've skipped straight past the awkward getting to know you stage into being comfortable with each other in our PJs. Finn is my spirit animal in that we can spend a whole Sunday in bed reading and only leave when we're in dire need for food. In my past albeit very brief relationships this was seen as laziness or some kind of reclusiveness when in fact I just love reading, dammit. So to have a guy who suggests a reading day as part of our schedule, well that's the type of man who has marriage material written all over him. Sometimes, our kisses do distract us and one thing leads to another but that just makes the time more special.

'Oh, I nearly forgot! I have a surprise for you!' I go to the hall table and bring it back.

He opens the small package and throws his head back laughing. 'A sword pen? I'll treasure this for the rest of my life.'

'Trust me, I know how mighty it is.' I giggle.

The TV is on in the background as we chat about the week just gone.

I make popcorn and we settle down with our fancy champagne and cheap microwave food. All the important food groups covered for a Friday night anyway. Draping my feet over Finn's lap I relax back and sink into some mindless TV.

The nightly news comes on as I go to ask Finn what movie we should stream when my mother's face flashes up on screen. I choke on my popcorn and try and cover it with a cough.

'You OK?'

I nod and gulp my champagne to get the kernels down. *What is she doing?*

The reporter, one of Astor's own, asks my mother about the future of Astor News and Media, and she replies, 'Our daughter Ellie is preparing to take over the company. It's all she's ever wanted. She'll be one of the youngest CEOs of a billion-dollar business. Ellie's been dreaming of this day since she was a toddler. She was bred for it.' What! *What is she doing?* So much for allowing me to follow my dreams . . .

'God,' Finn says, shaking his head. 'She makes her sound like a racehorse. *Bred for it.*'

'Mmm,' is all I manage. Is this a ploy by my mother to get my attention and inspire me to come home?

Finn grunts in disgust every time my mother speaks about me. The story drags on and on with Mother assuring the reporter things are going to expand under my tenure. Just what is she playing at?

'Maybe she's just a proud mother,' I say not wanting Finn to do any digging into the Astor family. His eyes are glued to the screen as if he's fascinated by it all, no matter how much he seems to disagree with what she says. 'Let's pick that movie,' I say and try and prise the remote from Finn's hand. He doesn't notice and instead uses it to gesticulate wildly.

'I hate to sound bitter, but I hate this kind of thing.'

'Oh, hate what exactly?' I raise a brow.

'Here's your classic case of a woman born with a silver spoon in her mouth. This Ellie person has probably never had to work a proper day in her life; she's just a figurehead there. She'll have had every advantage her privilege provides and just like that, she's going to be promoted to CEO of a billion-dollar company? It's so hard to break into that cut-throat world of media and here's a princess who's got it all at her fingertips. It's wildly unfair.'

If only he knew! It's hard not to bristle at the sentiment but I can't exactly stick up for myself either. Finn has no inkling of what the so-called princess life is truly like. How that woman's world is anything but glamorous! All the advantages I've had mean absolutely zero to me. Less than zero. It pains me to hear him be so judgemental. It doesn't seem like the Finn I know.

'Before you judge her, Finn, think of the People Library . . .' *What do you see when you look at me?* 'I bet her life is nothing like you think.'

He cocks his head. 'Maybe.' His voice is clipped. Why does this irk him so? I bet it has something to do with his background and upbringing. He can't see any struggle other than his own. *Most* people would look at the life of Ellie Astor and be envious – but *that* Ellie is a puppet on a string.

The air in the room grows heavy with unsaid words and I have the first suspicion that our different backgrounds have the ability to come between us, if the truth doesn't first. Now I know how he'd feel if I tell him I'm Ellie Astor! Tell him I'm the privileged princess who has never had to work a day in her life . . .

We can't seem to find a way back to each other for the rest of the evening and Finn soon makes his excuses to leave. I don't want the night to end on a strange note but I'm out of sorts seeing my mother on TV and wondering what it means for me. I'm desperate to call Teddy.

I kiss Finn goodnight and shut the door, with a heavy heart, and go to find my mobile.

'You saw it?' Teddy says forgoing a hello.

'I did. Finn was here too and made some pretty quick judgements about how I've been handed it all on a platter.'

'You're kidding? Though I suppose most people outside of Astor have no idea what it's really like, what our life entails. How'd you manage to bite your tongue?'

'It wasn't easy. But what *could* I say?'

'Nothing without giving the game up. And you know Mum's only going to continue sharing the good news about Ellie Astor, young, bright female CEO taking over this magnificent company because she was born for this role.'

'Finn said she spoke about me like I was a racehorse.'

Teddy lets out a barrel of laughter. 'I like this guy more and more. It does sound like that. Like you've been bred specifically to be *the face of Astor.*'

'But that's the thing, Teddy. He's not going to like me when he finds out the truth. Is he?'

'If he doesn't it's his loss. If he's the one for you, he will at least let you explain and no one could argue with your reasons why, surely?'

'You didn't see his expression. Like he was disgusted by this spoilt little rich girl.'

'*You're* disgusted by it and you *are* the spoilt little rich girl.'

'You've got me there.'

'How's the library going? Are you going to get there?'

'The first People Library experiment session was a huge success. I'd bet the library had never had so many bodies in it. We're getting closer but still a couple of hundred off – which seems like so many, considering it's already September. I have to hope the next three sessions bring enough new members. Even if it doesn't, Teddy, it's changing people already. Harry did such a good job of telling his story – there wasn't a dry eye in the place. The human books, the ones who've been relegated to the sidelines for so long, have banded together and formed friendships. We caught up for canapés afterwards and my face hurt from laughing so hard. I've never felt like this before, free to be me, to follow my own path. It's going to be awful if I do have to come home. Do you think there's any way Astor can survive without me?'

'I'm not sure, Elodie. I'm just not. Mother is emphatic that the media can only be handled by one of us, and she's still not keen on that being me. I'll do for now, but long term she wants you.' He lets out a frustrated growl. 'It's ludicrous. I've tried everything I can to convince her. Even Dad has tried. She's adamant that you're the only face that people trust. Selfishly, I'd love you back too. Together, we could start shaping Astor into the company we've always wanted it to be, couldn't we? We could do big things, but I need your help. You think you're just a figurehead, but it's obvious now just how pivotal your role is here.'

'But what if I don't want that, Teddy?'

'I know, I know, that's why I said I feel selfish. I wish there was a way you could do both, but I don't suppose there is. And things with Dad are a worry. He says he's fine but David has told me he's been back at the cardiologist's office every few days.'

'What's that about?'

'Dad says they're just monitoring it. But who knows for sure?'

I sigh. I've got a lot to lose if I leave Willow Grove. But how can I leave my family in the lurch when they need me too? 'I shouldn't have started things with Finn. As much as his comments upset me tonight, he's a great guy with a good heart. Now I've gone and messed it up by lying about myself.'

'Aww, Elodie, you've only lied about your name . . .'

'It's more than that though isn't it?' I don't want to think about it and what it means for me right now; my head is spinning as it is. 'Aside from Mum, how's things at Astor? Dad said you've taken on some extra projects.'

'Elodie, it's my dream job. Every day, I ease myself in a little more. I'm building relationships with the executive team, trying to prove to them I'm there for the right reasons this time and I'm reliable. A lot of them have opened up to me and shared what they'd like to see happen at Astor, how we can improve workplace culture – we've got a great team if only we could manage them ourselves. They've got so many amazing ideas but no one is brave enough to speak up in front of Mother because of the risk of being shot down. I see us here together, Elodie, making these big changes, and making Astor a place people enjoying work at again. After much wrangling, I've taken over the book bar expansion projects, working alongside Marco. It's enormous fun planning a five-storey bookshop and matching the levels with cocktails, spirits, wine, beers and bubbles. You'd have got a kick out of our meeting.'

It's so good to hear his passion for the job and the changes he wants to make for the staff. Maybe, together, we can achieve what we set out to. But it's not Willow Grove and my heart lies here.

'I'm proud of you, Teddy. Keep doing what you're doing.'

'Will do. Let me know when you've got the membership numbers.'

I exhale. 'Yep.'

*

Monday rolls around fast. Probably because I spent most of the weekend alone in bed reading. Finn was busy visiting one of his sisters and things are still a bit strange between us. It's like he's taken a step back. It's so subtle I don't know whether

I should mention it or not. I figure I'll leave things be for now, and gauge how he is when I see him at the library today.

It's Alfie's turn as a human book and my nerves make my belly swoop each time I think of the little guy under the spotlight. I shoot up a message to the universe and ask that today goes well for Alfie. I walk to the library, the scent of honeysuckles perfuming the air.

Alfie's waiting out the front with Jo and Harry. I check my watch. They're so early!

Harry is giving him a pep talk. 'Just be yourself, little man. That's all you have to do and you'll charm them all.'

'I'll try my best, Harry.' His face is grave.

'You OK, Alfie?' I ask as I fumble for the keys. 'You're quite early. You could have had a bit more of a lie-in.'

He gives me a robotic smile. It looks all wrong on his face. 'I'm. Fine.'

I open the door and we go to my office. Harry calls out that he's making tea and a hot chocolate for Alfie.

'Sit down and let's have a talk, yeah?' I say and hunt for the biscuit tin. Sugar will surely help this situation. I hand it over to Alfie but he shakes his head no. 'I'm. Fine. Elodie.'

'Something tells me you're a bit nervous, though, which is perfectly understandable.'

He shakes his shiny mane of hair. 'What if the person who borrows me is one of the bullies from school?'

My shoulders relax. 'Oh, Alfie, I hope you haven't been worrying about that all morning? I'd never let them borrow you! They've had their chance at making friends with the world's cleverest boy and they *blew* it! No, no, your borrowers are all lovely kids. Don't you worry about a thing in that regard OK?'

It hurts to think he's still carrying around scars left from those children. While he's usually bubbly and happy, it's clear the abhorrent treatment he's received for being deemed different has left its mark. If all goes well today, perhaps we need to schedule some parents to 'borrow' Alfie so they can see the effect bullying has on a little psyche. 'And remember, Alfie, you're in control. One word from you and it can stop right there.'

'You think I'm the world's cleverest boy?'

'I sure do. I don't know anyone as clever as you, Alfie. Not only clever but funny, charming and a joy to be around.'

He gives me a proud smile. 'Thanks, Elodie.'

'Here comes Harry with your hot chocolate.' While they sit around and chat, I excuse myself and get to work. I give the carpets a quick vacuum. It's become a morning ritual and one I find quite soothing. I do my best thinking while the machine is humming nosily beside me. Once that's done, I empty the bins. Who knew I'd become a fan of cleaning and sorting? Back home, we had a crew who did all those tasks, but I relish doing them myself. I check everything is in order for the People Library. I switch on the library computers and boot up the antiquated lending system.

Back at my desk, I'm checking membership numbers as Jo pulls me to one side for a chat. 'I'm doing the right thing, aren't I?'

I stash my paperwork. 'You are, Jo. Remember it's an experiment and we can shut it down anytime. My money is on Alfie surprising us all with how well he handles it. Doesn't he always?' Her face is pinched as if she's still not sure this is the right step. I feel it too. I want so much for this to be a way for Alfie to make friends, but we won't know until we try.

She bites her lip. 'I just don't want him talked about all over town in a derogatory way or anything. Or laughed at. If he gets flustered and stims, you know? Or he might put his headphones on and go blank. I don't want it to make things worse.'

'And if that happens, it's the perfect way to show his potential new friend what he does when he needs to regroup. Alfie shouldn't have to hide that side of himself to suit others, right? He's perfect just the way he is, stimming and all. I'll be right there. I vetted all the borrowers carefully for Alfie. They're all similar ages and have some degree of understanding about autism. As much as I want Alfie to make friends organically, I also want him to feel secure being in the spotlight so we can help foster some early friendships if we can. It'll be up to Alfie to see how he gels with them.'

'You're so right. Why should he have to hide that side of himself? That's a part of who he is.' She runs her hands through her hair. 'I've never thought about it like that before . . .'

The sugar has worked its magic as Alfie bounds over. 'Look at all the people!' he says, happily. Outside a line snakes around the corner out of view. Finn knocks at the front door and I motion for him to come in. He's press after all. He approaches us and says a friendly hello. What was I expecting, a great big hug in front of everyone? Still, he doesn't give me a special look, a clue to how he's feeling, which concerns me but there's no time to fixate on it. 'Hey, Alfie,' he says. 'You remember me from the *Chronicle*, right?' Alfie nods. 'Would it be OK with you if I take some photos of your first session?'

'Sure, my best angle is slightly left of centre. It makes me look more mature.'

Finn and I exchange a look and I have to bite my tongue not to laugh. He really is the bees knees, this extraordinary child.

'Left of centre, got it.'

I bend down to Alfie's level. 'Do you need anything before we let them in, Alfie?'

He taps a finger to his chin. 'Maybe my headphones. If it's too loud, then what?'

'Yes, it will be louder than normal, because there's so many people who want to visit the People Library and see about borrowing our very special book today. To counter that, we've set you up in the cubicle at the back. That way it'll be quieter, and you can tell your story without needing your headphones, but take them just in case, yeah?'

'OK, that makes sense. Do you want to learn the hand signal in case I need to abort the mission?'

'Yes I'd love to. Do you have one for abort the mission and one to tell me you're OK?'

Alfie shows me both hand signals, and I realise I've seen him use them with his mum before. They're quick ways of communicating that Alfie needs help without having to say it. Jo's such a good mum and has no idea how amazing she is. This bright little boy is a credit to her.

'OK, I'm ready.' He thrusts his hands deep in his pockets.

Maisie comes over and asks Alfie if she can give him a hug. Maisie has been anything other than supportive of the People Library experiment but she has a soft spot for Alfie, like the rest of us . . .

Alfie confirms she may hug him, which is basically Alfie dipping his head into her upper arm, rather than any arms tangling around one another. 'I'm proud of you, Alfie.'

'Thanks, Maisie. Keep those biscuits coming when I give you the signal. And don't forget the water. None of that sparkling stuff – it tastes like electricity and I can't stand it.'

She grins. 'Will do.'

'Right, ready?' I ask.

He gives me a nod. 'I'm going to wait in the room with Mum.'

'See you in a bit.'

*

ALFIE

'I'm Alfie and I have superpowers. No, really, I do. Not magical, not like Harry Potter or anything but go on, ask me a date.'

'A date?' Levi asks with a frown.

'Yeah, like November 3rd is a Thursday. June 5th is a Sunday, that kind of thing.'

'Ooh,' Levi says. 'OK, what about December 12th? That's my birthday.'

'It's a Monday.'

'A Monday? I wonder if Mum will let me have the day off. I'll ask her. OK, November 2nd?'

'Wednesday.'

Levi checks the days on his phone and smiles with admiration. 'How do you do that?'

Alfie shrugs. 'It's the way my exceptional brain works. It's called calendar counting and I find it easy. My mum says I'm *one in a million* and that she's lucky that I chose her out of all the mothers in this world. She reckons even though I always *throw her under the bus* – for the record I've never thrown her anywhere, and I especially wouldn't throw her under a bus because she'd probably die or have life-altering injuries – she still says she wouldn't change me for the world. I wouldn't change her either. Except maybe her job, which *sucks the life out of her*. Jobs are hard, so she says I have to study a lot so I can have a proper career where I don't need to *stand on my feet all damned day*. So, I study as hard as I can because I'm home-schooled.

'Well, it's called home-schooled, but I come to the library most days. I have my own cubicle here. Really, it should be called library-schooled. It's like it's my job, coming here every day, getting cleverer. Sometimes I wonder if my brain will explode, with all the facts I'm learning. But Mum says it won't explode, and she's usually trustworthy. My dad wasn't. *He couldn't keep it in his pants*. I don't know specifically what that means but it doesn't sound good.

'My favourite thing is learning about apex predators, sharks mainly. I'm scared of the sea because I don't want to be eaten by one but it's their home, so you take that risk if you swim there. I really don't like the feeling of the sand under my feet. It reminds me of sandpaper and I panic that it's scraping my skin off. It's not, Mum says, but I'm very sensory. I don't like loud noises; my clothes have to smell right and be made from a certain fabric. I don't know what that fabric is. I just know it when I feel it. My mum says it *drives her nuts* because I always have to choose my own clothes and sometimes it takes hours and hours. I tend to wear my favourite things until they're covered in holes and Mum says I look like a castaway, like I've been stuck on a desert island for a decade. Maybe she's being sarcastic but it's hard to tell. I really don't understand sarcasm. It seems so pointless. My castaway clothes always end up going missing, like I don't know she's ditching them. Now when I find the right clothes she buys me seven of the same, one for every day of the week. It's a better plan, I guess.

'At school, they said mean things, like we were so poor I only had one set of clothes. I tried to explain, I had seven sets of the *same* clothes but they didn't want to listen. And I think we *are* poor. We aren't rich – I know that for sure. But what's wrong with being poor? It would be worse to be mean, like they are. Mum cried when I told her what they said. I hate to see her cry. I'm always surprised by it and get confused about what to do. I find feelings hard to translate but when there are tears I know she's definitely sad. But tears can also mean she's laughing – one day she was laughing so hard she said she was *going to pee her pants!* She's a good mum. She's always laughing, crying or both.

'The things the kids say don't bother me as much as Mum thinks, probably because half the time I don't understand what they're implying. I want friends, that's all. But Mum thinks I'm going to be friends with the first person who comes along and what if that person isn't nice? I probably will be friends *just like that* but if they're mean to me, then I will end that friendship. I will ghost them. Have you heard of that? I really didn't understand how you could ghost someone, like does that mean you have to die to get away from them? But I googled it and ghosting just means you ignore them and pretend they're not there. It seems like a simple way to end things. I like that idea.

'I'd really like a friend I can talk to about sharks. I know a friendship has to work for both sides. My psychologist has explained all about social interactions and taking turns listening and talking. That's why the People Library is so fun, because those rules don't apply. Sometimes, I forget to listen to what people are saying because I'm waiting for my turn to speak and I have to hold on to the thought or else it evaporates and then it's gone forever. It makes it hard to talk because then I freeze up. So, if I do *talk over the top* of you, it's because of that. Anyway, so that's my story.'

'Cool. I like sharks and I'm scared of the sea too. My dad says it's the sharks' home so we have to be respectful of that. Hey, do you like pizza?'

'I *love* pizza.'

I'm debating about stepping in to arrange a catch-up for these little dudes but Alfie gives me the signal that all is well, so I leave it be. We can debrief later and I'll take my cues from him.

'Me too.'

Alfie grins. 'If you want you can come to my house and we can watch a shark documentary and eat pizza? It will have to be on a Sunday because that's Mum's day off. She doesn't let me eat frozen pizza because the preservatives will *eat my insides out*, but she makes a decent home-made pizza. She does hide a bunch of vegetables under the cheese, which is sort of annoying, but she chops them up so small so after a few bites you don't taste them as much. I have a highly developed palate, which she always forgets. But she doesn't want me to end up like my dad – *a heart attack waiting to happen*. So I let it go.'

'Cool, I'll ask my mum and I can bring my Lego.'

'Cool. I have a Lego shark.'

Oh to make friendships the way children do. Bonding so quickly and easily over sharks, pizza and Lego.

'Elodie is organising a Minecraft coding club, so we can also meet there if you want?'

'Yeah, sure. Want to build a world together?'

'An underwater world?'

Levi grins. 'Totally.'

If I leave here tomorrow, I will forever be grateful for meeting Alfie. 'You'll have to let me know how it goes,' I whisper to Jo.

'I didn't know he knew about the vegetables on the pizza.'

'He's like baby Yoda.' I love that she focuses on that and not the hilarious things he said about her. 'Are you happy for him to continue with this today?'

'For sure – he handled that like a pro.' Her eyes are glassy with tears and it's hard to look at her and remain composed myself. Little man Alfie has the world at his feet, if only the world would give him a chance to show just how special he is.

Finn snaps a photo of the boys standing together, going just left of centre to catch Alfie's 'good side'. Once the boys sort out a date for pizza and say their goodbyes, Finn takes Levi aside to interview him on his experience borrowing a human 'book'.

It's fascinating to watch the way Finn interacts with the young kid, making him laugh so he relaxes into the interview and answers the questions candidly. Finn would make a great dad – not that I'm anywhere near that particular stage in our relationship, especially as things are still oddly tense between us.

When Finn's done and has said goodbye to Levi I wave him over.

'Can we chat?'

'Sure,' he says, stuffing his iPad into his backpack. 'Here?'

I glance around. The library is packed and Maisie is still busy signing people up. She sees me looking and waves me over to help.

Finn clucks his tongue. 'Get the new members sorted first. I'm going to do this article now so I can get it published as quickly as possible. What about we meet tomorrow after work when things are a bit quieter?'

I give him a loose hug, wanting to connect in some small way again. 'Perfect, let's do that.'

I hurry back to the queue and help Maisie with memberships and queries about borrowing the human books. I'm quietly thrilled when some new members ask about volunteering to be a human book for the People Library too.

'Really?' Maisie says when a woman called Charlotte asks about joining as a human book. 'Have you *seen* what they have to do? They have to let all those skeletons fall right out of the closet – think about it, Charlotte, is that something you want to be part of?' Maisie's voice is taut with disgust. Where's the happy Maisie gone to this time? What's provoked this? While she hasn't been super supportive of the experiment, she's hasn't been her usual vociferous self lately either.

'There's some things I need to get off my chest,' Charlotte says. Aha. This is Charlotte from the crochet club – the Charlotte who wouldn't let Sofia join. Perhaps she wants to right some wrongs? I search her face for answers, but it's closed off after Maisie's comments.

'We'd love you to join, Charlotte.' I rifle through the papers on my desk and find the expression of interest sheet. 'Here's some more information about it. Fill it in and return it to me at your earliest convenience and we can get going. It's not for the faint-hearted but our human books have so far found the experience liberating.'

Maisie crosses her arms, and tries to catch Charlotte's eye, but she doesn't meet her gaze. Charlotte takes the proffered paperwork, mumbles a thanks and backs away.

'Maisie, what was that?' I hiss. 'For this to work we need new human "books" so we can attract new "readers". Are you trying to put everyone off who asks?' I thought we'd mended some bridges but it seems Maisie isn't about to change overnight.

Maisie grunts. 'If you let this experiment continue, do you know what's going to happen?' She doesn't give me a moment to respond. 'You're going to have everyone airing out their dirty laundry and before you know it, there's going to be this great big divide in town. Things were just fine before you came along; everyone knew their place. Now you've got Homeless Harry waltzing around like a B-grade celebrity. Sofia hasn't even shared her story yet, and she's suddenly the woman of the minute . . . everyone's talking about her cooking and her castle. The world has gone mad!'

Everyone knew their place? I close my eyes for a moment, not sure how to attack this. 'Maisie, come on. You know *why* we're doing this. Even saying everyone knew their place is offensive. Did Harry know his place, sleeping out in the elements? Did Alfie know his place not feeling welcome at school? Did Sofia—'

'Stop, stop, I get it! You'll have anarchy on your hands when everyone in town turns on one another – that's what I'm saying.'

'That's not going to happen!'

'Isn't it?'

I let out a frustrated huff and then paste on a mechanical smile. 'Right who was next?' I say. I feel waves of hostility emanate from Maisie but I don't give her the satisfaction of acknowledging them.

Chapter 19

Learning not to judge a book by its cover at Willow Grove library

The Chronicle by Finn Ford
Thursday September 8th at 8.47 a.m.

The People Library experiment heads into its second week with local home-schooled child Alfie volunteering to share his story. Alfie has a unique ability to calendar count and wowed his borrowers with his superpowers, of which there are many. Head Librarian Elodie Halifax says, 'We started this initiative in the hopes that we'd save Willow Grove library, but more importantly we've discovered that these stories needed to be told. Our brave human books have bared their souls in an effort to share their unique histories and complex lives. It hasn't been easy for them to open up but they've done so in the hopes that locals will understand their plight and see the folly of judging a book by its cover. Small towns are known colloquially to be a hive of gossip and these human books know that too well, being the subject of such talk for too long now. It's time to flip the script, and talk to them, rather than about them. The People Library experiment has proven that given time and a safe place to share their stories everyone deserves a new beginning. Everyone deserves to be listened to. Only then can we begin to heal as a community, by coming together and supporting the vulnerable among us. Instead of judging them, let's hear their stories, and help them.'

So, the question remains, do we judge a book by its cover and can we collectively change our thinking in order to become a more coherent and tolerant town? Surely, we understand that we need to put former preju-dices aside and open our heart and minds for those who need us most.

Turn to page 2 for interviews and photographs with Alfie and his first borrower, Levi. And if you'd like to sign up to borrow a human book join here: www.willowgrovelibrary/memberships

He's managed to sum it up perfectly again. On page two, Alfie's shiny happy face virtually jumps from the paper. The shot of him and Levi, arms slung over each other's shoulders is enough to make me weep, knowing Alfie's desperate need for a buddy. Finn's interview with Levi about his experience is adorable. He talks about wanting to learn more about Alfie's superpowers and how he thinks his ability to calendar count is more magical than Harry Potter will ever be, because Alfie is *real*.

I fold the paper in half while I wait for my takeaway coffee at Beans, the local coffee shop. In the small café, almost everyone holds a copy of the *Chronicle* in their hands, and there's a real buzz in the air about the article. I catch a few people pointing at me, figuring out I'm the Elodie from the article. I give them wide smiles and a little wave, hoping they'll approach me if they've got questions.

An elderly woman in a red coat wanders over to me. 'Hi, Elodie, I'm Pat from the gardening club. I love what you're doing for the library.'

'Nice to meet you, Pat. Maybe you'd consider joining and borrowing a human book yourself?'

She slings her handbag over her arm. 'Yes, I'd like to. I'm keen to hear Sofia's story. I might have been quick to judge her, you know.' She dips her head as if she's embarrassed. 'I heard all the rumours and I thought I'd steer well clear. You don't want to be seen making friends with people who've got that kind of reputation; otherwise next minute you'll be the one on the outer, if you know what I mean?'

Small-town politics! The downright meanness of everyone listening to scurrilous rumours and ignoring a person in case their own name gets sullied. It's hard not to shake my head at such a thing, but it happens everywhere. Here you happen to know the names of those on the edge because it's such a small town. 'I understand,' I say. 'But that's what we're hoping to change.'

'What you said about the community coming together and supporting the vulnerable really touched me. And it also made me feel a wave of shame too. I call myself a Christian and yet I stood to one side and watched this happen. I intend to do better, to be better and I wanted you to know that.'

'Thank you, Pat. I'm so happy to hear you say that. It doesn't take much to make these changes and I know it's already working. Our human books have enjoyed the experience and are already feeling more welcome in the town than they have in years. Like you, I'm learning too and intend to be better.'

'You've done a beautiful thing. But one word of warning.' She glances over her shoulder as if to make sure no one is listening in. 'Beware of Maisie. She's telling some tall tales about you. I'm sure they're not true, and if there's one thing we've learned from all of this it's to take all this gossip with a pinch of salt. But still, she doesn't appear to be very positive about her experiences with you and it's building momentum in some camps.'

Oh bloody hell, Maisie. What now? 'Thanks for the warning. Maisie has had a lot going on lately but I'll have a word with her.'

'Well, she's got her reasons, I suppose. She loved her gran, you know. And her passing away like that, so recently, it knocked her for six, it did.'

*

Back at the library, it's my turn to track Maisie's every move. Why is she talking about me around town? I thought when she finally opened up to me that we'd connected, and things would improve.

She's half-heartedly restacking shelves, shoving the books in like she wants to be anywhere but here. I flinch every time I see a book shoved so roughly. I don't know whether to pull her up on it or if that will make matters worse, knowing that *she's* been gossiped about in town, that someone told *me* about what she's been up to. Will we ever learn?

I decide to leave it be and try and work it naturally into

a conversation later. I go to the computer to check the member-ships. We're getting close with 147 to go. My mobile phone rings so I snatch it up to find it's Teddy calling from the Astor office.

'Dear sister, I held my first board meeting today!' Happiness springs through the phone line.

'Oh, wow! How did it go?'

'Father said he was proud of me, and Mother gave me a nod of approval.'

'Teddy, you must have impressed the hell out of them to warrant such high praise!'

'Right? And I got invited for a week in Ibiza with my gang of unruly mates and I turned them down. It was easy enough to do – the work here, it galvanises me somehow. I feel alive, compared to before when I had nothing to do all day, and nothing to focus on.'

This is a huge milestone for Teddy and a turning point in his life – I can feel it. I only hope they don't pull the rug from under him by changing their minds. 'I'm so happy for you, Teddy. I knew you could do it. It's in your blood!'

'Well, long may it last.'

'How's Dad doing? Any better?'

'If I didn't know better, I'd say he visited one of your ashrams and got enlightened. While he's still visiting the cardiologist every few days, he looks as fit as a fiddle. It's bloody weird, to tell you the truth. Maybe it's that he's lost a fair chunk of weight and taken up yoga. Catching him doing the downward dog is a sight I'll never unsee.'

I laugh, picturing such a thing. 'He's taken up yoga! Our father?' While Mum subsists on green tea and thin air, Dad is a purveyor of the good life. There's not an oozy stinky French cheese he hasn't tried. As far as exercise goes, he subscribes more to the 10,000 steps a day policy and that's as far as it goes. A bit like myself, really.

'Yep. Yoga and meditation.'

'Just . . . wow. I'm truly lost for words.' Is this genuine though, or is it a sick man trying hard to right the wrongs of living a frivolous lifestyle for too long? Something irks me about the whole situation. Dad finally taking his body into account, with diet and exercise, sounds like a man whose heart is in trouble.

'You and me both. Hey.' He lowers his voice. 'They read about the People Library experiment. They thought it was genius. They seemed almost . . . like they were *proud* of you.'

I take a moment to process it all. 'Huh,' I manage. 'They're really softening in their old age.'

'I know, I know. It's hard to believe. But things *are* suddenly different. They want me to attend a few more social events with the promise I won't drink. They told me they knew I hadn't touched a drop in over six months. Did you tell them, Elodie?'

'I did.'

'Well, that seemed to sway them, and I promised them I could be trusted with their baby and most of all I want this to be my future.'

My heart swells with hope. 'What did Mum say to that?'

'*You'll do until Ellie returns.*' And the hope bursts like a balloon.

'You can do this, Teddy. Go out and wow them! Get me off the hook.' It feels like they're teetering on the edge of trusting him. He needs to continue to show them how suited he is to corporate life.

'I'm trying, I really am. Last week I felt completely hopeless, but things are looking up. My confidence is back and I need to keep showing them I'm committed.'

'I know you are, Teddy. That's all we can do. But do let me know about Dad. I'm not convinced he's as well as he says he is.'

'Will do. How's it going with that man of yours? Did you tell him yet that you're the princess on TV?'

'No. I'm worried. Things have cooled off with Finn. He's been acting strangely since that day we saw Mum on the news. He was supposed to come over for a chat but cancelled last minute. Said something about being swamped at work. He has been busy doing all the People Library articles, but surely he can still snatch an hour to see me? It feels . . . like it's over before it really began.' The idea casts a pall of sadness over me.

'I'm sure you're reading too much into it. Wouldn't he say so if he knew who you were?'

Would he? Finn is polite to the extreme. I think he'd just quietly back away. 'I don't know. It reminded me of that French girl you were with, the one who dumped you as soon as she found out you were an Astor. Remember her? I get the same cooler vibe from Finn – I mean it's subtle but it's there.'

'Oh, Giselle in Paris? Only liked the idea of me playing the part of a penniless poet while I was on a gap year. Little did she know that was just me trying to fit in. That *really* blew up in my face. Who'd choose a pauper over me? It beggars belief!'

'Teddy, you're missing the point. Finn is of the same ilk. He's come from a humble background and I sense he's got some hang-ups about the haves and the have-nots. I get the feeling he knows I'm Ellie Astor, or something. And he's like

Giselle in that he doesn't respect the idea that I've been handed everything on a platter, even when that's really not the case.'

'So have a talk to him. Be upfront.'

'How though? I can't exactly ask him.'

'Yeah you can. Just ask why he's been acting differently lately. Say you noticed things have changed and is there any reason why – make it light-hearted if you need to. Say you're probably not thinking straight because of all the excitement with the People Library lately but have his feelings changed? Be *you*, Elodie. You don't step around confrontation; you tackle it head on.'

He's right. I usually do but here I've had to tread carefully. Like with Maisie and look how that's turned out. She's waging a war about me behind my back. 'Yeah,' I say still not convinced.

A dark-haired boy comes to the desk holding an envelope.

'I have to go, Teddy, but let's talk soon yeah?'

'Sure, talk soon.'

'Can I help you?' I say to the boy.

'This is for you and I'm not to say who it's from, Finn said.' He puts a hand to his mouth and muffles a 'Whoops.'

I grin and take the envelope. 'What a mystery. Who'd send such a thing?'

'No idea, lady.' He grins, spins on his heel and leaves.

Inside the envelope is a card that reads:

> *Whatever our souls are made of,*
> *his and mine are the same.*

I'd know that line anywhere. It's Emily Brontë's *Wuthering Heights*. But what does it mean? I glance to the front door, hoping to see Finn. Perhaps, I need to find the book itself? I take the card and head towards the shelves to search for *Wuthering Heights*. Then I remember I put it on the display table with a range of other classics. When I find it I prise the book open and another cards reveals itself. Is this a scavenger hunt? The next card reads:

Not all those who wander are lost.

If he's testing my knowledge as a librarian then he's going to come up short because I know my classics inside out! I find JRR Tolkien's *The Fellowship of the Ring* and the next clue pops out.

*It's no use going back to yesterday
because I was a different person then.*

My stomach sinks. Is this his way of telling me he's figured out who I am? It would be just Finn's way, showering me in clues to let me down gently. I hurry to find Lewis Carroll's *Alice's Adventures in Wonderland* to see if the next has any hidden meaning.

*And now that you don't have to
be perfect, you can be good.*

Is that a reference to my old life, the woman with the silver spoon who has had every advantage and still wasn't happy? Or is he just being an old-school romantic? I wish I knew for sure – so many things feel up in the air lately.

I know it's a John Steinbeck quote but I can't remember

which book. I find the section and flick through *Of Mice and Men* and find nothing. I try *East of Eden* and another card falls out. My heart is pounding, not knowing what exactly this all means.

We are asleep until we fall in love.

This one stumps me. Who said this? And what does the underlying message mean? That he knows who I am but he's in love with me? The books have all been classics so I flick through them in a mad panic, managing to catch Maisie's eye, who frowns at me, as if I've lost it. Which I probably have.

I get all the way down to T when a card falls out of Tolstoy. Aha, it's from *War and Peace*, a book I've never been able to get through. Maybe I should try again . . .

It reads:

They say it better than I ever could. Love Finn

The same young boy finds me crouched by the shelves and hands me a posy of wild roses. 'He said to meet him by the river for lunch if you've got time.'

I nod. Have I got time? I suppose I'm entitled to a lunch break. I usually eat at my desk, but I have to know what this all means.

'Maisie, back in an hour.' I don't wait for her supercilious scowl, I grab my bag and go.

*

Finn sits on a picnic blanket, nose pressed in a book. When he hears my approach he looks up, a smile lighting his face. 'You solved it in record time.'

'Was your little spy watching me?'

'Of course; otherwise how would I know if you cheated and googled the answers?'

I laugh in spite of it all. 'What does it mean, Finn?'

Confusion dashes across his face. 'What?'

'What does it *mean*?'

'You don't know?'

Am *I* talking in riddles here? 'I *think* I know, but I'd like you to be honest with me and come out and say it.'

'A man can't be a romantic? You're going to make me face you and say the words, already? I thought a slow burn was the way to go with matters of the heart.' He holds up a romance book. 'I've been researching these things.'

'What?' Confusion reigns.

'What I've been researching these things, or . . . ?'

'No, I mean what does it all mean? Why did you do that? Things have been so quiet between us. I felt like you'd stepped back a bit.'

Finn drops the book on the blanket. He plucks grass as he gathers himself. When he speaks again, he gazes into my eyes with such longing that it makes my heart stutter. 'I haven't felt this way before, Elodie. I sensed there was a distance between us too, so this was my way of showing you how I feel, through literature that you love so much. I'm wholeheartedly still in this. And I hope you are too.'

Have I read too much into it all? Certainly seems that way. But I know how crafty Finn is, and it could also be his way of telling me he knows and he's OK with my past, by using the words of others. Again, I can't really ask him without giving the game away. If that's the case it's the most romantic way to show me that he cares and he loves me for who I *am* not who I *was*. Dare I risk say how I feel? I'm usually so guarded with men but Finn isn't any man. 'I really like you a whole lot.' *Oh my God, Ellie, are you five?*

But baby steps and all that.

Finn throws his head back and laughs. Even his laugh is beautiful and melodious. Is that how you know it's love when everything the man damn well does is like music to your ears? 'I really like you a whole lot too. There's one more thing.' He leans in to kiss me, and I forget about the world, my lies and everything besides the sensation of his lips against mine. I wish I could press pause, and stay like this forever.

Chapter 20

PETE

'I'm known as Pilferer Pete, and to be honest the name hurts. I mean, there's no question it's true. I steal; I steal a lot. And I never really knew why until I met Elodie the librarian. She stopped me in the supermarket one day and said she thought she understood me and why I do what I do. At first, I thought she meant that she understood I stole food because I needed to eat. But I thought about it more and that seemed too easy a guess for someone to stop you in a shop and speak up like that. I *don't* steal because I need those things, not really. So, I spent some time thinking about the reasons why. It didn't take long to figure it out.

'Around town my family have always been known as "bad apples". I hear the whispers, "Here comes Pilferer Pete, from a family of bad apples, that guy. Would steal the coat off his mother's back if he could." And on it goes. When you hear that kind of thing, over and again, you begin to believe it. You begin to act a certain way because it's expected of you, you know? In a way, I'm playing a part that they've created. When I figured that out, I was floored, I tell you, *floored*. It was the first time in years that I realised I could change. I could be a whole different person. But would the town ever change their mind about me? Could I outrun the name Pilferer Pete? That's the big question, right? And it plagued me, leading up to doing this. What if this experiment failed? What if me sharing my story made my life even worse? Then what?

'I got to know the other human books. Sofia invited me to her house – it's a castle really and she didn't hide away the silverware, you know? She trusted me implicitly. And I thought, if she can trust me with all those fancy things in her house, all those valuables sitting there, maybe others can too. I can change and I'm going to prove it to everyone. I just need a second chance. And if it fails and I'm still known as Pilferer Pete, it won't matter because I've made other human book friends, and they get it. They get me. They have their own problems so we've bonded over that. And they're damn nice people too. For the first time since I can remember I've got people to talk to, people who care about me. As if I matter. If nothing else changes, then I'm grateful to know them and Elodie and Finn.

'But you know what I think? I think this experiment is going to change the whole town, and then maybe the whole world. I'm used to standing off to the side and watching people and I can already see the mood is different. Old wounds are healing. And what else can you ask for? I guess there's one more thing, though. There are the dreams we all have.

'I got so small I didn't feel like I deserved to dream. Like who did I think I was? Now I see it clearly. You have to dream big because no one can do it for you. I have a goal, a plan I want to work towards. I've always wanted to be a gardener, to plunge my hands into the earth, feel that connection to something greater than me. There's something satisfying about helping things grow, don't you think?

'So that's what I'm going to do: I'm going to get a job, even if I have to start at the very bottom. In fact, I'm going to *insist* I start there because then the only way is up.'

*

On Monday, Charlotte returns to the library with the People Library expression of interest sheet all filled out. 'Thanks, Charlotte. I'll have a read of this and let you know.' I want our human books to be interesting and to be able share something other than local gossip, but I'm not quite sure Charlotte's story will work if she doesn't tell it truthfully. I'm hesitant after her crusade to ruin Sofia's reputation. She writes that her story would be about regret.

'What's specifically do you regret?'

She swallows hard. 'So many things, where do I start? I treated Sofia poorly because of my own bad judgement. Then I tried to get as many people as possible on board to ostracise her.'

'Right.'

She surveys the carpet, not able to look me in the eye as if she's genuinely embarrassed about what she's done. 'Since borrowing the other human books I see now how sharing these things can ease the burden. I've lived with this for so long, it's like a disease eating at me from the inside out. But I'll gladly carry that burden because the way I treated Sofia was disgraceful so I feel by speaking up and owning my mistakes in such a public fashion, I might help prove to Sofia that I'm truly sorry. I have to at least try, for her sake.'

'And you're sure sharing this is the right thing to do? I want you to be certain about your decision.'

'I've given it a lot of thought. And I can't hide behind the lies anymore.'

'Well, then if that's the case I'll add you to the list. We'll let you know ahead of time when your slot is. And if you'd like to be interviewed after and have photographs in the paper Finn's the man to talk to.'

'In for a penny, in for a pound.'

I smile as she walks away. We're almost halfway through September and things are looking up. Not only are locals engaging with the human books, but so many of them are keen to share their own stories too. It's still too soon to tell if we'll get the membership numbers but we are definitely on the right track.

Chapter 21

'Argh!' I scream as I mount the kerb and slam on the brakes.

'It's OK! You're doing great,' Finn says, but his pallor is deathly white. 'Just go a little slower around the bends.' It had been his bright idea to teach me to drive when I confided in him I'd never sat behind a steering wheel before.

'Are you sure? I feel like there's a distinct possibility I could write off your car.'

'This old thing? Gah.'

This old thing is actually a relatively new Saab, the very definition of what a reporter would drive. Quick enough to zip to a story, respectable enough to own. At this stage it doesn't have any dents or scratches and I'd hate to be the one to mar the body.

'Come on, Elodie. It's only a car. It's not a living thing. So what if you bump into something? It's fixable.' God, he's lovely. That's the type of person Finn is, to focus on the positive, to think of a car as just a lump of metal that takes you from A to B.

'OK. I'll try again but if I damage it, I'm paying for repairs and I won't have you arguing about it, yeah?'

He shakes his head. 'Drive the damn car, lady. I'm hungry.'

I laugh and reverse off the pavement. I'm supposed to be driving us to lunch in the next town over to get some miles under my belt, but my hands quake and my legs shake and I'm not sure I have it in me. 'Can we have lunch at Willow Grove pub instead? My shout?'

'You scaredy-cat.'

'Meow.'

'OK, we can have lunch at the pub, but you're not paying.'

'Fine we'll go halves.'

'It's my shout – I invited you.'

'Can you stop arguing with me so I can drive?' There's a couple of cars behind me, tooting in frustration.

'I can.' Finn sticks a hand out of his window and motions for them to go around. 'Let them pass so you don't feel the need to drive at Formula One speeds again.'

'You're no fun. Driving at Formula One speed makes me feel *alive*!' I joke.

His eyes go wide. 'Until you're *not* alive. I don't want to be the bearer of bad news but we don't have a roll cage, helmets or fire-retardant driving suits.'

'More's the pity.'

'OK, Lewis Hamilton, get going. Warm-up lap pace, please.'

I jerk and bunny hop, crunching the gears with a groan. He's going to need a new gearbox at this rate. When we get to the pub, I turn into the driveway around the back that borders the park. 'Ooh look, there's Pete,' I say, waving to him and inadvertently stalling the car.

'Close enough to the lines,' Finn says and gets out of the car. Probably safest. 'Hey, Pete!' he calls out.

'Is he gardening?' I step over the flower border to investigate.

'Hey, Elodie, Finn,' he says, wiping his hands on the back of his jeans before shaking our hands.

'What's all this then?' I point to a rubbish bag and gardening tools.

He wears a proud smile that's enough to break my heart. 'I spoke to the local constabulary about helping out in the community for a bit. Pay my dues, sort of thing. They suggested I could do a bit of work in the park. Pick up rubbish, neaten the beds, sweep up the leaves that seem to fall nonstop, odds and ends . . . I've been working alongside the gardener Leon, whose been showing me the ropes.' He gives an embarrassed laugh. 'It might lead to a job, who knows? But the experience will help with whatever the next stage is.'

I give him a hug. 'Pete, that's great news! You're on the way to living those dreams.'

His face goes scarlet, but he says, 'Yeah, I hope so. I had some making up to do. Honestly, I know I've been let away with a lot. People turned a blind eye to what I was doing. The only way to show that I've changed is to prove it. So that's my plan. And I've been speaking with the therapist Finn hooked me up with, which has been really helpful.'

I glance at Finn who just shrugs. He's like a vault at times.

'The therapist suggested I get out of my comfort zone and own up to my mistakes. It was hard putting myself out there. I was scared the local constables would take one look at me and laugh, you know? But they didn't laugh, they said I was a good man for trying to turn my life around and that they believed I could do it. In the streets people keep saying hello, 'cause they've recognised me out of the paper or heard my story at the library. I've joined an online support group too. And that's helped a lot knowing I'm not the only one who felt the same compulsions but is making a go of it. It can be done.'

'I'm dead proud of you,' I say, grinning at him.

'It's thanks to you, Elodie, for starting this whole experiment. Without you, things would never have changed.'

'I'm not sure about that but thank you. And I look forward to catching up with you at Sofia's after she's had her turn as a human book.'

'Me too. Can't wait.'

We say our goodbyes and head into the pub for a cosy weekend lunch. I love these lazy Sundays with Finn, where there's no rush, nothing to do except be with each other and enjoy a nice meal before returning home and curling up in bed together. Tomorrow, it's Sofia's turn as a human book and I can't wait to see what the sessions manage to do for her. But right now, I focus purely on the man in front of me, willing our food to arrive quickly so we can go home and snuggle. Light rain falls, as my love for Finn blooms.

*

Later that evening I get a text from Teddy. I go to Finn's bathroom to read it privately.

Dad back in hospital. Cardiologist said they're monitoring because of one abnormal ECG. Whatever it was the following ECGs were normal. Dad said it's a lot of bother over nothing but I wanted you to know.

I knew his whole health kick was too good to be true.

I text back: *Should I come home?*

Teddy replies: *No, he told me not to tell you.*

Worry sits heavy in my belly. The only thing I can do is get this library saved and then go home and see what's really going on.

Chapter 22

SOFIA

'I'm going to be honest, I did want to kill him at times. There's plenty of land to bury the body and no one would have been any the wiser. But that's not in my nature! Kill him with kindness more like. I loved my husband, probably too much. Easy to look back with hindsight and see how he tricked me. Love-bombed me, they call it these days. Made me feel like I was the only woman in the world, and at my age, it was quite a heady thing. When I found out he'd emptied one of my accounts, I guess I knew, but I didn't want to face it. I figured there must have been an explanation that would make sense.

'And there was. An addiction to gambling! *That* I could work with. I felt that he'd fallen down the rabbit hole of gambling and that it wasn't his fault. Addictions are never easy, are they? I told him the best way through this for our marriage was if I cut the money off – but I supported him emotionally and encouraged him to find a job. If he wanted to gamble away his salary, then that would be his choice.

'But he had to prove to me he could stand on his own two feet. I wouldn't be his cash cow. Little did I know he'd steal from the council! That made matters a hundred times worse. When they found out, he up and left, just like that. Took the money and ran. I found out later, there was no gambling addiction, just the thrill of fleecing people and hightailing it. I believe in karma though and I know one day he'll be caught – but I had to eventually let it go. Otherwise I'd be the one turning bitter.

'It was the fallout in town afterwards that hurt so much. I understood very well how they'd fallen for his charm – didn't I do the exact same thing? But they kept me at arm's length. Stopped me from being included. Spread so many malicious rumours about me that I wanted to sell up and leave. I've never felt so alone. And all because I loved a man who betrayed me.

'Do I forgive them now? I'm getting there. That's due to this experiment and finding my people with the other human books. And with Finn and Elodie. Elodie is someone mighty special. Without her, I'd have only lasted another summer before selling up. I'd given myself one more year and if things hadn't improved I was going to leave. Head to France and buy a lovely little chateau there.

'Now I can't even think of such a thing. I've got honest-to-goodness friends! Finally! We're a motley crew, that's for sure, but we've formed a deep friendship because we were all out of favour, all outsiders, if you will, and there's no forgetting that. We can forgive, sure, but those hurts will always be there. Now we have each other and that's something I'll always cherish. We have our own little family of human books. I have people to cook for – that's all I've ever wanted. To be able to pour my love onto a plate. I delight in them. It's like having a ready-made family. And who knows, maybe one day I'll find love again. It's not impossible, is it? Is there someone? Well, it's too soon to tell but let me just say, there are some special people in my life and even if it doesn't amount to anything it's enough for me that they're there, in my kitchen with me.'

I stand off to the side, listening. I smile at the idea that love just may be on the menu for Sofia. And I'll make certain I look for clues at the next dinner party. I sense it's one of the books, so that can only be Pete or Harry.

I leave her as her borrower quizzes her more and go to help Maisie at the desk. The crowds have dwindled but only slightly.

We sign up more members and chat about upcoming programs. Maisie seems happier than ever. I put it down to the fact it looks like we just might save the library. Once we've caught up I check the membership total and we're only fifty-five short of our goal. It's in sight!

'Maisie, we're only fifty-five memberships off saving the library!'

She double blinks. 'Wow.' Her forehead wrinkles. 'Never in my wildest dreams did I imagine it was possible.'

'There were plenty of times I doubted it too,' I say with a laugh. 'We just might keep our jobs yet.'

'I'm not sure if I'm happy or sad to be honest.'

It's my turn to show surprise. 'Why?'

She gives a loose shrug. 'I sort of liked everything how it was before.'

How it was quiet, relaxed and a pace so slow she could nap? Or something else? 'But isn't this better? We'll have new books every week, new members and events. The possibilities are endless.'

'You wouldn't understand,' she says and walks away with what I'm sure are tears in her eyes. Her grief is always just below the surface and I make sure to give her some space.

Maisie's on my mind for the rest of the afternoon so when the day ends, I head to Sofia's house wondering if she can shed any light on the matter. When I arrive, I'm surprised to find Harry sitting in the garden, soaking up the soft sun and the book *I Am Pilgrim* in his hands. Aha, Harry is the potential paramour! They'll make a great pair and be the perfect antidote for one another and all they've gone through. It looks as though he's enjoying the book by the speed he's flicking the pages so I don't disturb him; instead I go around the back to the kitchen door and knock.

'Hey, Elodie! Come inside, I'm baking some bread.'

I motion with my head to Harry outside.

'Oh.' She blushes. 'It's early days yet, more a companionship thing but I've invited Harry to stay in the guest house on the condition he shares meals with me whenever he likes. It gives me someone to cook for . . .'

'Aww, that's so sweet! It'll be nice for both of you.'

She kneads the dough, her apron dusted white with flour. 'If it wasn't for the human library I'd never have known about his plight. Never have met him. I was so caught up in my own little bubble I didn't even know there were others just like me facing the same problems. Harry's a stubborn old man though. He didn't want to take over the guest house. We had a fair amount of back and forth about it but in the end I was honest and said being here in this great big castle is lonely. Lonelier than I could ever imagine and knowing he's close, even if we don't live in each other's pockets, provided a sense of security to me. Besides, we'll be coming into winter soon, and between us I can't stand the thought of him out in the cold like that. There's plenty of room here so why not?'

'It's a great plan that will suit you both.' I bet Harry fought long and hard about it though. If there's one thing he's got in spades it's pride. Sofia did well to convince him it was for her benefit as much as his. Could love blossom? Only time will tell.

'It is.'

I sit on a stool opposite. 'Did you hear that Charlotte has registered to be a human book?'

Her eyebrows shoot up. 'She did?'

I nod. 'You should borrow her. She might surprise you.'

Sofia wipes her hands and flicks the kettle on. 'Hmm, I'll think about it. Old wounds and all that jazz.'

I go to the cupboard and take out three mugs. I'm sure Harry could use a nice warm brew to accompany his book. 'I understand. Have a think about it and let me know if you want me to reserve her for you. Speaking of old wounds, what's Maisie's story, do you know? We seem to take one step forward then two backwards. And I just don't know what to do about her.'

Sofia unearths the biscuit tin. 'Well, I guess it's the fact that Agnes Bitterweather was her gran, so she's dealing with her grief and the fact things have changed so much at the library.'

'Wait, what?' I gasp. 'Agnes Bitterweather was her gran?'

Sofia stops in her tracks. 'Didn't you know?'

I fall back onto the stool, my mind spinning. 'No, how would I know? She told me her gran died but she never said it was

Agnes.' I'm shocked silent. No wonder Maisie has acted like a truculent child with all that going on.

With a shrug Sofia says, 'Oh, I figured Maisie would have told you as soon as you arrived. She's not exactly backward about coming forward, that girl. Agnes died right after she retired. Except I found out recently she didn't *actually* retire.' Sofia pulls a face. 'Her hand was forced. So I'm presuming Maisie is stewing in all of that and feels a sense of loyalty to her grandmother. Even if she *did* agree with all your changes she probably feels guilty admitting it.'

'Jeez, Sofia, now it all makes sense! For a town that prides itself on gossip, I seem to be the last to know. Who forced Agnes's hand?'

Sofia grimaces. 'The council. They weren't happy with her employee performance review or something.'

I take a mug of steaming-hot tea from Sofia. 'But why? I've looked over the finances and she did everything she could to cut costs and make the library viable.'

She pulls out a stool beside me and opens up the biscuit tin, which is full of home-made jammy dodgers. 'I don't want to speak out of turn. I've learned *that* from the People Library, and it's just gossip I've overheard . . .' Her voice peters off as if she doesn't want to say anything more.

I place a hand on her arm. 'You can tell me, Sofia. I won't take it as gospel, but it might help me understand Maisie a bit better.'

Sofia pulls a face. 'OK, well like I said, this is just the usual chitchat down the grapevine, but word is she was fired because there were a number of complaints about her.'

'For what?'

'She wouldn't let everyone in the library – she had certain rules, like how they were dressed, and who they were. It riled a few people up.'

I remember back to Harry and how he wasn't permitted entry. 'Right. Well, no wonder Maisie took my arrival so badly.' I take a biscuit from the tin, unable to resist the strawberry scent of jam.

'Yes, quite unfortunate in this instance. She'll come around.'

I take a bite and the biscuit crumbles all over me. I give Sofia an apologetic wave. Will Maisie come around? If only I knew. 'I don't know if she will to be honest, Sofia. But I'm determined to work it out with her.'

Sofia motions for me to wait, while she takes tea and biscuits out to Harry. When she returns she says, 'So how are you and Finn going? Don't think *that* hasn't been discussed about the place.'

I'm so distracted about Maisie I answer without thinking. 'Oh, where to start. I'm falling for the guy, no two ways about it, but I'm not sure there's a future. I'm not sure how long I'll be able to stay in Willow Grove.' My dad springs to mind. He hasn't answered my calls, which is so strange. He usually hates texting, says his fingers are too wide for the tiny keys but has used that as his method of communication lately.

Sofia's expression registers shock and I realise my mistake.

'Why wouldn't you stay? Aren't you so close to saving the library?'

I quickly backtrack. 'Yes, yes, we're very close. What I meant was that nothing is guaranteed yet, that's all.' I let out a tinkling little laugh. 'Don't want to count my chickens and all that. If we don't manage to save it I'll have to leave I suppose, have to move on to another library . . .' Do I need to start sowing the seeds of a reason I might just up and leave? The thought of such a thing makes me choke up so I turn away and fidget with my bag.

Sofia still notices and gives my back a rub. 'Never mind, dear. We'll save the library, don't you worry about a thing.'

Chapter 23

CHARLOTTE

'At first, all we knew was a new couple had purchased the castle and had it completely restored before they arrived in town. Who has that kind of money? We all wanted to know. It wasn't long before he introduced himself. Jacob was the most charismatic man I'd ever met. His silky voice, the way he talked, I believed he could do no wrong. We didn't see much of his wife, Sofia. I don't know why. But Jacob kept popping up, wowing us with these grandiose stories about how he'd made his fortune, how he was this hotshot in finance. Made a bunch of money on Wall Street, retired early and ended up in the UK. We took the bait, all of us.

'It was up to me to approve him for the treasury job. My job was to check the references, do some digging to make sure it was all above board, but I didn't. I still kick myself every day about my stupidity. He spun a story about how that part of his life was over – you know the millionaire high-flyer finance guy who'd made his money and run. He claimed that if his former colleagues knew he was taking a lowly treasury job in a small town, they'd think he'd squandered all his money away or something! It makes me sound so naïve in hindsight, but the way he spoke was almost hypnotising. I didn't want to embarrass him by calling his references over a town council job! And I was so grateful we had this mastermind working for our treasury! I figured we were the lucky ones, with his knowledge and skillset, he was over qualified for the job so who was I to make checks on him? What if he changed his mind in the interim? No, it was best to get the ball rolling. The treasury was in dire need of sorting out, and there was no time to waste.

'At first the spreadsheets were a wonder – he'd made magic out of mud! He told us what to cut back on, what to fund. Told us that we overspent on council wages – that didn't go down too well, but we listened. We followed his orders. To find out later that he'd fooled us all! Jacob didn't have a penny to his name. It was all Sofia's. The Wall Street gambit was a lie. He'd never been in finance. Once upon a time he'd been an electrician but lost his licence for dodgy practices – no surprise there.

'When I confronted him he said he had a gambling addiction. It was no problem, he had accidentally used the wrong account, is all. He had some trouble accessing money from his US banks, but he'd get a wire transfer and it would be paid back in full. What sort of finance whiz accidentally uses the wrong bank? Alarm bells were ringing so loud I couldn't hear myself think. He begged me to keep quiet, the money would be there the next morning when I returned to work. That was the longest night of my life. I should have vetted this guy. The hammer would come down on me. By the time I pieced it together it was too late. The money was gone. All of it.

'The next day arrived and I was at work before sunrise. Of course, he didn't show up. He was gone already. Gone while

I lay in bed the night before, guilt roiling in my gut. He left everything, just like that, including his long-suffering wife. The fog lifted and I went into survival mode. Self-preservation at any cost. I was so damn angry, so I turned that anger in Sofia's direction. I'm ashamed to say, I led the pack when it came to her not being included in anything. I made up the worst rumours about her and they caught fire and exploded. I didn't want to see her face and be reminded of the terrible choices I'd made.

'I don't think Sofia will ever forgive me, and rightly so. But if I had the chance then I'd admit my part in it all and apologise for my behaviour. It wouldn't be enough but it would be a start. The only person to blame for him dazzling me with make-believe is myself. When Sofia repaid the money, I should have celebrated. I only managed to keep my job by the skin of my teeth because of her. Because she stipulated that as long as no one was fired because of him she'd repay every single penny. And yet I still made her pay, in other ways. I'm ashamed of myself. I should be on my knees thanking that woman. And you know, I'm going to try hard to prove to her that I've changed. And I'm sorry. I'm so truly sorry for the hurt I've caused. There's no excuse, just a million apologies.'

*

I have a moment spare to call Teddy, so I head to a cubicle. Dad still won't answer my calls and Mum's phone always goes to voicemail. For two tech-savvy people, it's odd. But I have good news to share, and I want my brother to be the first to know. 'Hey, Teddy! I have great news! We just hit the target of 507 new members and well ahead of schedule too.' I check the date.

'September 26th, not too shabby is it?' For the longest time the October deadline didn't seem achievable, and now here we are! 'I'm so thrilled I almost want to crack a bottle of champagne. In fact, I just might because this calls for a celebration. *Champagne for one and all!* Although it'll take me all week to fill out the funding paperwork . . . But it'll be a labour of love.'

There's silence at the end on the line so I press on, wanting Teddy to realise how hard this was to achieve. 'For a while, I didn't think we'd get there but it was the human books that saved us, saved Willow Grove library! This will be a town *with* books forever more!'

'Wow, that's great timing actually. I mean congratulations and all but I was about just about to call you. Dad had another abnormal ECG. They're still trying to get to the bottom of it. Mum is not coping too well but is still coming into work at sunrise before going back and forth all day to visit him.'

'Neither of them are answering my calls. Is this why? What's the big secret?'

He sighs. 'They've been arguing incessantly about you. Dad wants to let you live your life in Dullsville but Mother is insisting that Astor will crumble without your magical touch. You're the face, Elodie!' His voice is heavy with frustration.

'Is it the stress of me being away that's causing this?' Dad has never defended me against Mum before; he's always followed her almost in awe and I'd hate to think I'm the reason for this.

He pauses for the longest time. 'I'm sure it's not that,' he says but his words are hollow. 'Or not only that at least.'

Tears streak down my face at my predicament. 'Be honest, Teddy. This is serious. If Dad is sick because of the stress of me leaving and him having to argue on my behalf, then I have to come home. I can't let his health deteriorate because of a choice I made.'

'Urgh, this is all such BS. Mother is the one who needs to pull her head in here. *She's* the one causing all this undue stress! I don't know what else to say, Elodie, except maybe you better come back, at least for now, until we know more about Dad's condition.'

'OK, I'll get back as quickly as I can.'

He lets out a sigh of relief. 'Are you sure?'

'I'm sure,' I lie.

*

That Thursday I'm with Finn at Fuoco, trying my level best to appear happy when inside I'm slowly dying. It might be one of the last times we'll be together like this before I have to leave. Do I tell him who I really am? I don't want to ruin this evening, I want to hold on to the memory of him, soak him up so it can last in my mind for as long as it can. Once I've submitted the funding paperwork, then my time here will be over. It's still so hard to comprehend.

Donatella is buzzing because Finn's write-up has done wonders and the place is packed. He's got a way of writing that makes people believe. Our conversation is stilted because I'm close to choking up every time I picture leaving him. Leaving this extraordinary life. When he finds out it was all a lie will he forgive me? Or will he assume the princess didn't want the pauper life and the experiment was just a way for me to pretend to be one of them?

'You're quiet tonight.' Finn brushes his hand over mine. 'Is everything OK?'

I gulp back a lump in my throat. 'It's been a long week. I need to hide under the covers and devour a book and a tub of ice cream.' If only it could be such a quick fix.

He groans. 'I wish I could join you.' Finn's off to London for the weekend to celebrate his sister Frankie's surprise engagement. 'But I'm keen to meet this guy that Frankie's fallen for. It all seems a little too whirlwind for my liking.'

'Ever the protective brother,' I say with a smile.

He gives me a cheeky grin. 'She's already given me a list of things I'm not to ask him.'

'But you'll ask anyway?'

'Of course!'

We finish up and wave goodbye to Donatella who commits to a launch hug instead and knocks the wind out of me. 'Come back soon, yeah?'

'For sure,' I say, my heart breaking just that little bit more. I've grown to love these people I call friends. London will seem so empty without them.

Outside the autumnal rain comes down hard and, like the gentleman he is, Finn hands me his jacket to drape over my head while he gets thoroughly drenched. We dash to the car and he offers me the keys. 'No thank you! Even Lewis Hamilton would baulk at driving around in this weather!'

Finn drops me off home, and we kiss a thousand final goodbyes. At least that's what it feels like. 'You sure you won't come to the engagement party?' he asks. 'They'd love to meet you.'

I shake my head sadly, unable to fight the feeling of gloom that's settled heavily in my heart. 'No, it's a family celebration. I'll wait until the next one.' If it's time to start cutting ties, I don't want to be making any new ones.

Finn dashes back to his car and drives away slowly on the

uneven road. As I wave him away, I realise I've still got his jacket on. It's a sopping mess anyway so I decide to wash it for him so it'll be fresh upon his return. I check his pockets to make sure there's nothing of value in them and find a stack of handwritten notes. I pop them on the bench and put the jacket in to wash.

Once that's done, I take the notes, which are stuck together as one and damp with rain. Could I gently prise them apart and dry them out? I'm concerned they could be important notes for a story and will be unreadable if I don't do something now.

I slowly pry them apart and start to place them in a row on the table. When I see what's written on them shock jolts me out of my morose mood.

Ellie Astor is Elodie Halifax?

There are also printouts of pictures of me at Astor premieres, and my Astor bio. There's a copy of my résumé for Willow Grove library. Highlighted is my experience with Henry Ackley, and then a note about how Astor published his memoir, and how I'm linked to him. Just how did he get a copy of my résumé? I suppose the council would have it on file after my interview. It wouldn't take much for Finn to wangle his way in there with that charming smile of his.

The notes are scribbled as if written in haste.

Ulterior motive for the People Library experiment? Will eventually come out that the great Ellie Astor is the mastermind behind it – for what reason? In order to become more famous/well liked? Do Astor plan to buy all the public libraries – is this a plot to make even more money/have control?

Befriends all the outcasts on purpose? Not because she's genuine.

Check whether she is a librarian or not? Is her paperwork fake?

Wants to write a book about how she personally saved a library from being closed/good PR/Astor name again? Testing for one of those 'undercover employer' TV shows?

Look into Astor more. What are their future plans? Expansion into Willow Grove perhaps? But what? Where and why?

I'm crushed as I read them all. How could he think so low of me? There's more but I don't have the heart to read them.

By the looks of this, he's been suspicious for quite some time. There's dates and times on each note, going right back to a month ago. How has he been able to look me in the eye and lie like that? I slump. He wasn't who I thought he was – and I guess he feels the same about me. There's nothing else to do except start packing my measly number of belongings. My family needs me and that's a lot more than I can say about Finn. Isn't it always the way? The Astor name ruins everything eventually but I really thought I had a chance here, to step away from it and prove myself. I guess I failed again. I may as well give in to it and live the life my mother wants . . .

Chapter 24

Friday morning, I dash into the library over an hour late. Of all days to sleep in! I stayed up far too late the night before, cleaning the cottage and making sure everything was in order before leaving the keys in the letterbox. I'll have to email the landlord later and let them know, but first I want to get out of Willow Grove.

'Maisie,' I say, finding her in the office waiting for the computer to boot up.

'You're so late. What gives?'

I take a moment to catch my breath. 'Never mind that. I need you to file the funding paperwork. It's all done, it just needs delivering to the council.' I rifle though my desk and find the file and hand it to her.

She frowns. 'So if it's all completed why don't you take it there? Is this because you don't want to walk in the rain? Because if so, I don't really want to either. I have a very low immune system.'

My head pounds. I don't have the patience for this. 'There's no time. Listen. I need you to step up, OK? Please lock up the library for ten minutes and take it there right now. You can take my place as head librarian, until they sort something else. I'll . . . I'll email them later and put in a good word.'

'What why?' She sits ramrod straight.

I fight back tears, as sadness and anger vie for position in my heart. I need to leave before I change my mind. Before one of my human books comes past and I lose whatever composure I have. 'I'm leaving. Something urgent has come up. I have to leave Willow Grove but *please* don't let all our hard work go to waste. You're going to continue to make great changes here. I believe in you, Maisie, even if you don't believe in yourself sometimes.'

She narrows her eyes. 'Why are you being so nice to me when I've made it so hard for you?'

I give her hand a reassuring pat. 'We all have our reasons, Maisie, why we act a certain way. I know your gran was the previous librarian here. I really wish I'd known sooner, and I would have tread a little more softly. I understand why you kept it to yourself, though, and again I'm really sorry for all you've been going through – it can't have been easy having me come along and trample over her memory, making all these changes. Apply for the head librarian job and do her proud, Maisie. Maybe that's how this is all meant to pan out.'

She wraps her arms across her body as if holding herself in. I'm surprised when tears spring in her eyes. 'I'm so sorry, Elodie. I should have told you straight up who she was to me. It's just that it hurt to see you come in and take over, as if the work my gran had done wasn't up to par. She worked here for so long, taking over when the place was a disorganised mess and she got it back in shipshape using her own blood, sweat and tears because even back then there wasn't enough money for this place. No matter how many times she appealed to the council, they wouldn't listen. Instead, they kicked her out like she was nothing. All those years amounted to *nothing*.

'Yeah, I know she came across as hard. She had strict rules about dress code and who could come in here, but that was only because she wanted to preserve what was here. She didn't want people coming in, dusty from work and marring the books – because she knew she couldn't replace them. I know people saw her as this bossy sort of witch but they didn't know her reasons. It was always about the protecting the books.'

'Is that why you were so shocked when I set up a table to sell some of them?'

She nods and wipes away a fallen tear. 'Yeah, Gran would be rolling over in her grave. Who'd sell these precious books before we knew we could replace them?'

Maisie's behaviour begins to make a lot of sense. Why didn't I see her motivations came from a deeper place?

'I'm so sorry, Maisie. Your gran sounds like she only wanted to protect this place, and like the human books, she was judged unkindly because no one knew the real person behind the façade.'

'Are you always this understanding?'

I shake my head. 'Of course not. Really, we're all the same and trying to make the best of things. Look, I have family problems too – that's why I need to leave. If anyone asks, please explain that it's a personal issue and I had to go. I hate to go, but I'll be leaving my heart here in Willow Grove.' I dig in my pocket for a wrinkled tissue, losing the fight to remain composed. I turn away so she doesn't see me cry – Maisie has enough on her plate right now without me adding to it. I quickly gather my things.

Part of me is suspicious about the timing of Finn's sister's surprise engagement party and his sudden need to leave Willow Grove. Maybe I'm overthinking it in my panicked state – but that same old worry surfaces, that people are only out for one thing when it comes to the Astor name and he's a reporter after all. All his notes, his investigations must mean something. Is he planning some sort of exposé that will catapult him into the world of investigative reporting? Was I his ticket out of here all along? It doesn't matter, I need to go and be with my father. I can put out any fires when I get to London. I heft my bag over my shoulder and go to leave. I give Maisie a quick hug and head for the door.

'Wait, Elodie!' She rushes to me. 'I'm so sorry about everything. I really am . . . I . . .'

'Don't be sorry. Get that paperwork in as soon as you can!' Members are milling about so I need to get out of here as fast as I can before one of them stops me for a chat. I hail a cab, screw the expense! I don't want to run into anyone I know catching the train and I have a sense my resolve might weaken. Alone with just the driver – at least I can cry in private. I'm sure most cabbies have had a woman bawling over a man many times before.

'To Central London please.'

My phone rings and Finn and Maisie's names flash. I send them straight to answerphone and then switch it off.

Maybe Willow Grove wasn't meant to be. I'll always be proud that we pulled together to save the library. Isn't that enough, that I achieved what I set out to do? I did it under my own steam without using my name or connections. That only leaves Finn's betrayal. He always seemed too good to be true with his wholesome smile and sparkling, inquisitive eyes. The old-school romance was a farce, after all. It came so naturally though, how would I guess? My chest is tight and I find it hard to catch my breath. Is this what it feels like to have your heart broken . . . ?

*

DONATELLA

'My papa regrets leaving the hills of Sicily. He doesn't say it in so many words but I can tell. He plays this hauntingly sad Italian music that reminds him of his mamma, God rest her soul. Moving here, he thought he'd being living this great British life. Everyone prospers here, or so he thought. And for a while Tony's Pizzeria was popular. But like a lot of small businesses around here, things slowed down. Money became tight. We had to use cheaper ingredients for our pizzas and that's one thing my papa doesn't like doing; for him quality is everything. If he starts cutting corners, where does it end?

'My biggest worry is that one day he'll announce he's returning to the homeland. But things are hard there too. Papa's been sending money home to the family ever since I was little and I know he wishes he had more to share with them. That's why I pushed him to update the pizzeria. Fuoco was my dream, but I did it for my papa. I thought that no one could resist a new pizzeria, modern furniture and an updated menu. But it backfired. People didn't understand. Was this the same owner, why all the changes, why is the menu more expensive, where have their favourite menu items gone?

'Oh, I cannot tell you how bad I felt when our grand opening was a bust. There were more staff in the kitchen than guests in the restaurant. I was queasy with worry. Had I made a huge mistake? Would Papa now leave? I only wanted to make him proud, show him that I knew what was needed in order for us to survive and be able to help more back home. I tried everything to get people through the doors. Buy one get one free pizza nights. Free home delivery. Complimentary focaccia. Five-pound children's pizza. Live music Mondays. Nothing worked.

'But then Finn did a write-up for the *Chronicle*. He interviewed Papa and I. We told him our story, starting all the way back in those dusty hills in Sicily. Why Papa came here, what his dreams were, and how he trusted handing his beloved pizzeria over to me – the next generation with Sicilian fire in my blood. I talked about how our family always had to take chances to make a better future. How hard it was for my papa to leave his country in the hope things might be better here. And how disheartening that was when it looked like it would all fail, after so many years of work. What had we done, really, except update a tired old pizzeria. Even back in Sicily things change, but in Willow Grove they lay dormant for so much longer. Why? What is it about change that people are suspicious of? I felt so alone when we opened Fuoco and there was no support. I felt so abandoned by the locals.

'Once the article published I held my breath and waited. I thought I'd die if nothing came of it. It didn't take long. Within a few days our old customers returned. They hugged Papa and thanked him for sharing his food with them for so many years. They talked about the sacrifices he made to try for a better life and how lucky they were he chose Willow Grove to settle in. Some apologised, saying they didn't know things were so bad, and they'd make sure to support us from now on because they didn't want to lose us back to Italy. Soon, we had new faces too. I don't know what the future holds, but Papa has stopped playing that sad old music. He's back to pickling olives. Telling me I'm not using enough yeast in the dough. And that's how I know he's happy, that he doesn't regret leaving Sicily. But he misses it. And he always will.'

Chapter 25

I get dropped off at Astor News in the hopes of catching Teddy. It feels like the longest Friday ever, going from the quiet of Willow Grove to the bustle of London, all in one day. I'm not ready to see my parents yet but I want to check in with my brother and ask him about how Dad's health is. I peek in on a meeting where he's taking centre stage. Teddy looks like the corporate dynamo he's always wanted to be, in his dapper suit, wearing his charming smile. All eyes are on him, their expressions rapt as if he's a god, and instinctively I know he's where he's meant to be. None of the staff have ever stared at me like that because my heart wasn't in it, not like Teddy's is. Before too many people see me, I try to sneak out to go wait in his office but as I close the door, someone behind me taps me on the shoulder.

It's Dinesh from finance, one of the happiest people I've ever worked with. He's forever smiling and has a wicked sense of humour. 'Oh wow, Ellie, the ashram totally agreed with you. You look . . . great!'

I know he's lying because I spent the better part of the hour's cab drive in tears. 'You even lie with a smile, Dinesh. That's quite a skill.'

He waves me away. 'So how was it? Are you enlightened?'

The tears threaten to start again. It's Dinesh being nice to me and pretending all is well because he's too polite to point out the obvious. Will the tears ever stop? What if I never set foot in Willow Grove again? Never see Harry, Sofia, Alfie and Pete. 'Enlightened is now my middle name,' I say. 'I'll fill you in soon. I'm coming off a red-eye – that's why I look so shocking. Can you tell Teddy I'm in his office when the meeting is over?'

'Sure, sure, when you're back on track let's catch up for dinner.'

'I'd love to.'

It seems inevitable that I'll have to return to Astor, if only for my family's sake. But it'll have to be on my terms. I'll insist Teddy is to take the helm if this promised retirement is to take place, and if not that he take my previous role and I then answer to him. He's clearly proved himself capable, like I knew he would. But being back here leaves me cold under the fake brightness of the fluorescent lights, the stale recycled air. Back in this hectic city with its wildly fast pace. It's so different to the sleepy, relaxed atmosphere of Willow Grove where everyone takes time to stop and have a chat. The town became a better version of itself after secrets were shared and apologies accepted. And that's all down to the people who live there.

Sneaking into my old office, I turn my phone on and it goes haywire with alerts. There's text messages and missed calls from so many Willow Grove residents. Is Finn's exposé out already? Surely even he couldn't work that fast, unless he's been writing the article about me the whole time? I check the

Chronicle social media pages; there's no new posts on any of them. I google my name. Nothing.

I flick back through the texts, looking for clues to how they all know but they're all same versions of the same thing.

Come back, Elodie!

We need you!

You're part of this town now and forever. We don't care who you are or who you were because we know the real you!

How could Finn *do* this to me?

I keep scrolling until I find one from the man himself. It reads: *I need to see you.* I delete it. Before texting Teddy to let him know I'm in his office in case Dinesh didn't catch him.

*

JO

'Honestly, I didn't think the People Library idea would work for Alfie. But I wanted to let him try. I'm fully aware that I have to let go of the reins a little but it's so hard when people aren't always nice. You can think a person's nice and then they'll show their true colours by making an off-the-cuff comment like: *You should teach your son some manners,* when Alfie doesn't engage when spoken to. That sort of stuff makes my blood boil and I'm always ready to go on the attack for Alfie.

'Straight away, I knew Elodie was one of the good ones. There was something really genuine about her. Alfie was busy telling her that her hair colour washed her out and she laughed it off but not in a fake way – like she really truly thought it was hilarious. That made me trust her, and I don't trust easily. She has Alfie's best interests at heart. Alfie warmed to her immediately. He didn't stop raving about her for the first entire week – she got him some shark posters and gave him his very own library cubicle. Like, who does that? Just instinctively know what he needs? Not many people, that's for sure. It made me happy Alfie has someone here to watch over him. I'm especially careful where Alfie's concerned but having both Elodie and Maisie here makes things better for our little family of two.

'It's just us, you see. I'm not sure if you've heard Alfie talk about his deadbeat dad? You have? Well I'm not going to apologise for that. He *is* a deadbeat. He left us early on and never looked back. But he's the one missing out. Alfie is the best kid in the world, despite the fact he's constantly blabbing about things I say in private. I used to find it mortifying when he'd spill one of my secrets, things I said on the phone or to friends not knowing he'd hear. But my little man has super sonar hearing so I've learned to keep my lips zipped unless I want all and sundry to hear. He doesn't mean any harm by it and these days I find it amusing. I guess I'm so used to it. When he told a woman at the bus stop her stockings made her skin look like KFC chicken, I couldn't help but laugh. He's right; they did. She had a go at me about raising a boy without manners, that old chestnut, but how can you explain when they go on the attack like that? I want to yell and scream, don't be such a judgey McJudgeface!

'But Alfie doesn't like it when I fire back. Instead, I wrap my arms around him and tell him he's the best boy in the world and his manners are impeccable. I always want to reassure him, it's not *him* who needs to change, it's them. I hope he never changes because he's perfect just the way he is. Sorry, I don't mean to cry. It's hard talking about him without getting emotional. I'm so damn proud of him, that's all. I know all mums are proud of their kids, but Alfie has had so many things thrown at him, and he wakes up every day with a smile on his face and sees the good in people. We could all be a little more like Alfie in my humble opinion.'

Chapter 26

'You're really here!' Teddy says, standing at the door of his office. 'What made you come back so soon? I thought you needed extra time to submit the funding paperwork?'

I step around his question and say, 'I'm in awe of you, Teddy! I peeked in on your meeting. You had their full attention. Let me tell you right now, they never looked at me with such open adoration. You're doing something right.'

He gives me a rueful smile and comes in and sits opposite me. 'You're back now though, so I guess that means you'll take over once again.'

I shake my head. 'I don't think so, no.'

I try to rearrange my expression to something akin to Zen, as if I don't have a care in the world but I must fail miserably because Teddy knits his brow and says, 'What's wrong? Is it the idea of being back at Astor?'

I take a deep breath, willing the words to come out unhindered. 'They know who I am. I've had countless messages from them today.'

Surprise flicks across his features. 'They? Who are they?'

'The locals in Willow Grove.'

'What?'

'How on earth did they find out?'

'Finn. I found all these notes in the pocket of a jacket he loaned me. They were truly malicious, like he was piecing a story together about me the whole time under the guise of dating me. I'm so hurt by it. I honestly believed we had something really special, and to find out it was all a lie . . .' It's enough to make my toes curl just thinking of it. 'He told me he used to dream of being an investigative reporter so I guess I'm his ticket to that. He'll probably go straight to Mogul Media with it.'

Teddy's face falls. 'It might *not* be him.'

'Come on, Teddy. It was all there in black and white. I'm so bloody heartbroken about leaving Willow Grove like some kind of guilty person. Rushing off without saying any goodbyes. I mean, I knew I'd have to leave probably at any rate, what with Dad being sick, but I wanted to do it the right way.' I don't say that Finn has hurt me more than I care to admit. I'm a fool for opening my heart to him. That guard I built up was there for a reason.

'I'm so sorry, Elodie. I really am. What do the messages say from your Willow Grove friends? Are they out for blood?'

I scrub my face. I'm exhausted right deep down into my bones. 'They're all supportive messages, telling me to come back, that it doesn't matter who I said I was.'

Confusion flashes in his eyes. 'So, isn't that a good thing?'

'Yes but I didn't want them to find out like that. And what if Finn sells his exposé to Mogul Media, then what? Mother will never let me forget that my first foray into the world ended in disaster.' There's a knock and the door swings open.

'Hey, Mum, Dad.'

Mum wears a look of triumph on her face. Dutiful daughter returned home and ready to work.

'The ashram did nothing for your complexion,' Mum says, deadpan.

'Did you just make a joke?' If there's one thing my mum isn't, it's a jokester.

'Trying to.'

I survey my dad, who does look as fit as a fiddle and not a man whose health is deteriorating. Could it be that changing his lifestyle has worked so well? 'Dad, you look great. When did you get out of hospital?'

'Yesterday. Honestly, darling, I'm fine. I'm sure one of the doctors has a crush on me and my ECGs are in fact perfectly normal.'

'Really?' I arch a brow.

'Really. Ask your mother.'

'She does seem to hang around him a lot. I might get her fired.'

'Another joke?'

'Sort of. Anyway, we're just so thrilled you're home and you've got that little library project out of your system. Now the real work begins. We're all set to announce you as the head of Astor—'

I hold up my palm to stop her. 'Not going to happen, Mum. You've known for years that Astor wasn't my passion and yet you wouldn't listen. I became a robotic version of me, working from morning to night, and when I shared with you my desire to leave, to have my own life, you shut me down as if what I wanted for my own life didn't matter. You're *still* doing it.'

She appraises me regally, like a cat would. 'I see that we've pushed you too far, Ellie. I didn't realise how punishing your schedule was until I started doing it. And I promise we'll change that. Teddy can take over a lot of that.'

'*What do you see when you look at me?*' I ask, just like we asked at the People Library.

My mother blusters. 'What do you mean? I see the face of Astor! I see a bright, young woman with the world at her feet. A female CEO who'll take the company to new heights.'

My shoulders slump. 'That's what you see in me, Mum? *Really?* You're projecting what *you* want, not what I want. You want me to fit into this mould you created, a mould that is identical to you! But I'm not you, Mum, am I? We're not even remotely similar. But I love you for all you are, and all you've done in your life, but mostly I love you because you're my mum. I want you to love me because I'm your daughter, not because of what I can do for the company.'

She continues, her voice softening a fraction. 'I love you as my daughter, of course I do! I never meant to make you feel like what you wanted didn't matter, Ellie darling. You always were such a daydreamer, always had your nose pressed in a book, like the day could slip away and you'd barely register that. I felt by pushing you, you'd eventually see just how much you could achieve. Realise your full potential.'

'I'm not *like* you. But that's OK. We don't all aspire to work crushingly long days, with back-to-back meetings, incessant phone calls and emails. Events most evenings.' I look at Teddy and it's glaringly obvious to me. 'Teddy thrives on that high-pressure, high-octane environment. Not me. You chose the wrong offspring to take over Astor.'

Teddy clears his throat. 'Thanks for the vote of confidence,

Elodie. You're right, I do thrive on it. It's all I've ever wanted to do.'

Mother sighs and does a strange little laugh. '*That's* becoming abundantly clear. I chose you because you weren't like Teddy! Teddy who went missing for weeks on end until his money ran out. Teddy who was in the press for his decadent lifestyle. You seemed like the safer bet. And I *really* love the idea of women taking over the world one CEO at a time. But it's slowly dawning on me that the person for the job *is* Teddy. You need an almost frenetic energy to do what needs to be done – to make those high-stakes decisions on the spot. He's proven he can do it. At the back of my mind is the worry that he'll eventually explode from the stress and then where will we be? What if he starts drinking again?'

'What if he doesn't? What if you foster a better work-life balance at Astor? Why does it always have to be all or nothing with you?' I pepper my mother with questions, hoping she'll see that changes need to be made here. One person does not need such crippling responsibility.

She shoots me a surprised look. 'I've never thought about it that way before. It's such a fast-paced industry, we have to work quick to break the latest stories, trump our competitors, so it's always felt like we needed to keep our fingers on the pulse, and go go go.'

I give her a sad smile. She's put so much pressure on herself for so long because she's been so worried control might slip from her fingers and the company will suffer if she looked away for a minute. 'There's a whole team of people who can help. It doesn't always need to fall directly on your shoulders, or Teddy's when he takes over.'

'I'm not sure—'

Dad cuts her off. 'She's right, Dorothea, she's *right*. Teddy is the best person for the job and he won't let us down.'

Teddy and I exchange a smile. Have we convinced her after all this time?

'But you and Teddy as a team! You'd make a formidable pair. I could rest easy, knowing you had each other, if I did decide to take things a bit slower.'

Teddy and I grin. She's tenacious, I'll give her that. 'Still a no from me. Ideally, I'd love to follow my dreams, and they aren't here at Astor.'

'What will you do instead?' Mum asks.

'Well, that I don't know. We managed to get enough members to save Willow Grove library, but then I got into a spot of bother.' I tell them about the notes and the potential threat of an exposé by Finn.

I wait for her to shriek. But she doesn't. 'Let's get one of our own reporters ready with a rebuttal. We'll spin it exactly the way it played out. You wanted to save a small-town library but you knew no one would take you seriously if you used the Astor name, so you used your real surname in order to achieve your goal. It was an experiment and it worked, and you hope to see People Libraries popping up all over the world.'

I give her a warm smile. Who knew my mother had a heart this big? We've got a long way to go but it's a good start. 'Thanks, Mum. I like that idea. I can work with one of our reporters and help flesh it out so it's ready to go when we need it.'

She takes out her phone and scrolls through her contacts. 'I suggest using Roger. He's the best one for this. You've got his email?'

'Yes, I have. Thank you.'

'So what next then, Elodie?' Teddy asks.

I contemplate it, but it's an easy choice. 'I'm going to get a job in another library, somewhere, somehow. I'm going to rent a cottage and make it mine. And I'm going to spend time at the weekends reading until an entire day slips away.' I grin at Mother.

'We hope you'll still visit,' she says.

'Always, and I hope you'll visit me. I can make a mean frozen pizza.'

'We can eat beforehand, I suppose,' she says and laughs.

And just like that I'm finally free. It's all thanks to the People Library showing me the way . . .

Chapter 27

MARY

'Jacques saved me, really he did. Before I met him I was in a toxic relationship, and each day it grew worse. The air was electric with tension that only I could feel. I'd wait for it, the put-downs, the snide comments, the gaslighting. I kept picturing the rest of my life, and a feeling of dread would sit heavily in my heart. When he began screaming his insults, I knew I had to leave. It escalates, doesn't it? Once the screaming didn't have the same effect, it'd be his fists and then where would I be? I had to get away from him, but first I had to plan it so I could make a clean break. I did some extra waitressing shifts, saved my pennies. When I had enough I hightailed it out of there. Did a bit of solo travelling, picked up some work along the way.

'I'd been gone about a year when I met Jacques on a Contiki tour. I was still so wary. The last thing I wanted to do was get in too deep with another man – what if he was the same and then I had to run again? But Jacques had this quiet persona. He was so patient, so gentle that I figured I deserved to be loved. Deserved to at least give it a shot. I couldn't spend my life running from people who show me any affection. We started dating. Things progressed slowly, while others around us were hooking up left, right and centre – you know the phrase: what happens on a Contiki tour, stays on a Contiki tour!

'But Jacques was different. He took it slow, he romanced me. He borrowed a kitchen in some guy's house in Mexico of all places and made me a proper French meal. You can fall in love with someone that quickly. It was the way he showered me with love, expressed through his food. Jacques isn't a man of many words, but I know he loves me more than anything. Instead of saying the words *I love you*, until they have no meaning, he'll bake me brioche, even though he's worked late in the restaurant. Or he'll bake profiteroles for my birthday and write love notes on glazed opera cakes. That's the way he says it, by *showing* me. I'm the opposite. I'll scream it from the rooftops. I shake him awake and jump on him to get his attention.

'When he asked me to marry him, he wrote it in the sand at a beach in Baja. Even then, he couldn't say the words, but I found it more romantic that he wrote them like that. I've got a photo of the words in the sand, whereas if he'd said them they'd have blown away in the wind. Gone forever. We're trying to have a baby, but it's hard, isn't it? When we both work so much and then we're dead on our feet afterwards. I keep thinking of spiriting him away. Taking him back to Baja, but we have this *other* baby, the award-winning bistro, so I'll wait. I know it'll happen when the time is right. And until then, I'll keep waking up to fresh brioche every Sunday, knowing I'm one of the lucky ones but only because I made that choice years ago not to settle for second best . . .'

*

The next day, I'm back in my townhouse, feet up on the coffee table as I scroll the internet and still find no mention of my name, or anything about Willow Grove. The *Chronicle* social media pages haven't been updated either. The absence of a story worries me more. Just how big an exposé is he writing? Perhaps he's gone to some other national with it and they're taking their time, getting it fact-checked and approved by their legal team.

I get a text from Sofia: *Darling, please come back! The town isn't the same without you. You've made Willow Grove into the place I always dreamed about living in. A tight-knit community where everyone has everyone's back despite a squabble here and there. No one cares you're Ellie Astor. Maisie is beside herself with worry about the library slipping away under her hand. Will you at least take my call? I miss you so!*

There's a Teddy-style knock at the door, banging so loud you'd think the place was on fire. I go and let him in, shocked to find Finn standing behind him.

'What . . .'

Both men walk inside before I can think to slam to the door. 'Hear me out,' Finn says, holding his hands up as if in surrender.

I'm so mad at Teddy I feel like my head is about to explode. Now Finn's getting a good peek around my townhouse. I'm sure he's calculating just what to say in his article about the extreme wealth on display here. The princess in the penthouse.

'Teddy, how could you do this?'

He shakes his head. 'Come and sit down. It's not what you think.'

I glare at him but go through to the sitting room, arms folded defensively across my chest. 'Make it quick, Finn. I'm really not interested in anything you have to say to me.'

'The notes weren't mine, Elodie,' Finn says.

'Riiight.'

'I mean it – they weren't. When have you ever seen me take notes on a notepad? I use my iPad for work.'

'That doesn't prove a thing.'

Finn rubs his face. 'It was Harry who found the notes stashed away in the library. He took me to one side and quizzed me until my head spun in order to know if he could trust me with this secret. He was worried people would find out because he didn't know who the notes belonged to.'

'Who did they belong to then, if not you?'

Finn rubs the back of his neck. 'Maisie.'

'Maisie?' I feel a wave of betrayal.

'Yes. Look, Maisie's young; she made a huge mistake. She was out of sorts about the treatment of her gran and to her the blame fell squarely at your feet, albeit unfairly. I had a chat on the phone with her yesterday and she's distraught that your secret is out and that you left because of it. Whatever you said to her as you were leaving made her realise that you were in Willow Grove for the right reasons.'

'What I said to her?' I struggle to recall that fateful morning when I left the library in such haste. 'But then she had all this information about me. She'd done all that digging. Why?'

Finn takes a deep breath, and explains, 'When Maisie found out you were *the* Ellie Astor, the one she's seen wearing couture in the tabloids, the one whose life seems full of glamour from the outside, she got angry. She believed there was an ulterior motive to your arrival in Willow Grove. Then you suggested the People Library idea and Maisie had it in her head that it was some kind of scheme, and that you weren't doing it for the greater good of the community. After you said your goodbyes to her in the library she took stock. Just because you have a fancy last name doesn't mean you're any happier than the rest of us. She finally pieced it together: we all have dreams and yours was to live your life on your own terms. She's really upset, Elodie. She's worried everyone's going to blame her for your leaving. But she's been so brave and told everyone what she did and promised to make it better.' Now all the missed calls from Maisie make sense. She wants to apologise.

'No one cares what name you use, especially me! You've done such a huge amount of good for the library and the town of Willow Grove. Old wrongs have been righted. Hurts are beginning to heal. And it's all because of you. I don't care if you're Ellie Astor, or Elodie Halifax because I know the real you. The one who wants to change the world, to help others in every way possible. To let go of her privilege and prove herself on her own merit. And trust me, I know what it's like to start over, Ellie, and to want to run from the past.'

It's so much to process. 'I wouldn't know because you never really speak about your past.'

'Likewise.' He's got me there.

'So tell me.'

*

FINN

'I always wanted to be an investigative reporter in the bright lights of the big city. The thrill of breaking a story before other reporters appealed to me. It's like playing detective, piecing the clues together and finding the narrative that fits. But life had other plans for me, and my own dreams went on the back burner. Eventually, those dreams drifted further and further away until they weren't reachable anymore. I let the idea go and while it hurt I figured it wasn't that big a deal. People sacrifice a lot more than that every day.

'I moved to Willow Grove because it was just far enough away from the place I grew up so no one would know me, or my family name. Isn't it funny, that we both were hiding from our surnames? Mine's not a name linked with glitz and glamour, more disreputable. I'd hear people talking behind their hands: *There go those Ford kids looking for all the world like they're starving.* Or: *They should be taken away from her. She's an unfit mother.*

'To be honest, she was an unfit mother most days, but she tried her best to raise us, while being crippled by drug addiction. It controlled her life and she made so many bad choices under its influence.

'My kid sisters were always hungry and there was always a new baby on the way but no man in the picture.

'Being the oldest child, I felt like I had to step up and look after us all as best as I could. I had to protect them until I could get us all out of that cycle of poverty, of witnessing addiction before they fell into that trap too.

'While working two jobs I put myself through university and would then go home to cook and clean, make sure the girls were doing their homework. I'd iron their clothes and ask them to wash their hair. I wanted them to look presentable, to look like despite everything, our little family had it together. In the small town we lived in, everyone knew our mum and her struggles. She made great fodder for gossip. But not a single person ever reached out to help, to offer support – anything that might have made a difference. Instead, she was ridiculed as a cautionary tale. So, I made damn sure my sisters had everything they needed and weren't neglected in any way. Their lives were tough, carrying around the burden of that name, but they were tough too and they got through it.

'I finished top of my class at university. The job offers came rolling in. Prestigious newspapers wanted to hire me and I was so very tempted. My sisters urged me to take the job of my dreams in London but how could I? They were still in school, my baby sister in primary school at that point. I couldn't uproot them, and how would we all survive living in London together? The starter salary wouldn't stretch far enough to support that. And I couldn't leave them with Mum – not full-time. It wasn't safe.

'Instead, I bumbled around freelancing until I took the job at the *Chronicle* at Willow Grove. When the baby of the family went off to university, I knew I could follow my own dream once more. There'd be time now for me. The girls all have their own lives and are safe and secure.

'But I found my dreams had changed. The little town of Willow Grove has grown on me so much I don't *want* to pursue a job elsewhere. Why would I want to leave and fly around the world when everything I need is right there? That's the thing about dreams – they shift as you grow. I only have to look at my sisters and know those sacrifices I made weren't really sacrifices, they were my path and it led me to this point where I feel like I belong.

'People know my surname but they don't know my story so maybe it's time I rectified that. It's not that I'm ashamed of my past, not at all; it's that inherent need to protect my sisters that keeps me from sharing. After the success of the People Library, I see now that if we all spoke up more, if we stood up for the underdog, if we opened our own hearts then the world wouldn't be such a lonely place. My mum was so lonely her whole life, despite being surrounded by people. Her addictions drove her and she was stuck in that loop of guilt, fear and shame. That stigma that surrounded her. We never gave up on her, because we knew her heart, but society did. Would things have been different if someone, *anyone* had given her a helping hand? When she died, I was so conflicted but mostly I felt like she was free of that pain, that torment that drove her to drugs. I felt like she'd have a new beginning, whatever the next stage is after death. That was enough for me, to know that.

'And what I've learned is, you can't change the past, but you can change the future. Now all I want is the woman I love to know I'd *never* betray her trust, not ever. And she's got a whole town of people ready and willing to keep her secret if that's what she wants. Because that's what friends are for . . .'

'Jesus, take the wheel,' Teddy says through glassy eyes as he clears his throat. 'If that didn't move you, Ellie, nothing will. I need to visit this People Library and borrow them all. Good luck, you two. I've got a date with Louise tonight, so I need to get my preparations started. She loves a man with a manicure apparently.'

'She does?' I laugh, thrilled for him. I wonder what's brought on her change of heart? Teddy showing her he's just as ambitious as she is? That he really is capable of settling down? Whatever it is, I'm pleased for Teddy. Louise is a gem.

Teddy says his goodbyes. When he shuts the front door

behind him I turn to Finn. 'Thank you for sharing your story.' I struggle to find the right words. He's been through so much and you'd never guess such a thing. It makes sense now why he judged my life, the life he thought I had when he watched Mum's TV interview. He had to fight so damn hard for the most basic needs and to do that and go on to university and for the girls to have such happy, healthy futures too – it's a real testament to the man he is. 'I'm so sorry you went through all of that but it made you into the man you are today.' What can I say? I don't want to sound trite or drown him in platitudes. He's too good for that.

He gives me a what-can-you-do shrug but I know he'll always play it down. That's Finn, always more concerned about everyone else first. 'And I'm sorry that I thought you'd expose me. It's always something I've had to worry about. People befriending me for disingenuous reasons. It was so utterly liberating to be someone else in Willow Grove, and work under my own steam. But I feel like I've let everyone down, hiding under the pretence of being someone I'm not. Asking for their trust when I wasn't being honest myself.'

'That's just the thing, Elodie. You have been your true self in Willow Grove all along. You weren't lying; your name really is Elodie Halifax! I know you're genuine in your reasons. You didn't lie to me, to any of us. You can't fake what we have. I feel it deep in my soul that you're the one for me and I don't give a damn what name you use.'

'You're too good for me, Finn.'

'You haven't met my crazy family yet. They just might scare you off.'

I scoff. I bet they're just as lovely as he is. 'They're lucky to have a brother like you. I bet you shielded them from the worst of it.'

'I'm the lucky one. Without them, maybe I'd have gone off the rails. They are a handful and constantly call, text and email me but they do give good advice about matters of the heart.'

'They do? What did they say about *this* situation?'

He lets out a sigh as if recalling their advice. 'They told me to find you and explain and if that included hiring a blimp and flying it across the sky then that's the level I had to go to, to make things right. They understood why you jumped to conclusions, and they said I should have told you about the notes as soon as I knew of their existence. My keeping them secret was a mistake. Selfishly, I didn't want to scare you off. I thought I could make it all go away and no one would have to be any the wiser. After, I did a bit of googling into the Astor family, I understood implicitly, that just like me, you wanted to be your own person away from what society thought they knew about you.'

'How did you know that, Finn?'

'It was your smile in all the press pictures, so wooden, so fixed. The blank stare in your eyes. That's not the Elodie I know. The Elodie whose whole face lights up when she talks about books she loves, ideas for the library, the human books. That woman looks for all the world like she's discovered Narnia.'

Only Finn would read so much into photos of me and be able to translate their meanings as well as he has. Is it because his soul recognises mine? It feels as deep and spiritual as that.

'Really,' he says. 'We're not so different after all.'

He's right. We've both tried to escape the narratives of our surnames, those long twisty tales that were whispered behind closed doors, exaggerated, aberrations of the truth. I might have been running away from privilege and he from poverty, but the ends are the same. It's true: you can never judge a book by its cover. I knew Finn was a great brother, almost a paternal figure in his sisters' lives but I never would have guessed he put his own dreams on hold to make theirs come true.

'I feel like all these paths led me to you. I stumbled into Willow Grove for that very reason. Not just for the library, for the escape, but for you. You are the missing piece.' I remember of all his romantic overtures, the way he breathes life into me when we kiss. And I know I've found the one for me. All the walls around my heart dissolve and I know by letting go of what came before, that what comes next will be authentic.

'That's finally been found.' He takes me into his arms and makes me forget about the world and everyone in it. Breathless when we finally pull away he says, 'So will you come back to Willow Grove?'

'I've got a library to finish saving, haven't I?'

*

ELODIE

'I'm sorry I lied, I truly am. But there's good reason for it. My life had been orchestrated ever since I stepped foot in the offices of Astor News and Media, even before then if I'm honest. Everything was always about how we Astors were viewed. *Don't do that: the press will take pictures. Don't say that: it's bad for optics.* And on it went until the real me shrivelled up and died and instead I became this mannequin who'd smile for the cameras and say all the right things, while the real me had slipped away. Like our other human books, I felt that even though I was *right there*, no one could see me. I played the part so often I forgot who I was and what I wanted. It became robotic. And I lost my way.

'My escape was books, always has been. That's the place I go to feel alive. It shores me up, comforts me and gives me hope. If those characters can overcome adversity, then maybe I can too. You can imagine my excitement when the opportunity arose to save Willow Grove library . . . It was like fate had intervened.

'I've always believed library cards are a portal into another world and this was going to be my chance to prove it. My life was so colourless before I came here. When the People Library experiment began to have some impact, I felt as though maybe I'd found my place in the world. I *can* do something meaningful, I *can* help in some small way. I so desperately wanted to live the life I always dreamed of. Work for a living, learn to cook, to drive – all those simple things people take for granted seemed wildly exotic to me. And yes, cooking is quite the chore, but I know I've got Sofia right there ready to spoil me with Michelin-star-worthy meals if I can't take one more frozen pizza. I've got Harry to chat about books with. I've got Pete, teaching me how to grow my own herb garden. And I've got little Alfie to make a grey day blue. And I've got all of you, if you'll have me?

'I promise to work hard and make sure the library is a success now and always. And I promise it'll *always* be a town with books. Because without books, without that escape, the world is a lonely place. Well, that's what I thought until I moved to Willow Grove and met a very special man called Finn Ford. And now I get to live like a romance novel come to life. None of this would have happened without you all.'

The crowd in the library cheer. I'm overwhelmed with hugs before everyone heads to the lounge area for refreshments.

'So you're staying?' Maisie asks with a smile.

'If you'll have me?'

'No question! Alfie and his friend Levi have talked my ear off and that old computer went on the blink and there was another lot of problems that are above my pay grade.'

'We can work on them together.'

She scratches the back of her neck. 'I'm really sorry I went digging into your life like that. I could just tell you weren't who you said you were and I was curious to know why. When I found out you were *the* Ellie Astor, I saw red. I saw someone with more power taking over again. It reminded me of Gran, being forced into retirement after working here so long. I was never going to tell anyone. OK maybe I was until we had that chat the day you left. You were so nice, even then when you didn't need to be. I guess I was jealous too. There's me having barely enough money at the end of every week to survive, not enough to buy Alfie's fancy biscuits for him, and you swan in here for what I thought was some kind of experiment to see how the other half live before you go back to your fancy life.'

I give her a hug. 'I suppose it was like that in way, Maisie, but it wasn't to see how the other half lived; it was because I yearned for that life too. I wanted to meet people and get to know them under my own steam, not because of my parents' accomplishments. And trust me, that so-called fancy life is over-rated. I'm so much happier here.'

'I can see that now. And I'm sorry that I made your life so hard. I promise to do better.'

'We both will. Did you get the funding paperwork in OK?'

She grins. 'Not only that but they've approved it already. They've been following Finn's articles about the People Library and want to discuss you potentially doing the experiment in other libraries too.'

'If it helps save them, I'm all for it, but perhaps we can make them a dossier on how to go about it. I've found my place and I'm not leaving.'

'Glad to hear it!' Maisie says with a warm smile. 'Now I better help Sofia with the refreshments, or we'll have anarchy on our hands. Harry's daughters have travelled hours to get here for this and if everything isn't perfect with the set-up Sofia will never forgive me.' Harry's daughters are visiting? My heart expands with happiness for my friend.

It's wonderful to see such a change in Maisie. I know how hard it is to own up to mistakes. She's still so young and having lost her gran in the midst of it all added to her burden. I've got a feeling we might just make a successful duo, after all.

'So, I feel like the general consensus is that you've worked wonders here,' Finn says, wrapping his arms around me.

'Without the bravery of the human books sharing their stories, I'd never have been able to share mine. And what a waste that would have been for the man who stole my heart never to have known just how much I adore him.'

'Is this the part where we kiss?'

I laugh.

'I thought books were all I needed but it turns out romance is a lot better off the pages,' I say and kiss him hard like I mean it. I kiss him with every ounce of love I feel for the guy, knowing how lucky I am that a jumble of twenty-six letters led me here to him.

A Letter from Rebecca Raisin

Thank you so much for choosing to read *Elodie's Library of Second Chances*. I hope you enjoyed it! If you did and would like to be the first to know about my new releases, click below to sign up to my mailing list.

Sign up here: bit.ly/RebeccaRaisinSignUp

I hope you loved *Elodie's Library of Second Chances* and if you did, I would be so grateful if you would leave a review. I always love to hear what readers think, and it helps new readers discover my books too.

Thanks,
Rebecca

Website: http://www.rebeccaraisin.com/
Twitter: https://twitter.com/jaxandwillsmum
Facebook: https://www.facebook.com/RebeccaRaisinAuthor

Rosie's Travelling Tea Shop

The trip of a lifetime!
Rosie Lewis has her life together.

A swanky job as a Michelin-starred sous chef, a loving
husband and future children scheduled for an exact date.

That's until she comes home one day to find her husband's
pre-packed bag and a confession that he's had an affair.

Heartbroken and devastated, Rosie drowns her sorrows
in a glass (or three) of wine, only to discover the following
morning that she has spontaneously invested in a bright pink
campervan to facilitate her grand plans to travel the country.

Now, Rosie is about to embark on the trip of
a lifetime, and the chance to change her life!
With Poppy, her new-found travelling tea shop in
tow, nothing could go wrong, could it . . . ?

**A laugh-out-loud novel of love, friendship and adventure!
Perfect for fans of Debbie Johnson and Holly Martin.**

Aria's Travelling Book Shop

This summer will change everything!
Aria Summers knows what she wants.

A life on the road with best friend Rosie and
her beloved camper-van-cum-book-shop,
and definitely, *definitely*, no romance.

But when Aria finds herself falling – after one
too many glasses of wine, from a karaoke
stage – into the arms of Jonathan, a part of her
comes back to life for the first time in years.

Since her beloved husband died Aria has sworn off
love, unless it's the kind you can find in the pages
of a book. One love of her life is quite enough.

And so Aria tries to forget Jonathan and sets off
for a summer to remember in France. But could
this trip change Aria's life forever . . . ?

**A heartwarming, uplifting and hilarious novel
of friendship, love and adventure! Perfect for
fans of Debbie Johnson and Holly Martin.**

Escape to Honeysuckle Hall

A fresh start brings a second chance at love . . .

When Orly's boyfriend and business partner dumps her for a celebrity fling, she finds solace in tacos, tequila and tears. One terrible hangover later, she's packed her bags and swapped her London apartment for the overgrown grounds of Honeysuckle Hall.

After years spent catering to others' whims, Orly is going after what she wants: a simpler life, surrounded by nature. Her plan to set up countryside retreats for burned-out city dwellers means she soon has the social life she's been dreaming of – and gorgeous carpenter Leo is always around when she needs something fixed . . .

As Orly's new life blossoms, so does her friendship with Leo, and she wonders if she's finally found somewhere to put down roots – until she discovers a series of anonymous notes, warning her off. Was she wrong to trust Leo? Or is someone else trying to sabotage her future?

A heartwarming and humorous romance for fans of Debbie Johnson and Holly Martin.

Acknowledgements

Many thanks to my sister-in-law Joanne Mateljan for sparking the idea for this book! Bali is on me, well if it sells millions, that is! Love you lots, Jo Bear.

Thanks to team HQ for all the hard work behind the scenes. To my amazing editors, Dushi who brainstormed this idea and gave it the green light and Abi who helped me knuckle down and get it done, you're the best.

As always, thanks to my family for their patience and support while I write. And thank you, noise cancelling headphones, you are just as crucial!

To all the little Alfie's out there, may you shine bright and let the world change for you, and not the other way around. Thanks to my son, Will, for letting me fictionalise him for this book. Like the character Jo, I barely react these days when he throws me well and truly under the bus with his no-filter approach to life. Some of those doozies deserved to be shared! You're a rock star, and I love you just the way you are!

And Jax, thanks for the plotting help. I can't wait to see where the future takes you with your great big imagination. And thanks for my first movie credit, I'll take it!

Lastly, this is for you, Dear Reader.

Thanks for the support now and always, it means the world to me. I hope Elodie's story strikes a chord with you.

What would the world be like if we lost our precious libraries? A town without books, a place without words . . . is not a place I want to be.

I have faith that bookworms can unite and band together to support initiatives to save libraries, those hallowed old halls that house so much magic!

Dear Reader,

We hope you enjoyed reading this book. If you did, we'd be so appreciative if you left a review. It really helps us and the author to bring more books like this to you.

Here at HQ Digital we are dedicated to publishing fiction that will keep you turning the pages into the early hours. Don't want to miss a thing? To find out more about our books, promotions, discover exclusive content and enter competitions you can keep in touch in the following ways:

JOIN OUR COMMUNITY:

Sign up to our new email newsletter:
http://smarturl.it/SignUpHQ
Read our new blog www.hqstories.co.uk
🐦 https://twitter.com/HQStories
f www.facebook.com/HQStories

BUDDING WRITER?

We're also looking for authors to join the HQ Digital family!

Find out more here:
https://www.hqstories.co.uk/want-to-write-for-us/
Thanks for reading, from the HQ Digital team